Reinventing
Lindsey

Maggie Brown

BELLA
B O O K S

2019

Bella Books, Inc.
P.O. Box 10543
Tallahassee, FL 32302

Printed in the United States of America on acid-free paper.

First Bella Books Edition 2019

Editor: Cath Walker
Cover Designer: Judith Fellows

ISBN: 978-1-64247-035-2

Other Bella Books by Maggie Brown

I Can't Dance Alone
In the Company of Crocodiles
Mackenzie's Beat
Piping Her Tune
Playing the Spy
The Flesh Trade

Acknowledgments

Thank you once again to Cath Walker for her editing skills. From the perspective of a seventh-time author, it is easy to track my growth as a writer. With each editing experience I learn something new about putting my thoughts on paper, as well as mastering the intricacies of the computer.

Many thanks to Bella Books for their continuing support in publishing my books.

In this novel I explore the idea that romantic attraction is in our genes. And as a backdrop for this love story, I set it in the emerging world of digital robotics. It is our future. Society and technology are advancing so rapidly that it is now logical to assume that one day robots will walk amongst us.

About the Author

Maggie Brown is a writer who thinks wit and humour go a long way. Is she intelligent, model-thin, mega-super-intelligent? Hell no!

She is an Australian alien life form, who drinks too much coffee, sits too long at the computer, and sometimes is a hot mess when struck down with writer's block.

She hopes you enjoy her story.

Dedication

To my readers and family

CHAPTER ONE

Flowers—walks in the moonlight—chocolates.

Romance, in Daisy Parker's opinion, was essential in every relationship. While passion fuelled love, romance sustained it. And like fine wine, true love became better as it aged.

Yesterday's wedding had been the proof of the program, a real success story for their agency. Still revelling in her triumph, she entered the office with a little skip, brandishing the bouquet.

"You didn't?" Allison Marsden said with a chuckle.

"Yep, caught it fair and square."

"I presume they tied the knot without any hiccups," Allison asked as she pushed over the box of chocolates.

"All done and dusted. Another satisfied customer," replied Daisy contentedly, plucking a chocolate out of the pack. Lindt truffles were her favourites. "The ceremony was beautiful. The bride was gorgeous, and the groom looked like he couldn't believe his luck."

"So he should. This was one of your greatest achievements."

"You're not wrong." Daisy chewed happily, remembering the work she'd put into getting them together. It had seemed an impossible task at first to match her client with the woman of his dreams, for although he was kind and considerate he was hardly an oil painting. The bride on the other hand, was vivacious and quite stunning. Daisy had known all along that they were suited, maybe an odd match for some but well-fitted in her book. Their genes merged perfectly. It was simply a matter of giving them the opportunity to get to know each other.

"This will make you smile a great deal wider," said Allison as she handed her a folder. "We've hit pay dirt."

"Really? It's someone important?"

"Very. We've moved into the big time."

"O-kayyy…you've got me curious," said Daisy. She resisted the urge to peek. Still on a high, she wanted to savour the moment. "I'll read this while you're at the coffee shop and we'll discuss it when you get back."

She fondly watched her office manager disappear. Since the business was running so smoothly, she'd offered her a partnership six months ago. The success of the venture was as much due to Allison's hard work as hers. Three years ago, Daisy had left university with a master's degree in anthropology, keen to launch into her working career. What to do, though, had proved a problem. Tired of the tedious world of academia, a career in research or teaching hadn't appealed, thus narrowing her options. But one thing she had known—it was time to start earning some real money. She was sick of trying to stretch the budget.

Over the Christmas break, she'd mulled over the dilemma. Then during a night out with friends on New Year's Eve, she was idly watching people flirt when the idea struck. Human mating customs were so haphazard, much like a lucky dip. Singles flocked to bars to meet that someone special—God knows how many times she'd done that herself—but alcohol, while it stoked the libido, did little for true love. Only about half of those who left together would go on a date—the rest would go home, maybe have sex, and then move on. Few were likely to partner-up for life.

Online dating services had a better average, though were hit-and-miss to a degree: people could cheat the system with false information and airbrushed photographs. But what if, she reasoned, the guesswork could be taken out of the equation? Real matchmaking should go further, be more target-specific. The process should have at least a seventy to eighty percent chance of success within a year, with the likelihood that she could find everyone's perfect match eventually. To achieve this, a hands-on service could be offered that included tuition as well as a personalized introduction.

And who better qualified to do this than she was, having majored in human behaviour and sexual attraction of the species. It was all a matter of science; genetics played a huge role in mate selection. Some seemingly unusual combinations made very successful marriages: the tall mom with the short dad, the Barbie-doll princess with the football fanatic, the basketball star with the science nerd.

Contrary to common belief, romantic love was the most powerful of all human experiences, more compelling than the sex drive. She figured if she went about it scientifically, it shouldn't be too hard to get couples together. Proper grooming could be taught. Courtship followed distinct patterns that were easy enough to emulate: eye contact, smiling, preening, body movements and so on.

The more she thought about it, the more enthusiastic she became. A week later, she took the plunge, rented office space and advertised for a personal assistant. Her father, Richard, had huffed and puffed about throwing away her education. A woman with a post-graduate degree shouldn't discard it on a whim to be a common matchmaker. The more he puffed, the deeper she dug her toes in. Her mother, Sheila, had simply laughed, claiming that as an anthropologist she would have more fun working with the living than with the dead.

Daisy had been relieved when her mother gave her support. Her approval meant a great deal. They were the best of friends and although there was twenty-eight years' difference in their ages, they were sometimes mistaken for sisters. Both a tad under average height, Daisy had inherited her mother's perky upturned nose, soft fair complexion, and grey-blue eyes. Their chestnut hair was the same vibrant colour, though hers was harder to keep tamed than Sheila's which naturally sat in soft orderly waves. Daisy had been flattered when someone remarked she looked like Emma Stone, an actor she thought awesome. Though she secretly thought she looked more like an older version of Little Orphan Annie. Curly hair and a sprinkling of freckles didn't do much for sophistication.

Thankfully, her father eventually gave up his opposition in the face of their combined disapproval and the Marigold Matchmaking Agency was formed. An incurable romantic and movie buff, Daisy thought it only fitting to name her venture after one of her favourite films, *The Exotic Marigold Hotel*.

Allison had been one of twenty applicants to answer her ad and proved a real find. Her efficiency and financial nous made Daisy's transition to business proprietor virtually worry-free. They had worked as an effective team over the following three years. As paperwork was a matter of constant annoyance, she left that part in Allison's capable hands, while dealing with clients was Daisy's forte. She loved interacting with people.

Once their office was set up, it had been only a matter of a few strategically placed notices on social media and a trickle of people began to appear. It hadn't taken long to build up a client base. All ages and from a wide range of lifestyles, men and women sought her help: unmarried, divorced, single parents and bereaved. Some had either abandoned the nightclub scene, some were too busy with their career, and others just sick of dud dates. Most had tried Internet dating with little success. But all sought a stable happy relationship.

She gave each her personal attention, which meant as the firm's popularity grew the demands on her time increased. The Marigold Matchmaking Agency soon achieved a stellar reputation, due partly to their efforts and partly to the fact that they strictly vetted their clients before accepting them. Each applicant had to have a genuine wish to find a life partner. They weren't a shagging service.

CHAPTER TWO

The name on the top of the front page of the folder commanded Daisy's attention immediately: Lindsey Jamieson-Ford. She swung back in the chair, her mind racing. All righty—Allie hadn't exaggerated. This *was* big! But what would the principal of LJF Robotics want with a matchmaker? Anyone so wealthy could have her pick. Curious, she read on. The woman was quite serious, she wanted to get married and was prepared to pay very well for the agency to match her up with a suitable spouse.

The figure she quoted caused Daisy to let out a sharp whistle. It was as much as their agency had earned in the last two months and they weren't cheap. Their clients mostly came from professional ranks. The letter from Lindsey was terse and to the point. She asked to be their client, proposed what she was prepared to pay and requested a meeting the following Tuesday morning at nine at her home.

Daisy flipped through the data Allison had added. LJF Robotics had been a subsidiary of the giant Engineering and Electronics Corporation owned by her father, Warren Jamieson-Ford, until LJF began to make money in its own right. Then Lindsey went out on her own, making a name for her company by bringing prosthetics into the digital age. It was also rumoured that they were nearly to the production stage of an advanced humanoid robot.

Information about Lindsey herself was thin on the ground. From all accounts, she worked mostly in a laboratory at her home and rarely ventured outside the grounds. She was, to all intents and purposes, a recluse. Daisy reserved her opinion on that one. The woman could be going out in disguise—not all well-known people sought the limelight. A photograph was enclosed in the file, a snapshot of Lindsey with her father at the opening of an engineering plant in January three years ago. She looked pleasant enough but needed to upgrade her wardrobe. Her drab suit screamed dowdy. And who wore long sleeves in summer?

Allison entered with two cups and a box balanced on a tray. "A cappuccino and scrumptious strawberry cheesecake."

"Good-oh," said Daisy. She hastily cleared a space on her desk before she looked up with a smile. Allison was not only an efficient administrator, but also a good friend. She was as much a romantic sucker as Daisy, convinced everyone had a soulmate somewhere. A practical woman with a warm loving nature, she was happily raising her two teenage daughters with her husband Noel, in a quiet leafy suburb. Because her attractive mature features radiated competency and trust, Daisy had persuaded her to be the public face of their agency in their advertising promotions.

"What do you think about Lindsey?" asked Daisy, keen to hear her opinion. Allison had a good eye for detail.

"I've no idea. There's very little about her on the Internet. She's extremely private, no profile on social media. The only new information I managed to dig up, she was involved in a motorbike accident when she was twenty-one. But the extent of her injuries was hushed up."

"No ex-boyfriend?"

"There was one photo in a magazine with a young guy at her twenty-first birthday party. Nothing anywhere since." Allison gave a shrug and added, "The woman is very good at hiding her private life."

"Who was he?"

"A law student—Martin James Hickman. His father's a judge."

"What happened to him?"

"He moved to London and married over there six years ago. He's back in Australia, now an associate with his father's old law firm."

Daisy idly brushed crumbs off her shirt as she tried to get her head around the information. "She's in her mid-thirties. Surely she must have had somebody since then."

"Believe me, I've searched. I even rang a solicitor friend who had business dealings with her. Apparently, she doesn't date."

"Damn," muttered Daisy. "I hate going blind into an interview. I don't even know what type of man she's attracted to."

"Maybe she has someone in mind and wants our help to get him."

"It'll make it a lot easier if she has. Just so long as they're compatible."

"Are you going to her place as she requested?"

"I guess I'll have to if I want the business." Daisy was normally strict about meeting at private residences, a lesson she'd learned the hard way early in the piece. A middle-aged, obnoxious client had become obsessed with her and cornered her in his lounge with a passionate marriage proposal. It had taken her over an hour of cajoling to persuade him to let her out of the house. Even though she had laughed it off, the stress of the experience had lingered for months. She vowed never to put herself into that position again. They had a strict policy now that all appointments were to be held at her office.

"I agree," said Allison. "For the money she's offering, we should waive that policy. I've received three more applications this week. What do you want done with them?"

"Put them on hold until I meet with Lindsey. We'll know then how much time I'll need to spend with her."

"Okay," Allison replied, then continued in a motherly tone. "You know, it's about time you started to look after your own love life. When was the last time you had a date?"

Daisy gave a shrug. "Jonathon and I went to the Adele concert last week."

"You went out with the man next door? Are you changing sides?"

"As if. He had tickets to the show, so I said I'd go with him."

Allison eyed her thoughtfully. "You can find everyone else a perfect match but not for yourself. What kind of woman do you like, and more to the point, why can't you get her? You're an expert at it."

"I've backed myself into a corner," said Daisy with a scowl. "As you know, I needed to keep my professional life separate at first, which meant I had to fly under the radar for the first two years after setting up the agency. Casual dates only. It could have affected the business…I couldn't take the risk. Now Marigold is big enough not to have to pander to bigots, my workload is the problem. I can't get the hours or motivation to go out much. I haven't been out on a proper date for months. By the time I finish the day, I only want to curl up on the lounge and chill out."

"Maybe we should take on fewer clients. The agency is doing extremely well financially."

"Perhaps we should. We both need more time for our own lives. I know your family will appreciate it."

"They would, but you're the one who needs a social life." Allison looked at her curiously. "Where exactly do you girls go to meet someone?"

"We do most of our networking with parties and dinners. There are a couple of private clubs for women in town with many lesbian members. Then there are always chat lines, cocktail bars, and pubs."

"I find it hard to believe that you've never met anyone you were really keen on. You're so bright and outgoing."

"I played the field at uni," Daisy answered sheepishly. "Although I knew which side of the fence I sat on, I even dated a couple of guys. I thought for curious people that it was a rite of passage in their sexuality. For some past societies, it was normal, even expected, to explore both sides. It wasn't until I was twenty-two that everything fell firmly into place. I coasted along dating, partying, never getting involved. It was all a bit of a game. Then suddenly I got what the fuss was all about."

"What happened?"

"Bridget happened. She was a lecturer in women's studies and so hot she sizzled. As soon as I clapped eyes on her, whistles blew and fireworks popped. My libido completely went off the charts. I was a crushing mess."

Allison chuckled. "I'd liked to have seen that. What happened to her? Obviously, she's not still around."

"She was a player. After we indulged thoroughly in the joys of the…um…flesh, in six weeks she moved on to the next conquest." When she caught Allison's look of sympathy, Daisy grinned. "I wasn't hurt about it. We weren't suited at all, in fact if she hadn't broken it off I would have. She was an egotistical prima donna who was actually a bit of a dumb ass about sexual attraction of the species. She couldn't distinguish between the physiological and the emotional, but she did teach me a thing or two about my body."

"Really, Daisy, you're so analytical when it comes to this stuff."

"Years of study. I'm mature enough now not to go overboard with my emotions."

"One day you'll meet someone, and you won't know what's hit you."

"Ha! Not likely."

"We'll see," said Allison.

CHAPTER THREE

"Turn around...turn around."

Daisy snapped off the irritating Siri voice, ready to scream. The GPS had her running around in circles, and if she didn't find the turnoff soon, she'd be late. Not a good start, for from the precise tone of the letter, Lindsey Jamieson-Ford clearly expected punctuality at their first meeting. Frantically, she swept her eyes up and down the road. Not a damn signpost in sight. Suddenly she remembered the mud-map attached to the letter that she'd arbitrarily dismissed as old-fashioned. Quickly she dug it out from the bottom of her briefcase. After a quick scan, she realized she'd come too far. Just before the T-junction on the way back, she found the unmarked gravel track tucked away between a stand of trees.

Thirty metres in, she brought her red Nissan to a halt in front of a steel gate. Before she punched in the passcode, Daisy ran her eyes over the elaborate surveillance setup attached to the left column. Nobody would be getting in here without permission. Once inside the estate, she drove along an avenue of pines until a two-storey house came into view. When she gazed upwards through the windscreen to take it all in, a slice of sunlight shimmered off something hovering above the tree line.

She shaded her eyes, squinting through the glass. Barely definable against the backdrop of the cloudless sky, a small pale-blue balloon winked into focus. She recognized what it was immediately. A cinematographer client had given her a personalized tour of a film studio, explaining in detail the tools of his trade. The balloon was a Halo, the latest technology in the generation of drones used for taking aerial shots. Powered by helium rather than a motor, it was impossible to detect by sound.

Skittish that someone was recording her every move, she eased the car to a stop in the stone-paved courtyard. When she stepped out, a blast of crisp spring air sent goose bumps prickling across her skin, though they were not solely from the cold. The house was enough to make her shiver. Brooding and formidable, it looked more like a gothic fortress than a family home. Straight out of an Edgar Allan Poe novel. The front door was solid steel, the windows were cased with heavy screening and the outside walls a hard-grey slate. Ivy crawled across the building like thousands of waxy green tentacles.

After a twist to ease her bunched shoulder muscles, Daisy climbed the three steps to the front porch. She peered at the door uneasily. A huge brass dragon's head was attached with the doorbell embedded in its eye. When she pressed it, the camera above immediately swivelled to focus on her. *Wow, talk about paranoid.* She was tempted to give it a wave but desisted—Ms Jamieson-Ford probably didn't have a sense of humour. A moment later, the door swung ajar with a creak.

A short matronly woman in a floury apron stood on the threshold, gazing at her in surprise. "Can I help you?" she asked.

Daisy let out a relieved sigh. The woman looked pleasant and unremarkable. "Hi. Daisy Parker to see Ms Jamieson-Ford."

"Is she expecting you?"

Daisy rocked back on her heels. "This is Tuesday, isn't it?"

"Yes."

"Then I have an appointment at nine."

"I'm sorry. I wasn't told to expect you. Come along then. She's in her office."

Daisy trotted along behind her up the hallway, at a loss to understand why Lindsey hadn't mentioned her appointment to her staff. Then all thoughts of her mysterious client disappeared as she passed an open doorway. She stared, fascinated. It was another world: the enormous room was like something out of a sci-fi movie. The whole impression was of space, with lounge chairs perched on tubular legs, oddly shaped lamps hanging from the ceiling and an entertainment unit that could have been on the deck of the Starship Enterprise.

On the far wall were images of spectacular land and seascapes, 3D holograms that slowly rolled over continuously like desktop images on a computer. To the side, a large curved ultramodern staircase wound up to the next floor. But most fascinating were the robots: one, humanoid in shape and size, was dusting the bookcase, while two small silver metal dogs zipped in and out of the furniture.

Unfortunately, she couldn't dawdle for a proper inspection for the woman who answered the door was waving impatiently for her to follow. "That's a private room. If I had known you were coming I would have shut the door. Come along. If your meeting's at nine, then you'd better hurry. You're already late and Ms Jamieson-Ford is very strict about time."

Daisy glanced at her watch. 9:06. *For shit sake!* Six minutes late and the help was in a tizz. Lindsey must be a time freak, which just narrowed down the eligibility field by half. Not many men wanted to be held to strict timetables. Women were mostly pliant, but from her experience males usually liked to be the boss, which definitely included *when* they did things.

There was no time for further speculation, for the door swung open and she was ushered into the room. Daisy sniffed appreciatively as she stepped inside. The air was tinged with the scents of leather and polish, which immediately recalled familiar images of cosy nooks in academic libraries.

This room was entirely different from the lounge she had just passed. While it was evident that most of the ground floor had been gutted and redesigned, the study had been left in what she presumed was its original state. It was a large room, the walls polished wood, with a bookcase filled with thick hardcover books—she guessed technical—set against one side. A vintage burgundy velvet armchair and love seat sat with a small coffee table on the other side. Technical drawings were tacked to a freestanding display board against the wall.

In front of an ornately carved arched back window, a solid mahogany desk dominated the room. Everything was perfectly in place on the top: paper, files, phone, and silver laptop. A gold-leafed desk set was impeccably aligned, while three pens and six graphite pencils marched in a straight row across the polished wood.

The woman in the high-backed leather chair behind the desk looked imposing, with a long unsmiling face, a thin straight aristocratic nose, and penetrating sharp eyes. Her brown hair was tied back in a tight bun, while a pair of thick black glasses sat on the end of her nose. Her dark grey jacket was spread open to reveal a plain white shirt buttoned up to the neck. Daisy went immediately into marriage mode—there was a bit to do here if she wanted to snag her a husband.

Lindsey's expression was neither welcoming nor discouraging, though Daisy knew she was being sized up. She waited for her host to make the first move. Finally, Lindsey pointed to the seat and said in a low polished accent, "Please take a seat, Ms Parker." Then with a smile, she turned to the small woman in the apron. "Thank you, Bernie."

"I'll be in the kitchen if you *need* me, Lindsey."

Daisy rolled her eyes at the emphasis on the word. Geez, did she look like some crazy psycho? She sniggered to herself—or maybe Cruella De Ville, here to pinch those little robot dogs? She waited until the cook disappeared out the door before she thrust her hand over the desk. "Hi, Ms Jamieson-Ford, I'm Daisy Parker."

It was waved away with an impatient flick. "There's no need for formalities. Call me Lindsey." She peered up at the clock on the wall. "You're late. If we're going to do business, then I expect you to be on time in the future."

Daisy blinked. Talk about an obsessive grouch. She'd have to lighten up or nobody would want her. Daisy made a point of studying her vintage Rolex before stating firmly, "Only by seven minutes. Your turnoff was hard to find…you haven't a sign. But be rest assured I'll be early in future." With a cheery smile, she launched into professional mode. "Now let's get down to business. Is there anything you'd like to know about the Marigold Agency before we begin discussing what you're looking for in a partner?"

Lindsey formed her fingers into a steeple and raked her eyes up over Daisy's face to rest on her hair. "Exactly how old are you? I was expecting to deal with someone more mature. What happened to that pleasant-looking woman on the brochure?"

"She's the agency's business manager, and for your information I'll be twenty-nine shortly."

"That old? You look about twenty." She gave a shrug. "I guess if you do the job properly, it doesn't matter what you look like."

Daisy curbed her temper. She was the boss of this show, not this antisocial woman. "You're right," she said briskly, "it doesn't matter at all because I've got the runs on the board to prove it. And lucky me for looking so young. Some people…" she swept her eyes slowly over Lindsey's face, "some people age far too quickly."

Lindsey actually smiled—slightly. "Tell me about yourself. I like to know the people with whom I have to deal," she said.

"We have an excellent reputation for helping clients. I have a master's degree in anthropology and started the business three years ago."

"That's impressive. I imagine your studies were the basis for this venture. Very innovative."

Daisy couldn't help feeling a little chuffed. She imagined praise was doled out in very small portions by this woman. She had learned from the beginning that clients didn't really care about her education, she was simply a matchmaker to them. It did give her ego a boost to have her academic achievements acknowledged. "I believe finding a mate can be achieved scientifically if a man and a woman are genetically suited."

"That's interesting. It's something I'd like to talk to you about in depth later. It would help in programming artificial intelligence. It never really entered my head to work with an anthropologist, but it makes sense," said Lindsey with a nod. "How do you start the process of matchmaking? I imagine you just can't pluck two people off the street and match them up."

"I've found that usually where there is attraction, there is a basis for compatibility."

"But not in all cases."

"No, not all," replied Daisy. "Lust is sometimes mistaken for something deeper, which is why I urge my clients to go through a courtship process."

"A bit old-fashioned isn't it. What about those who just want a permanent sex partner?"

"I've nothing against anyone living that way, in fact if that's what you want I say go for it. Is that what this is all about, Lindsey?"

Something flashed in her eyes—hurt, or anger or maybe it was fear—Daisy couldn't make it out, but whatever it was, it turned the eyes into sparkling pools of swirling colour. Daisy stared mesmerized. The eyes were extraordinary. The irises were a deep violet, shot through with flecks of gold and pale pink like facets of an amethyst. There was no doubt they were Lindsey's best feature.

Under the scrutiny, Lindsey shuffled in her seat. "Of course it's not the reason I'm employing you. Sex is a commodity you can buy like anything else in the world. I want a loving spouse, someone who cares about me. I thought I explained that in my letter."

Something about how she said those words about sex being a commodity and the way she was fidgeting with the paper clip on the desk, sent whistles through Daisy's brain. Somewhere in the past, Lindsey had paid for sex. She put it out of her mind—it was none of her business. "I know you did, but I have to ask all my prospective clients that question. It reinforces the end objective…to find true love. Now the first thing is to fill out a detailed profile." She took a folder out of her bag and handed it across. "I want you to write it by hand. The computer lacks the deep personal touch. It will take you some time, so I need you to do it when you're alone and I'll collect it next time we meet."

"How detailed?"

"It's very comprehensive, but if there are any things you're uncomfortable with I want you to leave them out. This isn't an exercise in Chinese water torture. It will help me understand who you are and what you expect from a relationship. It's amazing if you write it down how things become clearer. For example, some people want a partner at home keeping the household running, while others might love someone to share their workload. It's an individual thing that most couples sort out through compromise."

Daisy watched the expressions flicker over Lindsey's face as she thought it over. She had an interesting face, not pretty but intriguing. With a modern haircut, subtle makeup and more stylish clothes, she could look far less severe. As there was no question of money, it wouldn't be necessary to have off-the-rack clothes. An upmarket designer could do wonders for her. She'd have prospective husbands lined up to meet her. "So, do we go ahead?" she asked.

"I'm in."

"Good," said Daisy with a satisfied hum. With access to unlimited funds, this was going to be a cinch. An academic type would suit her down to the ground, and they were as easy as pie to handle. So unworldly. "We can do a bit of the groundwork today. Firstly, give me the profile of the man you think would be your perfect match."

The paper clip bent sharply in Lindsey's fingers as she averted her eyes. "I want a wife, not a husband."

CHAPTER FOUR

At her announcement, Lindsey expected the matchmaker to run. Instead, Daisy looked stupidly at her for a second before she broke into a chuckle. "Well, I wasn't expecting that one."

Lindsey shrank inside, fighting the nausea that hit when she was out of her comfort zone. And she was certainly out of that safe place now. Daisy Parker was daunting with her bubbly personality and pert appearance, a social butterfly who no doubt bonded with clients over exotic cocktails in trendy pub lounges. Everything Lindsey was not and didn't do. And now Daisy was laughing at her. When Lindsey first searched the web for a marriage broker, the woman on the brochure had drawn her like a magnet to the Marigold Matchmaking Agency. Her face radiated warmth and understanding, something Lindsey needed desperately.

The words seemed to stick to her palate before she managed to spit them out, "You're mocking me." She hurriedly scribbled out a cheque and pushed it across the desk. "That should be enough to compensate for your time. I'll buzz Bernice to show you out."

Daisy's face paled as she looked down at the cheque. "No… no…no, I didn't intend to insult you. You took me by surprise." She swept her hand through her hair and tugged a curl. "Oh God…I'm making a mess of this. I'd never laugh at you, Lindsey. If you want a woman to share your life, I'll find her." She slid the leaf back across. "Here, please…please take this back. Give me another chance."

Lindsey hesitated. Here was the perfect excuse to pull out, but if she did, she knew she would never have the courage to approach another agency. It had taken all her willpower to write the letter. She had no choice—it was Daisy or nobody. "I suppose I could," she said grudgingly.

"Thank you. I really am sorry. I didn't mean to offend you. Let's begin again shall we?"

Daisy looked so perturbed that Lindsey felt a pang of remorse. "I'm sorry too. I guess I overreacted." Then added anxiously, "Is it going to be a problem?"

"If you mean a problem because you're a lesbian, then absolutely not. Love is love. If you meant a problem to find you a wife, then no, it won't be. I'll just have to modify some of my teaching methods."

"You're going to *teach* me?"

"Oh yes. Everything that's worth having needs to be learned, and earned," said Daisy with a smile. "I want you to fill out the questionnaire before we start getting down to business. We'll spend the rest of the session today with an informal chat. Nothing deep and meaningful—just getting to know each other. Tell me about your work."

Lindsey let out a breath, pleased at last to be in familiar territory. "It's probably easier to give you a tour of the lab and explain things as we go." She gave a small cough. "However, there is a requirement if you're interested—you need to sign a confidential disclosure statement. Most of my projects are highly confidential."

"That's no problem. I'd love to see firsthand what you do."

Lindsey pulled out a form from the top drawer and pushed it across for Daisy to sign. "We've been working on artificial skin for prosthetic limbs and a device to link them to the brain. Our engineers are also designing a lightweight robotic suit to give mobility to the disabled."

"That sounds like exciting work. Are they near public release?"

"The skin...yes, and I've built a power unit that enables the person to control the movements of his or her artificial part. It's a tiny computer embedded in the skull, but with technology constantly changing there are always avenues for improvement. The suit is a work in progress for the team."

When they reached the end of the hallway, Lindsey pressed her thumb against the security keyboard and the steel door swung open. She was pleased to hear the gasp of surprise spring from her companion as they stepped into the lab. Her workspace was impressive, but the robot against the wall seemed to capture Daisy's complete attention as she knew it would.

"Wow!" Daisy gasped. "Now that really is something. It looks human."

Though she was determined to be nonchalant, Lindsey couldn't help feeling a spurt of pride. This project was her special baby. "You can examine her if you like."

"Her?"

"I think of them as part of my family," said Lindsey with a self-conscious cough. "I've made some robot animals, but she is only the second humanoid machine I've built."

"I saw as I came in. It looks like a man. So life-like."

"I am one of the leaders in the field, though I haven't shared this work publicly as yet or let anyone examine these prototypes."

"Of course." Daisy ran her hands over the robot. "It's... excuse me...*she's* covered in a material that feels like skin. Firm yet softly resilient. And the face, the hair, the eyes...she's bloody brilliant."

"There was a lot of delicate laser work in the small parts like the retina, hair follicles, and teeth. A time-consuming process but the result was well worth the effort," Lindsey added proudly.

"She's warm," said Daisy with a delighted grin, "like a real person."

"Her power unit maintains the body temperature as well as controlling the brain. I'm refining the central nervous system with electromagnetic patterns so she can mimic emotions with facial expressions."

"Like smiling and frowning?"

"Yes."

"I never imagined robotics had advanced to this extent."

"They don't belong to science fiction anymore. The first types were heavy, built with metal or a metal alloy. And though humanised, they were made to be non-threatening by quirky character traits and awkward movements."

"You're right," said Daisy with a smile. "Although in more modern films they tend to look much more lifelike, as in *Blade Runner.*"

"We are a vain species, are we not, to want something artificial to be in our image?"

"No," said Daisy with a quick shake of her head. "As an anthropologist, I can answer that one. It's not vanity, it's comfort in the familiar. People don't like anything too creepy or out of the norm. They accept things better if they feel they can trust something. Also, the general population responds better if they can communicate in a normal way, such as speech or arm waving." She looked at Lindsey curiously. "Have you safeguards in place in case they run amok?"

"You *have* been watching too many movies," said Lindsey with a chuckle. "Their movements only exist in conjunction with their brains, which are simply programmed computers."

"They can't learn anything other than the software they've been given?"

Lindsey dipped her hands into her coat pockets, careful how she answered. No one knew yet what she had accomplished with artificial intelligence. "If you're asking if they can think for themselves outside of their programming sphere…then no. But they have the capacity to be taught some complicated tasks like cooking."

"Ha! I bet it can't cook my mother's cheese soufflé. It always flops on me. Is this your only lab?"

"No, it's my private one. Our main facility is in the city. Once a week I commute to the building. I do lots of the designs, but we do have a team of engineers working on various projects."

"But not these robots?"

"No. They're special and I'm not yet ready to share."

Lindsey eyed Daisy as she poked around the lab for a further five minutes. She couldn't believe she had invited this stranger into her inner sanctum without a qualm. It was something she never did—in fact the only other people to have been there were Bernice and the most trusted members of her staff. Industrial espionage was a very real issue. But she had wanted to prove a point to this cavalier matchmaker. She needed to demonstrate that regardless of her personal hang-ups, she wasn't a failure at anything else.

When Daisy reached the open computer, Lindsey made a point of glancing at her watch. "As much as I'd like to continue our talk, I'm afraid I have to get back to work. When shall we meet again?"

"The day after tomorrow, if that suits you. That'll give you time to fill out your profile. Nine o'clock again?"

Lindsey winced as her anxiety flowed back. She hoped it didn't have too many intimate questions. "That'll be fine. I'll see you then," she said with a hint of gruffness. "I'll show you out."

After Daisy departed, she returned to her office, her mind reeling with images from the past that invariably rolled when she was stressed. She sat down in the chair, hunched against the chill wind of memory.

* * *

2004

Lindsey learned the hard way that rebellion came at a price.

At her twenty-first birthday party, the seeds of discontent that had been simmering for years finally sprouted. Up to that point, she had followed her mother's directives to the letter. How could she not? She had been told often enough that her mother's taste and ambition were far superior to hers. Ellen Jamieson-Ford had scrupulously mapped out her only child's life, from the clothes on her back to her circle of friends. Right from the time she could walk, Lindsey had been meticulously trained: her deportment was exquisite, her speech impeccable and her manners flawless. Unfortunately, she took too much after her big hearty father to be the delicate princess her mother longed for.

Her early teen years had been a nightmare. Gawky, bespectacled, her teeth caged in orthodontic braces and body yet to grow into her lanky legs, she was the proverbial ugly duckling. Then, contrary to the fairy tales, when she acquired breasts, straight white teeth and corrective surgery for her squint, she hadn't blossomed into a beautiful swan as everyone had hoped. She remained her father's daughter, a fact she was constantly reminded of by her mother. It didn't matter how brilliantly Lindsey excelled at her studies, she knew she would never be anything but a disappointment.

She accepted most things from her mother but eventually balked at her meddling in her love life. She hated that she insisted on choosing her dates. The most persistent of the socially acceptable suitors was Martin Hickman, a third-year law student. Her skin crawled when he touched her.

As the time approached for the first guest to arrive at her party, she said defiantly, "I detest Martin, Mum. I'm calling it off tonight."

Ellen barely spared her a glance. She replied quietly but forcefully, "You know his parents are friends of ours. I expect you to give the young man a chance."

Lindsey could not stop the hot sting of tears. She knew that voice too well. It wasn't a request but a royal command. At the imperious tone, something foreign in Lindsey stirred. It was her birthday and she was going to do what she damn well pleased.

She glared at her mother, a biting retort on the tip of her tongue. With an effort, she held her silence. Confrontation would only aggravate their already precarious relationship. Her mother in this mood was not to be trifled with.

After the final twist to her elaborate hairstyle, Ellen Jamieson-Ford peered into the mirror. "There," she said with satisfied nod, "that should do very well."

Lindsey studied the perfect coiffure for a second before she turned on her heels. On her way down the hallway to the grand stairway, she glanced at the grandfather clock. Six fifteen—the guests were due soon. As she descended to the ground floor, she was more conscious than usual of the grandeur of their mansion, with its panelled oak walls, tiered chandelier glittering over the spacious foyer, and intricately carved balustrades of the staircase. The ostentation didn't sit well with her personality. She was much happier in the kitchen talking to Bernice, their cook, than attending the frequent dinner parties at the long dining table.

Excitement and anxiety continued to swirl inside her as she paced the floor. Her friends were coming to the party and she was determined to have a good time. When the butler announced the first guest, she gulped down a glass of champagne before joining her mother in the hallway to welcome them. She balanced on the balls of her feet to relieve the boredom while she greeted her parents' stuffy friends. They were always the first to arrive. Soon the younger set began to trickle in, and finally, her best friend Kirsty appeared.

"Am I glad to see you, Kirsty," Lindsey murmured as she kissed her on the cheek. She gazed at her fondly. Kirsty was a standout, with spun-gold hair that framed an adorable pixie face and tumbled freely over creamy white shoulders. It was no wonder her hand was looped through the arm of the hottest boy in town, the captain of the rugby team.

"Happy birthday, Lin," Kirsty said and pulled a young woman forward by the hand. "This is my cousin Amy. She's on holidays and staying with us, so I asked her to come. I hope you don't mind?"

The air felt suddenly hot and sticky when Lindsey gazed at Amy. She was tall, about her height, slim with the long lithe muscles of a cat, dressed in a form-fitting black top with a turtleneck. Everything about her was appealing: her attractive spunky looks, her short spiky black hair and the confident way she held herself. Lindsey's heart gave a flutter as their gazes locked. The irises were a warm hazel colour, like autumn leaves. Amy gave a wink and grin, which made Lindsey feel as if she couldn't breathe. She pulled herself together and murmured, "Of course not. More the merrier. Come on in. Our crowd's out the back."

As she led them through the crush, Lindsey took another glass of champagne from a tray. She was going to celebrate whether her mother approved or not. Outside under the starry night, the younger revellers had already settled around the bar. When they stepped onto the terrace, Martin immediately appeared at her side and lazily threw his arm over her shoulders. As she shrugged it off irritably, she noticed Amy smile. She smiled back, unable to take her eyes off her. Amy was gorgeous, with the clinging top showing every contour of her small pert breasts.

Lindsey swallowed hard as a vivid image flashed into her head. The two of them were naked, pressed together on a soft bed in a dark room.

Trembling, she felt an exciting tingle spread between her legs. She went hot. This was her most guarded secret, why she disliked being touched by boys. Then when Amy took her empty glass and their fingers brushed together, the light cool touch on her skin felt like whispered words. From then on, Lindsey was lost in a haze of desire. As the bar became more cluttered and thick with noise, she was aware of nothing but the stunning girl in the turtleneck top.

Through the loud music and the babble of voices, she heard Amy murmur in her ear, "Wanna get out of here? My bike's outside."

Lindsey swallowed the last of the champagne in the flute in one gulp. "You bet," she whispered back.

"Come on then."

After Amy vanished down the stairs to the garden, she discreetly followed at a distance. A skitter of panic flared when she glimpsed her father on the front patio talking to an elderly couple, but they disappeared before she rounded the side of the house. Amongst the parked cars, Amy was already perched on a motorbike, a shiny blue helmet nestled between her thighs.

She handed it to Lindsey. "I always carry an extra one. You never know who wants a ride. Put it on and hop aboard."

The memories of that night still lingered as if they only happened yesterday. The wild ride on the back of the bike, her arms tightly around Amy's waist, her breasts pressed into her back. The first feel of a woman's lips, so soft she almost cried. How her body had melted into the embrace like candle wax touched by a flame. The feel of the slim fingers as they slipped into the moisture pooled between her legs and the exquisite pleasure as the pads skimmed over her clitoris. And finally, the roaring in her blood as her orgasm crashed through. She knew instinctively in the maelstrom of sensation that Amy had followed her into the sublime bliss.

But after they left the beach the memories were dark, shrouded in a horror that still haunted her. It was a removalist truck, they said…coming around the bend too fast in the middle of the road. After the excruciating agony on impact, all she could remember was the smell of disinfectant, white sheets, pain. A ventilator tube filling her mouth, a monitor attached to her chest. Pale faces staring down at her as the sound of *beep… beep…beep* echoed through the hospital room.

CHAPTER FIVE

"How did it go?"

Daisy gave a noncommittal shrug in reply to Allison's query as she hung her coat on the rack. "It's not going to be easy."

"You didn't like her?"

"It's not that."

Allison stopped typing and gave her a questioning glance. "Care to elaborate."

Daisy attended the coffee machine to give her time to formulate an answer. There was no doubt that Lindsey was complicated. She was tough, egocentric, very smart, but underneath the cold exterior there was also a hint of vulnerability. On first sight, she appeared a battle-ax. It wasn't simply her hairstyle or her severely tailored dark suit, but the look in her eyes, the set of her body, the twist of her mouth. Then she smiled and she became immediately softer, more human.

The scientist who showed her through the laboratory was an entirely different person from the brittle woman in the office. If Daisy wasn't mistaken, there was something attractive hidden beneath the façade, though she was going to have to drag it screaming into the open. Lindsey wasn't going to be a pliable subject. "Just let me say that we didn't exactly start off on the right foot. She was very prickly. I smoothed it over, but this is going to be a challenge. Lindsey has an extremely strong personality."

"You've had difficult clients before and it hasn't fazed you."

"Not like her. She's a very smart cookie. Super intelligent actually."

"So? Find her a super smart man."

"Ah," said Daisy. "There lies the problem. She wants a wife."

Allison sat up straighter. "Really? We haven't had a lesbian as a client before." She tilted her head with a sly grin. "This is right up your alley, you being of the same persuasion an' all."

A groan escaped from Daisy. "You're kidding me. People are people whatever their orientation, and she's not exactly Miss Congeniality. Then there's the fact lesbians aren't running around in abundance out there, so options are more limited. I just hope she's not too fussy and someone clicks with her. I'd say she relates to machines better than with people. She's even built a surrogate robotic family, one that does exactly what she wants."

"She sounds rather odd."

"She's…well…different. Not unlikeable though. I have a feeling I'm going to have to spend a lot of time with her, so put those new applications on hold until I sort her out. Now I'd better get to work with our other clients. Did Alan get back to you about his date with Sandy?"

Allison gave a thumbs-up. "All's going well there. They're getting on like a house on fire."

"Excellent. I knew they would suit each other. Okay, I'm going in to plan a strategy for Lindsey."

Once entrenched behind her desk, Daisy took out the Kentucky Fried Chicken box and began to munch through the chilli wrap and fries. With a last lick to clean the mayonnaise off her fingers, she wiped her hand with a tissue then downloaded the file. After another quick perusal, she set up a new page with the heading: *Lindsey Jamieson-Ford Project.*

On the first line, she typed *Personal appearance.* Then she added some pertinent points, excited that the budget was unlimited. Reinventing Lindsey was going to be fun.

> • *Hair (Make an appointment with the Boris salon's personal stylist)*
> • *Clothes (Contact designer dressmaker Nicolle Jane re fittings)*
> • *Makeup (get a range of cosmetics sent over from Chanel)* plus *a session with Andrea Ming their chief makeup artist*

Daisy clicked the save button and logged out. That would be a start—she couldn't really go on much further until she'd read Lindsey's profile. She didn't have a clue what type of woman she preferred, or whether she saw herself as a top or bottom, or if it didn't matter anyway. Finding a perfect match for Lindsey wasn't going to be as simple as pairing her with a man. Lesbians were more complicated—so many different types. As well, there were bisexual women who made equally as loving partners in a same-sex relationship, but they came with hurdles to jump over too.

After phone calls to shore up the appointments, she swung back in her chair to plan her course of action. She needed to snag an invitation to the Beauvoir, the most exclusive women's club in the city. With a hefty joining fee and then a yearly subscription of ten thousand dollars, their exclusive membership was made up of wealthy women at the top of their fields, many of whom were gay. She had been taken there once, entirely blown away by the experience. Unfortunately, her date, Carmen, hadn't impressed her nearly as much as the club had.

Carmen was one of the country's top models, a striking, slender woman with coal-black hair, large heavily fringed eyes, exotic high-slashing cheekbones and a dreadfully condescending attitude. One date with her had been enough for Daisy. As well as being annoyingly toffee-nosed, Carmen hadn't had the wit to realize Daisy wasn't interested in going to bed with her on the first date. She had declined an invitation to repeat dinner, which hadn't been taken well by the supermodel. Carmen's chagrin at the snub was fuelled she suspected, not so much as her desire for Daisy but rather that anyone could say no to her. However, since she was the only avenue she had to get Lindsey into the Beauvoir, she would have to eat humble pie.

Although she didn't intend to introduce Lindsey for at least three weeks, she figured it would be better to line it up now so she knew where she stood. Squaring her shoulders, she reached for the phone to invite Carmen for a drink. It would only be polite to ask the woman face-to-face for the favour, though she doubted she'd refuse considering how important Lindsey was.

* * *

Carmen, her long manicured fingers wrapped around the stem of a martini glass, was already perched on a barstool when Daisy entered the Hilton lounge. It was a pity, Daisy mused, that her personality didn't match her appearance. The model looked all class. Her dress was tastefully elegant, and with it, she wore a single strand of pearls, earrings to match and a slim gold watch. All very discreet and exclusive. Her black hair was swept off her neck, secured with a gold clip that was probably worth as much as the Marigold's monthly takings.

Carmen raised her glass in welcome. "I was early, so I started without you. What will you have?"

"A vodka and orange, thanks."

Once the bartender moved off with the order, Carmen skimmed her gaze over her slowly. "So, to what do I owe this honour? I thought you gave me the brush-off."

"It wasn't like that," said Daisy awkwardly. The woman had a knack of annoying her. She wished she'd tried another avenue to get into the damn club. "I told you we were very busy and I couldn't find time to date."

"Hmmm, I think that was just an excuse not to see me again."

At the snarky tone, Daisy quickly slipped off the chair. "This isn't going to work. I'm sorry I…"

"No…no. Don't go. I'm just annoyed you wouldn't go out with me again. I like you Daisy…a lot. You know that."

Daisy made a vague gesture with her fingers. "I really am run off my feet with the business, Carmen. I made a conscious decision to put my personal life on hold until I get a handle on things."

"Then why did you ask me for a drink?"

"Well…um…the fact is…I promised Lindsey, a very good friend of my aunt's, that I would try to show her the Beauvoir Club. I'd be super grateful if we could come as your guests one night. Not immediately…perhaps next month if you could manage it."

"Lindsey?"

"Lindsey Jamieson-Ford."

"The principal of LJF Robotics? My word girl, you *are* stepping up in the world. I'd be delighted to take her there." Carmen ran a fingertip lightly down her arm and her mouth quirked into a seductive smile. "Just make sure you come too."

Daisy grimaced. Why wouldn't the woman give it up? They didn't suit each other at all; their tastes were definitely not compatible. Carmen was a glitz and glamour queen, while she was a down-to-earth pragmatist. Oil on water. "I'll be there. Now drink up and I'll shout the next round. I'll get a plate of nibbles as well."

Surprisingly, the evening turned out much more pleasantly than she had anticipated. Carmen on her best behaviour was charming, with sly wit relating amusing anecdotes of the modelling industry. When they rose to go, they shared a hug goodbye. Daisy had to admit the scent of the delightful perfume swirling through her senses and the feel of a soft body was wonderful after months without the touch of a woman. As Daisy watched her sway away on her extra-high heels, she wondered idly if Lindsey would be interested in the model. She turned the key with a snap, cranky she'd even considered it. Carmen would eat the poor woman alive.

CHAPTER SIX

Lindsey stared at the fourth page of the questionnaire. The first questions had been relatively straightforward: her childhood, her family home, what she had achieved in life. Without a qualm, she hadn't mentioned her mother's domination or the accident. Instead, she'd focused blandly on her father, their garden, her studies and her business. The happy memories.

But this next page was far too personal, but too direct to gloss over. The sneaky matchmaker expected her to give in-depth details of her former relationships, including how she related to her parents. A total invasion of privacy. As much as she tried to ignore the questions, they brought back things she had tucked away in the darkest recesses of her mind. Years of therapy hadn't entirely alleviated her shuddering nausea when she had to relive those times.

Helpless against it, she pressed a fist to her forehead, riding out the roller coaster of fear that one day the world would see her as she was—unloved and unwanted by her mother, afraid of intimacy and half a woman. Who would want to love her then?

With an effort, she took a deep breath and then another as she had been taught. The panic faded until she could again focus on the page. The pain turned into anger. Determinedly, she tore the offending sheet out of the file and methodically ripped it to pieces. Her past relationships weren't up for discussion. They were none of Ms Nosy Parker's business.

When she flipped the second to last sheet over, she sighed with relief. Here was the question she wanted to answer and nothing too personal. *What do you want in a partner?*

With bold strokes, she began to write in dot points.

- *A mature woman between 34 and 42. (A little older wouldn't matter though)*
- *Kind+ considerate of my work hours*
- *Some knowledge of electronics/mathematics or at least an academic*
- *Moderate drinker*
- *Good time management skills (always to be on time)*
- *Tidy*
- *A homebody*
- *Someone who eats nutritionally balanced meals (no fast food)*

Lindsey chewed the end of the pen as she reread the list, then moved "homebody" up higher. The last person she wanted was someone expecting a fabulous social life because she had money. With a final look, she nodded, satisfied. That would do for the time being. Tomorrow, after discussion with Daisy, she might think of something else. She turned to the last page. There was only one question: *Why do you want a soulmate?*

She had to be honest here. It was a simple answer and the only reason she had forced herself to write to the matchmaking service.

She wrote *I'm lonely.*

* * *

Lindsey paced around her office, with almost painful anticipation for Daisy to reappear. She had handed over her questionnaire as soon as their meeting had begun, but instead of waiting until she had left the estate to examine the contents as good manners dictated, Daisy had immediately disappeared without a by your leave to the side terrace to read it. Lindsey felt nervous. In the cold light of day when she reviewed what she'd written, she could see there were huge gaps in the whole thing. She hadn't included anything remotely private or confidential. Little to reveal anything of substance.

To ward off the jitters, she hit the intercom button to the kitchen. "Bring us morning tea in ten minutes, please Bernie."

"Will do. I baked muffins this morning."

When Daisy appeared five minutes later, instead of taking the chair at the desk, she made a beeline for the lounge chairs. "Come and sit over here with me, Lindsey. It'll be more comfortable for a friendly chat. I don't like too much formality."

With no excuse at hand, Lindsey reluctantly settled into a chair opposite. She knew perfectly well what Daisy was doing. By making her give up her seat of power behind the desk, they were now on a level playing field. She forced herself to rest backward with legs crossed. Daisy merely smiled, but the glint in her eye had Lindsey worried. She could sense beneath the friendly expression the woman was annoyed.

"The flowers are pretty," Daisy began. "I had no idea you had such a glorious garden around the side."

"I like gardening," replied Lindsey warily. "It gets me out in the fresh air and I enjoy growing beautiful things."

"You've done a great job. Have you had the house long?"

"About ten years."

A sharp knock caused Lindsey to jerk upright. Embarrassed, she sat down quickly when Bernice appeared at the door with a tray mobile.

"Morning tea, ladies. Fresh blueberry muffins."

"That sounds divine," exclaimed Daisy. "I'm glad I only had a cup of coffee before I left."

"You may go, Bernie. I'll pour," said Lindsey.

"No…no, stay please Bernice, and have something with us," said Daisy. "Sit next to me. I'd love to get to know you."

"That's very kind of you, dear. It'll be nice to have a chat. We don't see many people."

Lindsey nearly snarled. The damn woman was interfering with her staff. When Bernice looked at her for confirmation, she could do nothing but nod pleasantly.

"Have you been here long?" asked Daisy as she buttered the muffins.

Bernice smiled. "I've been with Lindsey since she was born."

"Oh, my, you must love her very much to come with her when she bought her own home."

"She's like my own child."

"And of course, she needed help after the accident," Daisy added, then gave an appreciative groan when she bit into the muffin.

"Yes," said Bernice. "They were hard times until Lindsey could adjust. The loss of…"

Lindsey quickly clattered her cup sharply onto the saucer. To her immense relief, Bernice stopped blabbering out her private business. It had been a close call.

Lindsey glowered at Daisy. The hide of her—clearly, she had looked up old newspaper clippings and was fishing.

"Oh dear, I am going on. Would you like some sugar?" Bernice continued, a little more subdued.

"Yes please." Daisy popped a heaped teaspoon into her cup. "I have a sweet tooth."

"Too much sugar in your diet increases the risk of type two diabetes, cardiovascular problems and hypertension," muttered Lindsey.

Daisy stirred vigorously. "Thank you for those pearls of wisdom, Lindsey. I'm sure Bernice serves great nutritionally balanced meals. Lucky you for having such a wonderful cook."

Bernice beamed. "Thank you, Daisy. I love my kitchen. Do you enjoy cooking?"

"Like it—yes. Am I good at it—no," said Daisy with a laugh. "I often resort to takeaways when I'm busy."

"Then you aren't married, dear?"

Lindsey leaned forward in her chair, keen to hear the answer as a blush pinked Daisy's cheeks.

"No. I'm single."

"Never mind. I'm sure a pretty girl like you won't have any trouble finding a husband."

Daisy opened her mouth then closed it again. She merely nodded.

Lindsey relaxed back smugly. So—Daisy hadn't managed to find a partner for herself. How very satisfying to see the self-assured matchmaker off balance. Now she knows how it feels. They chattered on about herbs and recipes until Bernice rose to gather up the cups. "I'd better get back to work. It was lovely to meet you, Daisy."

"Oh, I'll see you again. I'll be in and out in the next few weeks working with Lindsey."

"You're a company employee? I didn't realize."

"A consultant. I'll be helping here for a while."

As soon as they were alone, Daisy turned to eye Lindsey. "You haven't told her, have you?"

"No. And I expect you to be discreet. This business is solely between us, no one else."

"We maintain strict client confidentiality. Does she know you're a lesbian?"

"Yes. I told her when she came to live with me. She's been very good to me and I didn't want to keep something like that from her."

Daisy lifted a hand to toy with a curl. "Well at least that won't come as a surprise. But you do realize don't you, that when you have your makeover, she's going to get a shock?"

Lindsey stared at her, alarmed. "What makeover?"

"The one starting tomorrow. I've made an appointment at eleven thirty for the Boris Salon's top hairdresser to style your hair."

"I didn't agree to that."

"If you want help, Lindsey, then please do what I ask. I really would like you to be reasonable about what I suggest. I have a lot of experience and a great success rate. I had to go ahead and make the appointment...he's hard to get into. I only snagged the appointment because there was a cancellation, but I can change it if it doesn't suit."

"I suppose the time is okay if you insist that I must have a haircut. Is it the only thing I have to endure?"

"Good heavens, no," exclaimed Daisy with a look that dared her to argue. "You're going to have a new wardrobe, new makeup and after the fashion statement is complete, the tuition will begin."

Lindsey bristled, prepared for battle. The moment had all the makings of a High Noon, but Daisy defused the situation adroitly by saying with a soft pleading voice, "I really would appreciate if you'd cooperate. I do this with all my clients. It's amazing how much confidence a makeover can give."

"Oh, all right. If I must, I must. How long will this business take?"

"I know you're a busy woman, so if we want to do the preliminary work quickly, then I suggest we meet every day until you're comfortable about going out socially. I'm putting myself at your disposal."

"I'm prepared to put my work aside for the time being too." Lindsey's gaze latched onto the folder poking out of Daisy's carry-bag. Curiosity got the better of her. "You haven't mentioned my questionnaire. Aren't we going to go through it together?"

Daisy gave an enigmatic half smile. "No."

"Oh? Then why did I have to fill it out?"

"I wanted to know about you."

"Well, some things are private. There weren't any lurid details you obviously wanted to hear," remarked Lindsey testily.

"On the contrary, it told me a lot. Now I do have a question that I really want you to answer."

"It's obviously not on the questionnaire."

"No. This is about your preference. It's nothing too explicit, but I need to know when I introduce you around."

"Go ahead then."

Daisy leaned over and took her right hand. "What kind of woman are you attracted to?"

At the feel of the touch, Lindsey's muscles tightened. As subtly as she could, she eased her fingers from Daisy's grasp. Then she blinked to focus on the question. "What kind of woman? Didn't I put that in my profile?"

"No, this is your sexual preference. What kind turns you on? An athlete? Butch? Femme? Political? In the closet, or out and proud? Do you want to be the boss in a relationship? Who is in your fantasies?"

Lindsey's jaw sagged, and heat blossomed into her cheeks. "I...I don't really have a preference. Um...no...wait. That's not strictly true. I like women who are on the feminine side...with curves." She fluttered her gaze over Daisy's torso and down her legs. "You know...your type of body...with nice breasts and hips. Older though."

Daisy gave a wry smile. "Oh, me when I'm grown up."

"Yes, but," she added more firmly, "I'm also attracted to the mind, if you know what I mean. I'll never be happy with someone who is vacuous or ditzy."

"I know exactly what you mean there. Do you prefer to wear dresses or pants?"

"I prefer pants, though I don't mind my suits with skirts or a simple-cut evening dress. I detest anything frilly."

"Good. That will be enough for today." Daisy handed her a slip of paper. "Here's the hair stylist's address. Will that time suit you?"

"That'll be fine."

"Great. Do you want me to pick you up?"

"No. I'll drive in. I employ a chauffeur. Joe also keeps the maintenance on the house in order."

"I'll see you tomorrow then. There's one last thing before I go, Lindsey. I want you to give me a hug."

Lindsey froze, unable to think of a way out. She hadn't touched anyone but Trisha intimately for years. With a swallow, she edged forward and gave her a tentative squeeze. Before she could get away, Daisy pulled her closer until they were pressed together. After a last firm clasp, she murmured, "There. That wasn't so bad, was it? You're going to have to get used to touching people, Lindsey, if you want a wife."

CHAPTER SEVEN

The tension in Daisy's shoulders finally unknotted after she shut the door of her office. She rubbed her temples to relieve the headache behind her eyes. Talk about a difficult morning—understanding Lindsey was like peeling an extra-layered onion. The questionnaire made it clear the woman had some serious hang-ups. She had written only what she wanted Daisy to hear, a romantic version of an ideal childhood.

While her father was portrayed as a loving parent, only one passing comment had been made of the mother. From all accounts she was still with her husband, which meant Lindsey had a big problem with her. She was probably a mother from hell, though Daisy would have to reserve that opinion until she could find out more. The accident too was ignored, which must have been a pivotal point in her life. It was after it that Lindsey disappeared from press clippings. Even though for the last five years she'd made the Forbes' ten top Australian entrepreneurial scientists, there were no interviews recorded. And Bernice had said "the loss of." What did she lose? She seemed to have all her parts working. Maybe it was internal, like her spleen or a kidney. Or maybe it was someone dear to her.

But most disturbing was what was missing. Lindsey hadn't simply left out the answers, she'd torn out the page. And it was obvious she didn't like to be touched. Not that that was too odd; many people were reserved. But that, combined with the fact she had refused to fill out anything about relationships, sent alarm bells dinging. She had lots of work to do before Lindsey would be ready to hit the dating scene.

Daisy toyed with the idea that maybe she should let Lindsey go. It was going to be a hard slog if the woman didn't try to fit into the program. But she couldn't bring herself not to help her. Once she had accepted a client, it wasn't in her nature to pull out of the contract. But it wasn't only that. Lindsey pulled at her heartstrings. Those last words she had written had sealed the deal. *I'm lonely*. She knew the feeling, and everybody deserved to be happy. Daisy would just have to do her very best to find her a loving wife.

With a determined click, she opened Lindsey's file on her laptop and began to fill in the next stage of the program. After the hair appointment tomorrow and the shopping spree for a new wardrobe the following day, it would be the weekend. Whether Lindsey would be prepared to work through Saturday, she had no idea, though she doubted the woman took too much time off for leisure activities. But if she was willing, then it was better they moved on quickly. Daisy was a little dubious that Lindsey would see the program through, so it was advisable to begin the tutorials while the iron was hot.

Not that Lindsey would need to be taught the finer points in how to conduct herself in public. There was a subtle difference between those who were born to money and those who had acquired it later in life. No doubt, Lindsey Jamieson-Ford was a true blueblood. She was cultured, articulate, highly educated, and carried herself well. But while those attributes were admirable in polite society, they didn't get you a date. There was another silent language to show your interest in someone. For some people it came naturally, others had to be shown.

She typed in the pertinent points on Lindsey's profile from the questionnaire, chuckling when she came to her ideal woman. A boring goody-two-shoe. Nothing about style, looks, sense of humour—she was describing her robots. Lindsey had no idea who would make her happy or what made women tick.

And that was where Daisy came in. She was the dating version of Tom Cruise in *Minority Report*—correcting a looming disaster before it happened. Over the coming weeks, she would get to know what kind of personality would suit Lindsey and guide her in choosing the right fit. Naturally, sexual attraction had to be there as well, but that ball was solely in Lindsey's court. It would be a delicate dance to combine the two satisfactorily. She hoped it wouldn't be too long before Lindsey sighted the woman of her dreams.

Her good humour sprang back when Allison came in with two salad rolls and a cheery smile. "I guess you haven't had lunch yet."

"No. Great muffins for morning tea, though. Compliments of Lindsey's housekeeper who can cook up a storm. They melted in my mouth."

"Maybe you can grab one for me the next time." With a low grumble, Allison pushed aside papers to put down the tray. "I wish you'd tidy your desk occasionally."

Daisy swept an eye over it. Her latest files sat in untidy heaps around her laptop, yellow Post-it notes were stuck in a row down one side, while two framed photos of friends and family were arrayed on the other side along with a small vase of freshly cut yellow roses. "It's not untidy, just casual," she said, unable to contain a grin as the image of Lindsey's perfectly arranged desk flashed into her mind. "I know exactly where everything is."

"Hmm…so you say. Now, tell me what happened today. You looked in a mood when you came in."

"Lindsey's a real puzzle. After spending the morning with her and reading what she wrote on her profile, I'm more at a loss than ever to know what makes her tick."

"What kind of woman does she think attractive?"

"A mature me with your face."

Allison arched a brow. "Care to explain?"

"She likes my body type but in someone older. She only wrote to us because you were on the brochure. Apparently, you radiate 'kindness and maturity,'" said Daisy, hooking two fingers in the air to punctuate the last words.

"Really? That's very flattering."

"What's that smug look for? Don't tell me you enjoy being a lesbian pinup girl?"

"Ha! You're just jealous. I'm taking it while I can. Obviously, Lindsey has good taste."

Reflectively, Daisy rubbed her fingers with the serviette. "On the serious side, I doubt if she's socialized much doing ordinary things like catching a movie or going to the beach."

"Does she get out of the house?"

"To their main lab in town once a week, so I presume she has friends there. Or at least colleagues. Maybe she goes places with them. I would just love to talk to them, but that would be prying. I'll have to think of a way to get her to take me there."

Allison looked at her curiously. "You're really interested in this one, aren't you?"

"She intrigues me. On one hand she's cool and reserved, on the other she's this warm, vulnerable, and talented scientist."

"Now you have to answer the question we always ask before starting a new case. Do you think you can help her?" asked Allison.

"I think so, but it won't be straightforward."

"You don't want to invest a lot of time to find she needed a therapist instead. That'd be demoralising for both of you."

"I know she's got problems, but they're not insurmountable. It's not as though I haven't had difficult clients before," said Daisy with authority. "She really needs my help and I'm going to give it to her."

"Okay, you know what you're doing. So how are you going to go about it?"

"After jazzing up her appearance, I'm going to take her out. Can you get me a couple of tickets to *My Fair Lady*? Everyone likes that one. She's going to have to learn how to relax socially."

"I'll get on to it and see what else is on offer," Allison said. "Find out if she likes classical music—the symphony has a good program and I've season tickets you can borrow. If she's into modern stuff, I think Taylor Swift is doing a tour. Then there's always that country and music festival, though from what you've said about her it's not likely she'll be a fan. But you never know."

"Thanks. I'll ask her what she likes. Now I'd better check up on my other clients. Any problems?"

"None. Eliza took Dan home to meet her parents."

"Oh my, that is progressing at a rate of knots. Looks like we might have a match there."

"I'll manage the rest if you like. I'll let you know if something comes up that I can't handle." Allison popped their luncheon rubbish into the wastepaper basket and added as she stood up, "Lindsey's house is too far to be driving there every day. You'll have to discuss it with her."

Daisy held up a hand. "I will. It took me nearly two hours this morning in the traffic." She sat pondering that problem. Maybe she could persuade Lindsey to take an apartment in town for a week or two. She could certainly afford it.

"Best of luck with that one," she mumbled to herself.

* * *

Daisy made sure she was outside the salon before Lindsey arrived. On the dot of eleven thirty, a shiny black Mercedes-Benz purred up the street and stopped in front of the glass doors. She eyed it with approval. What was it about some cars? It looked gleaming and burnished, as if it was made of a completely different metal from a normal car. And how is it that they always find a park? She breathed a sigh of relief. So far so good. She'd turned up for the appointment.

"Hi there," said Daisy with her best smile.

"Hello," replied Lindsey, fidgeting with her handbag. "How long is this going to take? Bernice's cousin usually trims my hair at home."

"Oh," said Daisy with a vague twitch of her hand. "I shouldn't imagine too long."

Sebastian, the salon's principal stylist, was waiting to greet them as soon as they stepped into the foyer. A slightly portly man in his late forties, he was dressed neatly in a short-sleeved white silk shirt open at the collar, and dark pants supported by a pair of blue tartan braces. His medium-length textured hair was a mixture black and silver, a colour Daisy suspected, was achieved with a bottle rather than from age. After the introductions, he discreetly ushered them through the main salon to a room at the back.

"Wow!" was the first thing that came to mind as she gazed around the small beauty parlour. The premium luxury suite was decorated with quiet elegance, with fragrant candles sending an intoxicating aroma of jasmine into the air. It was set up exclusively for one person, with a plush leather seat for the cut, an exotic-looking basin for the wash and a padded couch for waxing and massage. A best-cut crystal glass sat with a bottle of sparkling water beside the seat. Two lounge chairs with coloured cushions were set against the wall for visitors. She peeped at her companion to see if she was impressed. Lindsey wasn't admiring the décor, instead was eyeing Sebastian warily as a mouse would a cat.

He must have twigged she wasn't there of her own volition, for he wasted no time in directing her to the seat. Then with a quick twist, he freed her hair from the tight bun. After the thick brown hair tumbled over her shoulders, Lindsey looked immediately younger and less stern.

"Hmmm," he murmured as he fanned out the strands with his fingers. "Beautiful. But not the style I think for you. We need…let me think…something shorter, more modern. More colour."

Lindsey winced but remained silent.

"When do you want me to come back?" asked Daisy.

"Not until two, unless Ms Jamieson-Ford would like a relaxing massage as well, then make it three."

"No massage," Lindsey said firmly.

"Shall I bring some lunch?" asked Daisy.

Sebastian looked horrified. "She will be well looked after."

"Okay, then. I'll be off." She flipped Lindsey a wave, ignoring her pleading look.

Out on the street, Daisy gave the entrance one last glance before she headed to the shops. What wouldn't she give to be pampered in that salon? Hell, it would cost a fortune. Every woman's fantasy and Lindsey looked like she'd been sent to a torture chamber. That woman seriously needed educating in the ways of the world. What was the damn point of having money if she didn't splurge a bit on herself occasionally?

Browsing in Myers, the time passed quickly—too pleasantly, for when Daisy thought to check her watch it was nearly two. She flew down the escalator, hurried along the street to the salon, panting as she pushed open the door. To her relief, Lindsey was nowhere in sight. She wouldn't be popular if she were late. With a nod to the receptionist, she found herself a spot on a seat by the wall to wait. When a stylish woman emerged from the back room five minutes later, Daisy craned her neck to see if Lindsey was behind her. But then something about the way she was purposely striding towards her, made her take a second longer look.

Daisy blew out a startled breath. *Holy shit!* The new hairstyle was incredible. This was a very different Lindsey. Sebastian had completely altered her appearance. The below-the-shoulder locks were gone, the hair now cut short in a chic two-toned black and white colour design. The underneath jet-black layer was cropped into the nape, while the platinum blond section covered her crown to her ears with a casual side-swept fling.

"You look fucking fabulous," exclaimed Daisy with a rush of emotion.

"Shall we go?" Lindsey merely shrugged as she stepped toward the entrance.

Daisy quickened her pace to keep up with her when they reached the footpath. "Hey wait. What say we have a cup of coffee before we head home? There's a nice café on the other side of the street."

"I was intending to leave immediately."

"Come on, Lindsey. I haven't had lunch and I'm dying to hear all about your experience in that dreamy salon. Please?"

Lindsey paused, looked across the street then back at Daisy who flashed a smile of encouragement. "I guess I could," she murmured.

Delighted, Daisy gave a tiny fist pump. Things were moving smoothly in the right direction. "That's great. I could do with a few minutes off my feet."

"Your hair really looks fantastic," said Daisy after they had settled into a corner table and ordered. "It should be easy enough to keep in the style, as well. But more importantly, what do you think of it?"

"Why is it so necessary for me to like it? You're the one who wanted me to have it," Lindsey said, regarding her steadily until Daisy squirmed under the unblinking stare.

"I did, but surely you can see how attractive it makes you. You look a different woman."

"Hardly," said Lindsey flatly. "I've always been plain. My mother told me that often enough, so I have no illusions to the contrary."

A wave of anger, and pity, surged through Daisy. What kind of shitty mother would tell her daughter she was unattractive? She leaned forward to scrutinize Lindsey properly. As she swept her eyes over her face, Daisy felt a warming flutter in her stomach. Well hello, the woman was actually quite striking. The hair, the newly shaped eyebrows and subtle makeup brought out the best in her features. Without her harsh bun and thick reading glasses she looked so much younger and softer. Her long-lashed, violet-flecked eyes contrasted appealingly with her ivory complexion, and as well, she possessed a natural grace and poise. Not pretty, for her features were too pronounced, but she was beguiling in her own way. Why hadn't she noticed all this before? With a more exciting wardrobe, she would look better still. Now if she could only get Lindsey to shed her insecurities, she'd have women falling over themselves to meet her.

"First thing…you are not plain. Far from it. Why your mother ever told you that is beyond me. Very few women are naturally flawless…most have to work at it."

Lindsey narrowed her eyes. "You don't have to boost my ego. I intend to do exactly what you tell me because I know you get results. I don't need to be flattered."

"It's a genuine compliment not flattery. You'll have to learn to accept one, because you're going to get quite a few."

"I doubt it, but thanks for saying it. What happens next?"

"Okay," said Daisy with a smile. "Tomorrow we're going shopping, so bring your credit card. You are going to buy some seriously expensive clothes, which will make you look a million dollars. We can find something other than those suits and black-rimmed glasses."

"Really? I want someone to share my life and enjoy some intellectual conversation, and you're worried about my choice of glasses?"

"Yes I am. No one wants to go out with someone who looks like a grumpy owl. Keep them for work, as they make you look scholarly. But they're not for play."

Lindsey looked at her in disbelief but didn't argue any more. "What's next?"

"Then we are going to spend the next two weeks, or however long it takes, to help you acquire the skills to attract, and keep, a life partner. During that time, you and I are going out to the theatre, movies, dining and every other place a lover would expect to be taken."

"You want me to go out on dates with *you*?"

"Yes, I do, whether you wish to or not. You're never going to make anyone truly happy, Lindsey, until you learn how to enjoy yourself."

CHAPTER EIGHT

Lindsey took several deep breaths before she said coldly, "It's easy for you to be blasé about enjoying oneself. I have no desire to share the details of my past but suffice to say I never had the opportunity to be a social butterfly like you."

"I've no idea how you gained that impression of me," Daisy said, clearly insulted by her tone. "I work long hours and am definitely not a gadabout who flits from one party to the next. In fact, apart from an odd date, I'm usually at home curled up on my couch with a good book."

"Okay, sorry, I stand corrected," she replied grudgingly. "If I agree to all this, I want to make it clear that my past and my present are separate. I don't discuss my mother and I don't expect you to pry."

Daisy screwed up her face. "I never pry. Anything I shall ask will have a direct bearing on your capacity to love someone. Past baggage can affect a relationship."

"Like what exactly?"

"Like if you have an ex or two lurking out there ready to sabotage your love life."

"Definitely not. What about you?"

"I beg your pardon?" replied Daisy.

"You're going on the dates with me. I don't want to find an irate man ready to shoot me. Quid quo pro with information, please."

"I'm single and free as a breeze."

"Good," said Lindsey. "I'll be happy to accompany you then."

Daisy opened her mouth as if to speak, but then turned to her plate and took a bite of her smashed avocado.

"You obviously have something else to say, so out with it," said Lindsey. As she uttered the words, she found herself distracted by the way the full lips wrapped around the fork. It was mesmerizing. Who would have thought the act of eating could be so sensual?

"Have I something above my lip?" The question startled her out of her silent thoughts. She flicked her eyes up to find Daisy peering at her quizzically.

"Umm…no. Just thinking. You wanted to ask me something else?"

"It would be easier if I didn't have so far to travel every day. You live the other side of the city and it takes me nearly two hours to get here. My car's as old as Methuselah and ready to die. I need to trade it in soon. Would you consider getting an apartment in the CBD for a few weeks or coming into my office to share the driving some of the time?" asked Daisy with a hopeful expression.

"I thought I was generous with your remuneration. It was to include travel."

"Don't worry about it…it was just an idea." Daisy turned her attention back to her meal with a half-hearted shrug. "I'll manage."

Something about the tone of those last two words made Lindsey feel that Daisy had judged her mean-spirited. Perhaps she was being a little unreasonable—it would certainly be efficient to eliminate travel time. As well, if she were magnanimous about this request, she might get a few more wins when it came to things she didn't want to be railroaded into doing. "I have a small cottage on the estate you could use."

Daisy glanced up quickly. "A cottage?"

"It's quite comfortable. My programmer stays there overnight occasionally. It has all the essentials: Wi-Fi and a study if you need to work at night. Also, a stove and microwave for breakfast. You can have your lunch and the evening meal with us."

"Thank you. That's very generous of you."

"Excellent. Then that's settled," said Lindsey with a nod. "If you come over tomorrow, you can unpack before we go on this… ah…shopping expedition. What time is the appointment?"

"Eleven thirty. It'll probably take most of the afternoon."

* * *

From her bedroom window on the second floor, Lindsey watched an older model red Nissan sedan sporting a dint in the left mudguard, jerk to a stop outside the front door. Her father, whose garage housed a late-model Bentley, an E-type Jag and a vintage Rolls Royce, would have said it looked like it was stuck together with superglue and ran on prayers.

It came as no surprise who owned the car. Daisy got out, briefly examined the front wheel, gave the tyre a kick, and plucked her phone from her coat pocket. After a brief animated conversation, she popped the mobile back in her coat and bounded up the steps. A minute after she knocked on the door, Bernice appeared and they drove off together to get Daisy settled into the cottage.

Lindsey sat down on the edge of the bed with a thud, wondering how she was going to survive this vivacious larger-than-life woman invading her quiet life. In fact, she'd had very little sleep worrying about it. What the lessons involved she had no idea, though it didn't sound as if she was going to enjoy them and she'd probably fail miserably. She had mixed feelings about the shopping spree as well. Buying new clothes was fine. All she had in her wardrobe were suits for work, shirts and pants for the lab, old clothes for gardening, and boxers for bed. Nothing to dress for Daisy's proposed dates. But she wasn't going to be cajoled into buying something too outlandish. That was definite.

After slipping through the shower, she fluffed up her hair with the blow-dryer in front of the mirror, just as Sebastian had shown her. Not that she would ever admit to Daisy, but she loved what he had done with her hair—in fact, the whole experience in the salon had been wonderful. As well as a scalp and face massage, she had been treated to a foot massage and pedicure. A very tasty lunch was served with a glass of freshly squeezed orange juice, while Sebastian, who had actually read her book on the future of robotics, conversed intelligently. So, with genuine enthusiasm, she promised to make a follow-up appointment in a month.

Bernice's reaction to the new hairstyle had been a little puzzling. After her initial burst of delight, she had fallen silent, teary-eyed. At a loss to understand the unexpected show of emotion from her usually composed housekeeper, Lindsey escaped to her study. She was happy to find Bernice was back to her old self as they sat down for dinner. When she explained that Daisy was going to stay in the cottage, Bernice eyed her in surprise and asked, "What exactly does she do?"

"She's a consultant."

"Of what?"

Lindsey launched into her prepared explanation. "She's an anthropologist, helping me program the robots. Since I never go out, I need to be updated in the social aspects of life in the city. Modern society is constantly changing. I'm going shopping for new clothes tomorrow."

Bernice gaped at her. "Do you plan to make escorts out of the robots? That's a bit ambitious. I thought they were to do simple household chores."

"That'll be what they'll be used for initially. Eventually though, they will be able to do much, much more. For example, take people places—blind, sick or elderly people who need help outside their homes."

"It seems to me you're putting the cart before the horse."

"Maybe it is a bit premature," agreed Lindsey airily. She took a bite of the roast and deftly changed the subject. "Oh my, this lamb is really tender."

The awkward silence from Bernice spoke volumes. It was clear that Lindsey's explanation, which she granted was a little weak but the only one she could think of, was viewed as ridiculous. To her relief, they never returned to the subject. Bernice didn't bring it up again either at breakfast, merely nodding when Lindsey had asked her to show Daisy the cottage when she arrived.

She heard the door open downstairs. Quickly, she buttoned up her blouse, put on her coat and took her brown handbag from its place on the side table. As she always did, she brushed down her skirt with her hand before exiting the room. Daisy was waiting with Bernice in the kitchen, their heads together in an in-depth conversation. As soon as she stepped through the door, they broke apart.

"Hi," said Daisy with a little wave. "Ready to go?"

Lindsey glanced at Bernice, noting her heightened colour. From the guilty look on her face, they had obviously been talking about her. She flicked her eyes back to Daisy. She was dressed in skinny blue jeans with ripped knees, a loose white sleeveless blouse, a wide brown belt and brown ankle boots. An outfit Lindsey would never have considered elegant, but Daisy looked all class. She felt positively drab beside her.

"I ordered Joe to pick us up here at nine thirty. That'll give us plenty of time to get into the city. He'll be here in five minutes."

Daisy handed over a piece of paper. "This is the address."

CHAPTER NINE

.

Nicolle Jane's showroom was on the fourth floor of an exclusive shopping block in the CBD. When the lift door slid shut, Lindsey's stomach churned. It was more a sensory overload—too much happening in too short a time for her to cope well. Daisy must have sensed her disquiet because she gave her back a light rub. "Are you all right?"

This time Lindsey didn't recoil from the touch, in fact she welcomed it. Daisy's presence was reassuring now she was out of her depth. "I'm fine."

The elevator opened to an all-white reception area. With a welcoming smile, a leggy elegant woman rose from behind the desk at their approach. "Ms Jamieson-Ford, please come this way."

Lindsey grimaced—the receptionist's eye-catching jewellery and impeccable makeup did nothing to allay her feelings of inadequacy. She trudged along as they were led down a corridor, the short walk punctuated by the clacking of the receptionist's stilettos on the floor. She allowed herself to relax a little once inside the showroom. It was plush, with a cream pile carpet, comfortable white suede armchairs and rows of bags and shoes that shouted *Prada! Armani! Versace!*

A woman appeared from behind a curtain that separated the room from, Lindsey presumed, the clothes and fitting bays. She air-kissed Daisy with a, "Wonderful to see you again, Daisy," and then turned to her. "Welcome, Ms Jamieson-Ford. I'm Nicolle Jane. I understand you're requiring a new wardrobe. It'll be our pleasure to assist you."

Nicolle looked to be around forty, her soft face radiating such warmth and understanding that Lindsey felt her tension ebb away. *Thank god, a mature compassionate woman.* "Please call me Lindsey," she murmured.

"I would be delighted to. Now if you could come with me, we'll take your measurements first. One of the girls will bring you a cup of coffee while you wait, Daisy?"

Lindsey was relieved Daisy wasn't accompanying them, for she needed to talk to the designer in private. Once through the curtain, she gazed around the large studio-like setting. Racks of clothes filled the brightly-lit space, neatly laid out for easy access.

Nicolle ignored the clothes, leading her to a private alcove. "Please…take a seat," she said with a warm smile. "Now this is how we'll proceed. After my assistant takes your measurements, we'll adjourn to the showrooms where models will show some of my labels. Once you've made your choices, you'll try them on. My tailors will make sure each item will be temporarily altered to fit you perfectly. They will make the changes permanent for anything you finally choose. Now, have you any preferences?"

Lindsey let that settle for a minute before she eased the words out. "I've had shoulder reconstruction after an accident which left a deal of scarring. I can't wear anything without sleeves."

"No problem at all. We'll limit the showing to articles with sleeves and those that cover the shoulders. Is there anything else you'd prefer?"

"Nothing too flashy. I like dressing conservatively, not too many frills."

"Of course. I've quite a few pieces in my collection that will be just what you're looking for. Many of my creations have tailored lines. Now come with me so you can be measured. You'll have to strip to your underwear but keep on your shirt."

Lindsey smiled at her gratefully and rose to accompany her to a workspace where a dressmaker mannequin perched. When Nicolle clapped her hands, a woman with a tape measure immediately appeared from a back room. From then on, it was all business for half an hour while the woman impersonally took every possible width and length.

Finally, Nicolle reappeared. "Well done," she said. "That's the tedious part finished, so now you may rejoin Daisy while I assemble the clothes. We've prepared a light lunch for you both while you wait."

Daisy was sitting back reading a magazine. "Hi there. How did it go?" she asked.

Lindsey sank down into the chair. "Fine. They're going to bring us lunch while Nicolle organizes the clothes. Afterward, they'll model them."

"Great. I just adore fashion parades."

"Why am I not surprised?"

"Oh, come on. Don't be such a grouch. You'll simply love these clothes." As if to punctuate that comment, a cork popped behind them. A young woman appeared with a tray of hors d'oeuvres and sandwiches, while another poured champagne into delicate flutes. Lindsey eyed the wine suspiciously. She only ever drank sparingly and rarely while doing business, especially at lunchtime. She hoped it wasn't a ploy to get her to buy more. Daisy, however, didn't seem to have any reservations. She was drinking it down with little hums, so not wanting to appear too stuffy, Lindsey took a sip.

When the flavour burst over her taste buds, she let out a moan of pleasure too. It was by the far the best champagne she'd ever tasted. No doubt, though, she'd be paying a small fortune for it. The cost of the hair salon had been enough to raise her now neatly shaped eyebrows. God knows what she'd be handing out today. She took a bite of a caviar and salmon canapé and gave it an A1 rating as well. "How do you like the cottage?" she asked.

"It's brilliant thanks. And I'll simply love the spa."

"I've one too." She didn't add that she had installed it to help with her rehabilitation.

"I just adore relaxing with jets of water thrusting against my body. Don't you?"

Lindsey sucked in a sharp breath at the image. "It is…um… nice," she wheezed out.

"Hey. Are you all right? You look pale."

"No…I'm fine."

Daisy took the bottle from the ice bucket and topped up their glasses. "Have another. They'll be starting soon."

Nicolle appeared from behind the curtain. "Firstly, ladies, I like to present our daytime collection. We'll start with office wear."

Like ringside seats at a prize fight, Lindsey swung her chair around to face the runway. Daisy had obviously settled in, lounging back with legs crossed while she clutched her champagne flute in one hand and popped a second dark chocolate truffle into her mouth with the other.

Lindsey looked at her disapprovingly. "Too much sugar is bad for your health," she said.

All she got back was a withering stare.

The model was impossibly thin, like a twiggy stick insect. She was dressed in a beige suit, the cut so exquisite it appeared an extension of her body. Her short, streaked, caramel-blond hair was casually stylish, her teeth whiter than white, and her skin had an expensive pearly sheen. Her shoes were so ridiculously high that Lindsey wondered how she kept her balance.

"Killer heels," murmured Daisy.

"Hello fallen arches," muttered Lindsey.

She had to admire Twiggy though, for being able to walk with such poise. It seemed effortless, lithe and smooth without taking up much space. Maybe it wouldn't be such a bad idea to seek a model's advice to help perfect her robots' gaits. They were still a bit jerky. With that thought in mind, she studied the walk. The neck and back were straight, the lower half of the body leaning slightly forward. As she moved with a distinct sway of her hips, she placed one foot in front of the other rather than planting them parallel to each other.

Lindsey surreptitiously pulled her phone from her coat and began to video the walk. When she noticed Daisy frowning, she poked it back into the pocket.

"You shouldn't be taking photos. It's a private collection," Daisy whispered, then said louder, "Do you like the suit."

What could she say? All her suits paled in comparison. "I don't think it'll look that good on me."

"Nonsense. Nicole's chosen all these outfits with you in mind. You can try it on." Daisy gave the designer a nod. Twiggy disappeared, replaced by another model not quite as thin but equally as flat-chested. This one glided gracefully, with a long sweeping swan-like neck. Her suit was entirely different, a looser fabric cinched tight by a silver chain. It looked spectacular on The Swan. Daisy didn't bother to ask this time, merely raised her finger.

For the next hour, the models worked through the business, casual, and evening outfits. Daisy gave the nod for all but four outfits—Lindsey had given up putting in her two-cents' worth. Then it came to the finale: formal wear. Daisy was a bit more discriminating here, choosing only three long gowns and one tuxedo.

"What? Not all the formal wear is good enough?" Lindsey breathed in her ear.

"They're worth a fortune," she whispered back.

"My God, the woman has constraint. Who knew?"

"One tux is enough for the time being. You'll bless me when you see the price."

Lindsey had no doubt about that. Her bill would be astronomical if she took half the clothes she was going to try on. Nicolle Jane would not be cheap.

Daisy poured more champagne and handed one across. "Here, finish this. You'll have to go try them on in a sec."

Lindsey eyed the glass dubiously. "I'm not used to drinking."

"Then you'll be very relaxed when you try on the clothes," came the airy reply.

"Just so long as I don't have to walk in those high heels."

CHAPTER TEN

At the sound of rustling behind the curtain, Daisy finished scrolling through the fashion blogs on her phone and readied for the action. She was peeved she hadn't been invited into the inner room, but Nicolle only let prospective buyers into that Aladdin's cave. Designers were very protective of their creations. Without a thought, Daisy reached for a third chocolate but reluctantly closed the lid. Perhaps it was time to watch her weight. Her jeans were getting a bit tight—the super-thin models with their waspy waistlines made her feel like the Incredible Hulk. Though, mind you, she couldn't imagine jumping their skinny bones.

When Lindsey appeared in the beige suit with an aqua blue silk shirt underneath and a slim silver chain around her neck, she could only stare. Wow! Eye-poppingly fantastic. Nicolle flashed a smug told-you-so look when Daisy gave her an enthusiastic nod. The show continued, with each outfit decked out with matching accessories and shoes. She noted the heels were only mid-high.

By the time they came to the formal wear, Daisy had only given five of the forty-odd pieces the thumbs-down. Lindsey was going to have a hard time choosing what to buy. She had remained stoic throughout, giving no indication whether she liked them or not. When she paraded the first outfit, she had looked embarrassed as she shifted from one leg to the other, but after that appeared to be on automatic pilot.

Every piece of clothing fit her perfectly. Daisy was particularly fond of the leather ensemble with the gorgeous Jimmy Choo boots, just right for when they'd hit the bars. And Lindsey in jeans looked a different woman—far more accessible. Then came the first full-length evening dress: a breathtaking fitted gown, with satin sandals peeping out from beneath the hem and elaborate diamond-drop earrings sparkling in the light. Timeless elegance. Lindsey looked so stunning Daisy had to blink away a few tears. She wondered why there were no sleeveless or strapless numbers, but that thought vanished in a cloud of pheromones when Lindsey appeared for the finale in a charcoal-grey tux.

God damn, the woman was a bona fide hottie. She'd have to fight them off with a stick. At that scenario, she felt a twinge of possessiveness but quickly dismissed it as a hormonal glitch.

After Lindsey departed with Nicolle to discuss which items to purchase, Daisy tipped her glass in a silent toast.

Goodbye dowdy Ms Jamieson-Ford.

Welcome sophisticated Lindsey.

Hello success!

To her surprise, she didn't have long to wait. Lindsey appeared in her old suit and carried four parcels. Disappointment surged through Daisy. She'd only bought four outfits—she had hoped Lindsey would've considered at least eight or ten. She prayed one at least was the fantastic tux.

Nicolle seemed more than happy enough though, radiant as she danced attendance on Lindsey. "It has indeed been a pleasure showing you my collection, Lindsey. I'm sure you'll be very happy with your purchases." Then to Daisy's surprise, she simpered, "You're most welcome to come back anytime. As

I said, it's been a real pleasure. And thank you, Daisy, for your recommendation. Drive home safely now."

Unable to contain herself, Daisy blurted out as they walked to the lift, "Which ones did you buy? Was it only these four? I thought you might have taken a lot more."

"Did you now?"

"Well, they all looked fabulous on you and there were selections for every occasion."

The arrival of the lift interrupted their conversation. Lindsey didn't seem to want to take it up again once inside, which left Daisy stewing. The black Mercedes-Benz was parked outside in the pickup zone when they emerged and she gave an exasperated groan when the parcels disappeared into the boot. *Shit!* She wasn't even going to see them until they got home.

"Well, out with it. Which ones did—" Daisy stopped at the phone ringing in her purse. When the ID showed Allison, she shrugged at Lindsey. "Sorry, I'll have to take this. It has to be an emergency, or my assistant wouldn't be ringing."

She pressed talk. "Hi, what's up, Allie?"

"We have a crisis. The wedding's only three days away and Jeanette's been crying on my shoulder for the last two hours," answered Allison, sounding exhausted.

"Crap. Where are you?"

"At the office."

"Right. I'll be there in five minutes."

Seething, she jammed the phone back into her purse. Jeanette was one of those prima donnas she hated. Everything was always about her. She was lucky to get someone like Ron but didn't have the wit to see it.

Lindsey eyed her, clearly curious. "Everything all right?"

"Trouble with a client…nothing too serious I hope. I'll hop out here. My office is only a few blocks away."

"A little detour won't be any trouble. Just give the driver your address."

After Daisy rattled it off, he swung the car into another lane.

"Would you like us to wait?" asked Lindsey.

"No…no. This will take some time, but thanks all the same. I appreciate it. I'll get a lift out early tomorrow. What say we start at nine?"

"That'll be fine. I'll wear one of my *new* outfits," said Lindsey, flicking a bit of fluff off her sleeve.

"Sooo…are you going to tell me how many of the clothes you bought or is it a big secret?" asked Daisy peevishly.

"The lot."

"The *lot*! You're telling me you bought everything?"

"Yes."

"Holy hell! That would have cost you an arm and a leg."

"It did," stated Lindsey primly. "But that's the end of it. No more dress shops, no more buying sprees. Nicolle has also supplied handbags and jewellery and is organizing a range of shoes from various designers to be sent out to try on. As for my glasses that you despise so much, she has arranged frames to try as well."

Daisy knew it was time to retreat. The lingerie and makeup would have to wait. After all, she had scored a victory today—no need to push it. "You're going to be really happy with your clothes, Lindsey. Nicolle is one of the leading designers in the country and her creations are popular with the…um…affluent set." She said conciliatorily, careful with her words.

"She has a definite flare. Have you any of her clothes?"

"God no. I can't afford her."

"Apart from her overpriced garments, I found Nicolle to be a very personable woman and most accommodating to deal with. Ah…here's your stop," said Lindsey with a wave of her fingers, and as Daisy was about to climb out of the vehicle, added, "she even asked me to have a drink with her one evening."

Daisy turned quickly to stare at Lindsey. "She asked you out?"

"Yes. For a drink."

"Huh! And what did—" The question died in Daisy's mouth when two sharp blasts from a horn pierced the air behind them. Quickly, she scrambled out the door with a "See you tomorrow." As she watched the Mercedes join the line of cars, she let out a snort. No wonder Nicolle had fawned all over her. Lindsey had just bought, without a blink, nearly a quarter of her summer collection, as well as accessories. What a coup for her label. The news would travel like wildfire through the fashion industry, raising Nicolle to superstar status.

And now she wanted to see Lindsey on a personal basis. That most certainly would have to be monitored. Not that she disliked the designer. On the contrary, she was a charming woman, but Lindsey was a babe in the woods when it came to dating and romance. This reinforced the role Daisy had to play. She needed to be vigilant with Lindsey in her quest for a wife. And being rich didn't help. There were plenty of gold diggers out there ready to stick their claws into her.

Now off her champagne high and feeling a bit jaded, she opened the office door. Dealing with this crisis was going to be a giant pain in the neck. When Jeanette spied her, her wailing increased a few decibels. Daisy, ignoring the hysteria, said firmly, "Calm down and tell me what the trouble is."

Allison dashed to the bathroom for another box of tissues after Daisy took her place on the chair in front the woman. When the sobs subsided into sniffles, Jeanette blew her nose with a loud honk and stuttered, "My parents flew over…*sniff*… from Perth today and Ron deliberately went off to the football. *Sniff.* They expect us both to have dinner with them tonight so what am I going to say to them?"

Daisy took a deep breath, wishing she could say what was on her mind. It was obvious why he had disappeared, and she didn't blame him. She had met the father once, an experience she didn't wish to repeat. But she was not in the mood to pander to drama, so she shot from the hip. "You know very well what the problem is. You've been putting your head in the sand long enough."

The red-rimmed eyes stared at her. "I don't know what you mean."

"Yes, you do, so face it. Your father controls your life and if you continue to let him do it you'll lose Ron."

By her expression, she could see Jeanette's mind was ticking away, formulating a plan that would probably involve her. "Would you—"

"Definitely not," said Daisy sternly. "This time you're on your own. I've finished with all this rubbish. Now go into the bathroom and wash up. You look like a wreck. If Ron does come home to take you to that dinner with your parents, as I suspect he might, then you don't want him to see you looking so frumpy. Just remember that your chances are running out. Tonight is the night you stand up to your father. Do you understand me?"

The pout dissolved into misery. "I guess, but it's going to be hard."

"If you don't do it now, you'll never get the courage." She patted her hand. "Just remember, when you're married they'll be living on the other side of Australia. Now off with you."

Without a word Jeanette retreated to the bathroom. When she emerged ten minutes later she looked a different person—certainly not the one drowning in tears when Daisy had come in. All traces of smeared mascara were gone and she'd added another slick layer of lipstick. After giving them both a long hug, she vanished out the door.

Allison plonked down on the chair with a long moan. "Thank heavens those theatricals are over. That woman is your worst nightmare. I pity her poor husband."

"Everything's a melodrama to her I know, and she's completely self-centred, but she genuinely does love him. If the father leaves them alone, they have every chance of a happy life."

"If you say so," said Allison eyeing her closely. "Your fuse was a bit short, wasn't it? I realize it did the trick, but I've never heard you so forceful with a client before. Something's gotten under your skin. Come on, out with it. What happened today?"

"All went really well," said Daisy and related the events of the day.

"So, she bought all the clothes. Nicolle Jane must be laughing all the way to the bank."

"I'll say. But that's not the end of it. She asked Lindsey out for a drink."

"Why, that's wonderful."

"I'm dubious about that, I doubt they're suited."

Allison's brow furrowed. "So? She's not going to marry the woman, she's just going to have a drink with her. Let them work it out."

"I will," snapped Daisy, "when Lindsey's ready for the dating scene."

"Okay, don't get your knickers in a knot. I got those tickets for *My Fair Lady* for Wednesday fortnight, by the way."

"Great. I'll take them with me."

"So…is it possible for me to meet her?" asked Allison.

"Tomorrow if you like. I was going to ask you to take me out there early in the morning. I came in with her today. I'll catch a cab home to my apartment tonight."

"I'll pick you up there about seven." Her eyes twinkled. "I'm dying to meet her. It's not often someone's able to get under your skin."

Daisy rolled her eyes. "Whatever."

CHAPTER ELEVEN

Lindsey woke up with yesterday's events churning in her head. The whole experience had been a pleasant surprise. She hadn't had a clue what to expect but the service had been faultless. Since the accident, all her clothes were sent to her house on appro and her suits were made by the same tailor. Now fourteen years down the track she was more than just a little rusty when it came to fashion—she was a complete pudding head. Thankfully, Nicolle had at once made her feel at ease and her opinion valued. Even though parading the clothes was a novelty, she soon tired of it and gained far more pleasure out of watching Daisy's face while she studied each item. She was like a kid in a candy store.

Nicolle was certainly an accomplished woman: good-looking, mature, considerate, and talented. An all-round attractive package. Lindsey was surprised when she'd asked her out for a drink, for there was no mistaking from the intimate smile that it was intended as a date. Though she was flattered, the invitation hadn't evoked any flutters in her breast, but it had been only good manners to accept. She had suggested they could organize something in three weeks' time, figuring Daisy's tutorials should be over by then.

After her morning shower, Lindsey went to the cupboard for her usual daywear but then hesitated. What was the point of paying a fortune for new clothes if she wasn't going to wear them? She dug into the shopping bags for the soft blue jeans, coral shirt, and suede boots. When she examined her reflection in the mirror, she had to admit that the rig-out looked very smart. There was no denying Nicolle knew her trade.

With a spring in her step, she went downstairs. Bernice was in the kitchen preparing breakfast and stared at her in astonishment. Conscious of her old friend's scrutiny, Lindsey plucked a grape from the fruit bowl on the table.

"Good lord, Lindsey, what have you done to yourself?" exclaimed Bernice.

She bit into the grape, feigning a casual air. "Just updated my wardrobe."

"That's an understatement of the year. You look…well…an entirely different person."

"I can assure you it's still me."

"I hadn't realized you'd grown into such a striking woman," said Bernice with a hitch in her voice. "You've been right there in front of me and I've never really seen you."

"Don't be ridiculous. It's the clothes and hairdo. We both know I'm sorely lacking in the looks department. Mother let me know that often enough."

"Yes, she did. And it was wrong, very wrong to be so cruel, especially to a child. That woman should have been strangled at birth."

Lindsey's eyes widened. It was the first time the elderly housekeeper had openly condemned her mother. "Why am I just hearing you say that now?"

Tears sparkled on Bernice's eyelashes. "I'm your employee and your mother's before you. It was never my place to criticise your family. As much as I loved you like my own, I hadn't the right to drive a wedge between you and your mother. I've held my tongue over the years while she stripped away your self-esteem one layer at a time, but now I wish I hadn't been so stupid."

"Don't go heaping blame on yourself. You were the one bright spot in my life, for though I loved Dad, he never had the fortitude to stand up to her. Besides, it wasn't all bad...I had my studies and my career, things she could never take away from me. I inherited Dad's genes there. Mother's social standing might have been impeccable but she hadn't the wit or aptitude to design anything."

"I often wondered over the years why she was so hard on you. Looking back, I think she resented your talent. You were a genius at making things from a very early age."

"Let's face it Bernie, it was because I never fitted the mould. All she ever wanted was a pretty daughter to parade around. Anyhow, I'm free of her now."

"Yes, you are, but one day you'll have to face her again you know."

"It'll be on my own terms when I do," said Lindsey firmly.

Bernice looked at her approvingly. "Well spoken. Just remember, time is a great leveller. She's a lot older now and you're a lot stronger. Now tell me why Daisy is really here."

"It's a...um...top-secret project I have in the pipeline. She'll be staying for a week or two."

"Well I think she's delightful. I can't imagine how she persuaded you to get new clothes and hairstyle, but good for her."

"Huh! She's bossy...make no mistake about that. Like a pesky kid sister."

"Oh, she's hardly that young," said Bernice. "She has an air of competence that only comes with experience." The chime of the doorbell made her turn toward the hallway. "Maybe that's her now."

Lindsey glanced at her watch. "It's only ten to eight. She's not due 'til nine. I'll get the door so stay there and finish preparing breakfast."

To her surprise, Daisy was standing on the porch with the attractive woman from the Marigold's brochure. Lindsey gave

Daisy a nod, conscious her new clothes were being studied avidly.

Daisy's companion stepped forward at once with a friendly smile. "Sorry to just lob up like this, but I've driven Daisy out and took the opportunity to meet you. I'm Allison Marsden, the other half of the Marigold Matchmaking Agency."

The hint of tension in Lindsey subsided. Allison had one of those warm faces that radiated empathy. "Hello. I'm very pleased to meet you. I was just about to sit down to breakfast. You've had a long drive and you must have left very early. Would you care to join me?"

"A coffee would be nice," replied Allison.

As Lindsey ushered them over the threshold, Daisy gave her a nudge with her elbow. "You look awesome."

Lindsey merely lifted a brow, leaving her to follow as she led them down the hall to the dining room. Bernice promptly appeared from the kitchen with a jug of orange juice. "Hello Daisy. Would you and your friend like some breakfast?"

"I'd love some, Bernice. I only had a cup of coffee before I left. This is my associate Allison Marsden."

"Hi, Bernice. Daisy told me you're a great cook," said Allison with a smile.

"One of my greatest pleasures. You'll have something to eat as well?"

Allison looked embarrassed. "Are you sure? I don't wish to impose."

"Nonsense, there's plenty. Sit down. I'll just throw on a few more eggs."

Lindsey, who watched the exchange quietly from the sideline, said sharply when Bernice bustled off to the kitchen, "Bernice isn't privy to our arrangement, Allison."

"Daisy did tell me. Naturally, I'll be discreet. Confidentiality is strictly adhered to in our business."

Catching the flush on her face, Lindsey backtracked quickly. "Sorry, that must have sounded judgemental. I didn't mean anything by it. I'm just a bit antsy about the whole business."

"I can quite understand that. It was a big step for you to seek our help and I'm sure it was a decision you didn't take lightly. I know how difficult it can be to meet people if your work takes up most of your time. We have many busy clients who prefer a more structured way to find a life partner."

"That does make me feel much better," replied Lindsey, soaking up the compassionate words. "I'm afraid my work has consumed me to the extent I've become quite a hermit."

"Don't worry. Daisy will have you out and about in no time."

"That I can believe," said Lindsey dryly. "What about you, Allison? Married? Children?"

"My husband Noel and I have two teenage girls."

"It must be wonderful to have a family."

Allison chuckled. "Now they're in their teens I think sometimes they're like Pod People. I'm the old ball and chain, solely around to stop their fun."

As Lindsey burst into a spontaneous laugh, Bernice called out, "Breakfast is ready. It'll be easier if you come in and help yourselves. The plates and cutlery are on the divider."

Lindsey watched them get up, content to wait until they were served. As business partners, the two women certainly seemed to complement each other well: Allison appeared calm and steady while Daisy had an energetic flair. And from the way they were clearly at ease with each other, there was little doubt they were firm friends. She felt a moment of extreme isolation. That was what she was really missing, a female friend, someone to confide in, someone who cared.

When her mind wandered back to Kirsty, she felt something knot in her stomach. After the accident, her mother had made sure their friendship ended. As Lindsey lay in the hospital for months enduring surgery, skin grafts, and rehab, her mother had forbidden visitors until Kirsty had simply moved on with her life. After graduation, she had travelled overseas, and they had lost contact completely.

With a sigh, she pushed back the chair and got her meal.

The room was quiet for a few minutes while they ate. Lindsey lifted her head from her bowl of yogurt and fruit to watch Daisy enthusiastically work her way through the large plate of ham and eggs. She'd never seen anyone enjoy food more.

She seemed to be one of the lucky ones with a fast metabolism, for although she had generous curves, she was carrying very little extra weight. Bernice was beaming at her, as she did with anyone who appreciated her cooking. There was no doubt that Daisy had a natural aptitude when it came to people. She already had Bernice wrapped around her little finger. And she did it so effortlessly. Lindsey felt a pang of envy. She'd been compartmentalizing her emotions all her life. She knew how to put fear and longing in a box and hide it away.

"I understand you're doing a lot of work on prosthetic limbs," said Allison.

"I am," replied Lindsey, pleased to be now on familiar ground. "My company's been working on the project for quite a few years now, mainly on artificial arms. We've come a long way in the field of neural interfacing. To put it in layman's terms, that's how the microelectrodes send signals to control the synthetic limb."

"Sounds like cutting-edge technology."

"Indeed, it is," said Lindsey. "Each prosthetic is a complex unit with its own artificial bones, tendons, and muscles."

"How do you replicate nerves?"

"There's no nervous system *per se*. Joints operate with fluid containing metal particles. A miniature computer in the brain sends magnetic impulses to move the elbow and fingers."

"Really? I had no idea. Not that I ever knew much about the subject…it is way out of my league. How far have you come with the cosmetic side of it all?"

"A long way. Our latest arms are made from advanced plastics, with a soft carbon-fibre overlay. They're coated with pigments to match skin tone, and we're quite adept now at adding details such as freckles, hair, fingernails, and fingerprints. The computer also keeps the limb the same temperature as the rest of the body."

"Wow! Are they available yet?"

Lindsey shoved her coffee cup aside and chewed her lip. The cost was the most frustrating part of her work. "Unfortunately, these limbs are extremely expensive to make. The average amputee wouldn't be able to afford the high-tech ones. We're working on it though. Like all technology, the prices will come down as we refine the product."

"So how do you keep your research funded?" asked Daisy, looking up from her plate.

"Those are our experimental lines. Our research laboratory is only one facet of our enterprise. We make cheaper three-D-print prosthetics and we also have a large range of digital software for the robotic industry."

"What's three-D printing?"

"It's the process of creating three-dimensional objects from digital files. Layers upon layers of material are laid down by a machine in horizontal sections until the desired object is finished. It's a simple technique: melted plastic filament is squeezed through a nozzle to create the virtual design."

Allison stared at her in disbelief. "And you make functional fingers and elbows like that?"

"Yes. It's the future," Lindsey said then added, "we do what we can to help the less fortunate. We have a fund set up for children who have had limbs blown off by landmines."

"I imagine there're plenty of those poor little ones. I—" Allison broke off when her phoned beeped a text. "Sorry… work calling. I'd better run. I'll drive Daisy over to the cottage and head back to the office. Maybe we can get together again and you can tell me more about your work. I find it fascinating. Thank you both so much for your hospitality."

Daisy rose to her feet with her. "See you in half an hour. Thanks for the great breakfast, Bernice."

After Lindsey showed them out, she watched them walk to the car. Before building her second robot, she had studied the female body in depth. Essentially, there were four basic shapes: hourglass, ruler, spoon, and cone. Allison was a ruler, tall and slender, while Daisy had an hourglass figure. Both women were very fetching, in perfect proportion to their build. Lindsey slid her hand down over her hip self-consciously. She was a cone, with a strong wide upper body, slim hips and long legs—to her mind, the least attractive of the body types.

As if on a magnet, her gaze automatically lingered on Daisy's behind as she bent over to open the car door. Lindsey moistened her bottom lip with her tongue and idly began to stroke down the length of her neck with her fingertips as she swept her eyes over her. Then embarrassed, she swung around sharply. What was wrong with her? She'd never been one to stare. But as she reached the door, she couldn't resist a sideways glance over her shoulder.

CHAPTER TWELVE

"Okay. What do you think of her?" asked Daisy when they pulled to a stop outside the cottage.

"She's nice. Serious, a little reticent, but very engaging. Not what I was expecting."

"Huh! She likes you. That was obvious."

"Give her a bit of slack. She's not used to someone like you."

Daisy narrowed her eyes. "There's nothing wrong with how I interact with my clients. Lindsey can be a bit scratchy when I ask her to do something."

"I imagine she could get brusque at times, but that's understandable. She's extremely bright and used to being the boss." Allison winked. "You didn't tell me she was so foxy. And that cultured voice. Whew!"

"You think she's hot?"

"She is, and you know it," said Allison with a grin.

"Handsome is as handsome does," said Daisy primly. "She can be flat-out stubborn if she doesn't want to do something. I have to be careful how I handle her."

"Oooooh. *Handle* her?"

"You're incorrigible," said Daisy with a hoot of laughter. "Come on in and have a look at this place. It's awesome."

She pushed open the gate and led the way up the path. Surrounded by a white picket fence, the quaint cottage was set in a colourful garden, with an archway of honeysuckle over the front entrance.

"Delightful," murmured Allison.

"Wait 'til you see inside. It's even got a fireplace and a spa."

"Well you fell on your feet, didn't you? This cottage-in-the-countryside-living is going to spoil you."

"Yep," said Daisy smugly. "I'll think of you when I'm relaxing in the spa at night with a glass of wine."

* * *

Gunmetal grey clouds floated across the sky as Daisy hurried down the lane to the main building. She wished she had been born in another era when courtship was much simpler, when everyone understood that dating was the precursor to marriage. It was so much more complicated now, especially with Tinder. The app had transformed the dating landscape into a game that fitted in your pocket and mimicked flirting at a bar. People were enticed into bed by a few text exchanges. You ordered a lover like you ordered pizza: swipe right and you were in. There was no dating—no relationship—no real human connection. You were no longer a person but a profile in a new singles' game where sex could be arranged instantly like online shopping. There was no need to know how to communicate.

One of their clients had spent two years searching for love using the app before coming to Marigold. She said initially she had enjoyed the experience of having such a wide choice of partners, but eventually the novelty wore off. Disenchanted with the shallowness of the process, she likened everyone on Tinder to the last people at a party trying to find someone to go home with.

Daisy could only shake her head. Love and commitment—there was no app for that.

As she neared the house, she concentrated on the next session with Lindsey, though not completely able to ignore her quivering stomach. Lindsey was such an unknown. It was anyone's guess how she'd take the coaching. At the front door, she adjusted her grip on her briefcase and rechecked the time. Right on schedule. Bernice appeared a few moments after the doorbell chimed and said with a bright, "Come in, Daisy. She's waiting in her office so go on through."

The desk lamp gave a lone glow in the otherwise grey room. Absorbed in something on the computer, Lindsey didn't look up so Daisy cleared her throat. When there was no answer, she plopped down in one of the leather office chairs, pulled out her phone and logged onto Facebook. She was tittering at an amusing video clip when Lindsey's voice echoed in her ear, "Shall we begin?"

"Oh, good, you're ready," Daisy said, switching off the phone with a flourish. "Let's sit over in the comfortable seats where we can chat. And can we turn on the main light?"

"Why not," Lindsey mumbled. She quickly rose, strode past Daisy to flick the switch and walked over to a burgundy armchair. "What's this going to entail exactly?"

Daisy sank into the love seat opposite. "Firstly, I'm going to outline a few things."

"Proceed."

"Relax, Lindsey. This is supposed to be fun."

"If you say so."

Daisy casually crossed her legs. "Firstly, I'd like to ask you a personal question."

"Oh?"

"Before you get upset, I need to know this. It's important you answer truthfully. How much dating experience have you had? This is solely between you and me. I am not judging you, but I have to know how much help you need."

Lindsey shrugged. "I used to when I was much younger. Now I don't date. Haven't for years."

"Right, then we'll start at the very beginning. I've devised a step-by-step dating guide I give to all my clients. The most important part comes from learning the essentials. Success is in the detail. Chapter one: how to let someone subtly know you're attracted to them."

"Is this really necessary? It's sounds rather juvenile."

"It most certainly is," Daisy persisted. "You might be socially competent but good manners don't get you a date. Body language is the fundamental part of meeting someone so you'll have to know how to show your interest. First off and the most important is eye contact. Be bold. Catch her eye."

"But what if she looks the other way?"

"If she does immediately, then she's probably not interested. But if she holds your gaze for a moment then it's a different story. You're in with a chance."

"Lucky me," came the dry reply.

Daisy couldn't help herself—she chuckled. "I know it sounds odd, but humans do have mating rituals just like animals."

"You're a regular David Attenborough." Lindsey lolled back in her chair and waggled a finger in the air. "Okay, let's say I've established she's a little keen by the way she peered into my eyes, so what do I do next?"

Daisy angled her head and said with authority, "You smile at her—only fleetingly though—then turn back to your friends or friend as the case may be."

"Why don't I give her a broad smile…or maybe a wink?"

"Definitely not!" said Daisy, wincing. "Too wide a smile and you're desperate. Wink and you are a player."

Lindsey sat up straighter in the chair. "Really? Sounds odd to me. I thought you just rocked up to someone and offered to buy them a drink."

"God no. That's a pickup line for a one-night stand. You're not after sex. Or at least, I don't think you are from what you've told me," Daisy said with a grin.

"Then how do I get to know her?" responded Lindsey, ignoring Daisy's quip.

"Ah," said Daisy with a smile. "When she looks at you again...which she will...you start the body language. Sit up straighter, play with your hair, lick your lips, straighten your top, fiddle with your jewellery and slide your fingers down the stem of your glass. While you're doing all this, flick a quick glance sideways over your shoulder a couple of times in her direction. Lastly...emphasise your best asset. In your case, it's your lovely long legs. Cross them, angling your body so she can see and later recross them to the other side. If you're wearing heels, dangle one off your foot."

Lindsey stared at her. "Are you serious? I've never heard such tripe in all my life. You think acting like a performing seal is going to interest an intelligent woman?"

"Correct."

"No woman with any brains would be taken in."

"Wanna bet?"

"Yes, actually I do."

"Okay," murmured Daisy, leisurely stretching out her body with a satisfied smile. "You're on. Tonight, we'll go out to a cocktail bar for a few drinks. The clientele is mostly professionals and it's popular with lesbians."

"You want me to go out to a *bar* with you?"

"Yep. Nicolle is sending the rest of your outfits today, isn't she? Those white linen pants with the beige blouse will go very nicely. Not the boots though. Heels, so you can...you know... dangle."

"I'd better write down it all down," Lindsey said with a harrumph. "I wouldn't want to forget one of the *important* instructions."

"I'll give you a printout you can study."

"You've a printout of this rubbish?"

"Yes, and a video. It's on a USB stick so you can watch it on the TV or your computer."

"I'll read the printout but I won't need to watch a video to grasp the finer points."

"You will," said Daisy in her no-nonsense voice. "A picture is worth a thousand words. It only goes for twenty minutes. We had it specially made, so shall we adjourn to your TV?"

"If I must, but it'll have to be the computer. Bernice might see the TV."

"Okay, set the laptop up on the coffee table here."

After Lindsey strode off to her desk, Daisy pulled the small table closer. She patted the space beside her on the love seat. "Sit here. That way we can watch it together in case you have any questions."

For a minute it looked like Lindsey would object, but she eased down with a huff and opened the laptop. When Daisy inserted the USB stick, a picture of a busy trendy bar flashed onto the screen. She gazed at it proudly. This had been their biggest office outlay by far, hiring a professional film crew to make the video rather than try themselves. The two lead actors, with the improbable names of Buck and Candy, were part of the package. Daisy was left to provide the venue and crowd. She sent off the script to the actors with detailed instructions, booked a bar for one Monday morning, then Facebooked friends offering free drinks for the three-hour session. They had been inundated with a rent-a-crowd.

With the cameras ready to roll, Buck had arrived first and immediately headed for the bar. Dressed smartly in fitting jeans, blue shirt, and a tailored sports coat, he looked dashing—perhaps too attractive for what she wanted. No woman in her right mind would knock him back. Even some of her lesbian friends had eyed him off. His face was rugged, his black hair thick and shiny, his nose classically straight and his mouth sculptured. Daisy, playing one of the bartenders, pointed to a beer sitting on the coaster when he sauntered over. He gave her a wink as he took the schooner, then sidled off to sit with a group of men at the other end of the room.

Five minutes later Candy arrived in a tight red dress. At least five-ten in her spiky heels, she looked dazzling with glossy mane of platinum-blond hair framing a heart-shaped face, her breasts spilling over the low-cut neckline. Daisy could only shake her head. The siren wouldn't have to try to get anyone's attention. She had an inbuilt mating call nobody could ignore. But as it panned out, she needn't have worried. They were consummate actors and followed the script to perfection, with just enough pauses for even the thickest client to follow their acting. She hoped Lindsey would deign to take notice of the moves.

With a few quick twists, Daisy steered the cursor over the start arrow. "Right, here we go. As you can see, the action is in a bar."

Lindsey gave a little titter. Daisy ignored her and continued, "That's Buck coming in now."

"He's extremely handsome. Which one's the woman."

"Candy will be in shortly. Buck has to settle in first."

"Candy? What sort of name is that? Sounds like a porn star."

"What does it matter? That's just her stage name," Daisy said, exasperated.

"You'd have to wonder at her intelligence to call herself that."

"Concentrate on what they're doing."

"Whatever."

"Here she comes now."

Lindsey, who had been lounging back in the chair, shot upright. "Good God! Why would she have to bother with all this stuff? She only has to crook her little finger and they'd all come running."

"Just look at the damn video," Daisy growled.

"Okay. I was just pointing out the obvious."

"They're playacting, Lindsey. Don't worry what they look like."

"How can I not help it? She's pretty much in your face."

Daisy held in the irresistible urge to chuckle. Lindsey lapsed into silence and relaxed back to watch, intent on the screen. When the last scene faded with the actors chatting quietly together, Daisy clicked it off. "Well…what did think?"

"Interesting."

"Do you want to watch it again? That's what you'll be doing tonight."

"I think I can remember it all," Lindsey said, eyeing her thoughtfully. "I watched you serving the crowd. You were very efficient. Have you had a great deal of experience at bar work?"

Daisy blinked, taken aback at the line of questioning. "I worked in a bar for a while to pay my way through university."

"Ah. That would have given you a great insight into human relations."

"I didn't need it. I majored in human behaviour and sexuality."

"Yes, but to see it firsthand in that environment would have been very valuable."

Daisy cleared her throat, at a loss to keep track of Lindsey's thought process. "So? How's that relevant here? What's it got to do with the video?"

"Everything and nothing," replied Lindsey. She dropped an arm on the back of the chair and began to pick absently at the velvet. "I've a proposition for you."

Daisy narrowed her eyes. "Go on."

"I'll do whatever you say without arguing if you do something for me."

"It depends on what it is. We both know it would make things so much easier if you cooperated, but I'm employed specifically to help you find a soulmate. It has to be my priority."

"I know, and I won't compromise that," Lindsey persisted. "But if you're going to stay out here for a couple of weeks, I imagine our lessons won't take up all your time. I want you to have some input into the software for my robots. Would you be able to help the company's coders?"

"I wouldn't have a problem. One of my post-grad courses was quantitative anthropology, which basically entails employing computer programs for pattern recognition within design and ethical data."

"Wonderful. Now I'm not asking you to work for nothing—the remuneration will be in line with a top programmer's salary. What do you say?"

"What exactly would you want? I imagine it has to be pretty detailed."

"Yes, it would. I want you to give them a personality with a thorough background of a middle-class person born and bred in this country. Go as deep as you can—popular culture, religion, ancestry and so on." She gave a wry smile. "Sorry, I'm telling you how to do your job. You'd know exactly what is required."

Daisy couldn't deny her spurt of interest in the proposal. The public usually perceived anthropology as the study of tribal people in remote areas where lifestyles were foreign and exotic, à la Margaret Mead. It was far from the truth. The science was more about how to communicate and socialise in the "here and now." It was a study of what makes a human being unique—language, culture, religion, genetic makeup, and environment. There was no doubt that to build a personality from a clean slate would be a fascinating challenge. But did she have the time? Granted she was living on the premises, but still her primary objective was to find Lindsey a wife. She couldn't ignore that.

"It's tempting, but I'm not sure if I can find the time. I'm not prepared to compromise our marriage contract."

"I wouldn't expect you to finish in two weeks. I would imagine it would take much longer, but maybe you could make a start. I'll run through what I've programmed myself, though it's only basic. I haven't the expertise in the field to produce an in-depth profile."

Daisy wavered. Apart from the appeal of doing something innovating using her academic expertise, working with Lindsey might not be such a bad idea. The woman had been an entirely different person when she had shown her through the lab, so perhaps it could be an avenue to interact with her more. They could get to know each other, become friends. She suspected Lindsey was just as much in need of a friend as she was a wife. And if they became close, it wouldn't be as uphill a battle to ease her into society.

"Perhaps you could email me what you've finished, and I can have a look," she said, not prepared to commit herself at this stage. There was the agency to manage as well, and even though Lindsey was paying extra well, their reputation depended on a flow of clients.

"You'll think about it?"

"I will, though bear in mind that we have to start socializing and I also have a business to run."

"Thank you," said Lindsey, all smiles. "After lunch, I'll show you what I've done. Let's adjourn to the dining room. Oh, sorry…I'm jumping the gun. Have you finished your lessons for the day?"

"I guess." Daisy knew she had been outmanoeuvred. Lindsey had moved on. Her demeanour had slipped from cynical client to genial scientist in the blink of an eye. Even her voice had changed. Now it was melodic and fruity, like a crisp full wine. She gave a wry shrug. "We better finish up about three though. I want to hit the bar by six. A lot of professionals like to have a drink after work."

CHAPTER THIRTEEN

As Lindsey nervously followed Daisy up the flight of steps to the Hazy Grape, she yet again wondered what had possessed her to take the silly bet. Public outings stressed her enough without the added tension of performance. When she hesitated on the top landing, Daisy quickly slid her hand against the small of her back. Her voice warm and encouraging like a primary school teacher urging on a struggling child, she ushered her through the door.

The place was alive with colour. There was bright art deco furnishings and vibrant wall hangings. The bar had a shiny copper tone, and behind it were rows of bottles shimmering in a multi-coloured display as they reflected the pendant lights hanging from a mirrored ceiling. Not that Lindsey was up to appreciating the décor. All she wanted to do was bolt back down the stairs, though there was no hope of that. Daisy had her sleeve in a firm grasp as she manoeuvred them through the crowd to the bar. "We'll get our drinks before we find a table," she said cheerfully. "What'll you have? They do killer cocktails."

"A vodka and orange will do," Lindsey muttered as she tugged the fabric free.

"A screwdriver and a margarita," Daisy called out to the bartender, then picked up a piece of cheese and an olive from a dish and popped them into her mouth. The service was slick, their drinks on the coasters in front of them within a minute. Lindsey automatically reached in her wallet for her credit card, but Daisy waved her away. "I'll get this one. Let's find a table that will give us a great view of the room."

Her eyes firmly straight ahead, Lindsey followed her to a small table in the far corner. It was the ideal spot to scan the people in the room. The club was on the high end of the scale, filled with executive types in power suits as well as those dressed for a night out. Daisy hummed happily while she sipped her drink. "We're in luck. There're quite a few groups of women without men."

Lindsey took a gulp of her vodka, needing the boost. The alcohol hit her stomach and she could feel the pleasant burn. "What happens now?"

"Pick a woman who's facing our direction."

"Okay," muttered Lindsey. She swept her eyes around the room and zeroed in on a sloe-eyed beauty with long glossy dark hair and red pouty lips. She snickered to herself. The woman looked as unapproachable as an iceberg in Antarctica—there was no way she'd even look twice at her. She pointed a finger. "There...the dark-haired woman in the black dress with the diamond-drop earrings."

Daisy checked her out thoroughly and nodded. "Right. Shouldn't be a problem for you."

"Rubbish. She's probably straight," said Lindsey sharply.

"Won't matter. A lot of women are bi-curious."

"Huh! If you say so. Okay, when do I begin?"

Daisy took another swig of her margarita. "Go to the bar for another round. Walk past her table on the way back and do something to catch her eye."

Lindsey hastily polished off the rest of her drink. She was going to need a load of Dutch courage for this. She forced herself to get up, skirting around the tables to reach the end of the bar. After signalling to the barman for a repeat order, she rested back to study the woman in the black dress. She was engrossed in conversation with three women—all looked in their mid- to late-thirties. From their designer clothes, jewellery, and mannerisms, they smacked of wealth and power. There was no mistaking that look. She'd seen it often enough at her parents' dinner parties.

Carrying the two glasses, Lindsey wandered toward their table then exaggerated a stumble as she reached them. They looked up at her with startled glances. Ignoring the others, she met her target's blue eyes. The woman didn't turn away at once but held eye contact for a fraction longer. *Bingo!* Lindsey gave her a slight nod before she moved on.

"Well?" asked Daisy when she put the drinks down.

Lindsey shrugged. "She held my gaze."

"Cool. Now do your thing while we talk."

"Won't the two of us being together put her off?"

"If you play your part properly, she'll get the message you're available."

Lindsey regarded her dubiously but refrained from any more argument. Just better to get it over with. She began with a slow sensuous movement, caressing the side of her throat down to the top of the collarbone. After sipping her drink, she teased the top of the glass with her tongue. As she talked, she fiddled with her hair, pouted with an occasional head toss, crossed and uncrossed her legs, slid a fingertip up and down the glass and played with her earrings. In between, she threw a couple of quick looks in the woman's direction. Aware she probably looked like a shameless vamp on the prowl, she quashed down her acute embarrassment. When she began to dangle a shoe off her toe, she snuck another look over her shoulder. The woman was staring blatantly straight at her. Lindsey raised the stakes, sliding a finger across the top of her cleavage while she swung the shoe in a slow circle.

She turned back to Daisy to find her staring at her chest, her face a rosy red. "Damnit, Lindsey," she whispered. "Tone it down."

"Too much?"

"Shit yes. Be subtler next time."

"Okay. What happens now?" asked Lindsey with a shake of her head.

"Go to the loo. She'll follow you."

"You think she's interested?"

Daisy groaned. "She wouldn't be flesh and blood if she weren't. You were so good *I'm* nearly ready to jump you. Now go."

Oddly aroused to think she had excited Daisy, Lindsey rose reluctantly from her seat. "Promise me you won't leave me too long with her."

"I won't. When you're ready to leave, pull your earlobe. I'll ring you and you can say there's a family emergency."

"Right, here I go." Lindsey resisted the urge to dash through the crowd, though the tension in her belly increased by the second as she slipped past the tables. On the way, she risked a glance at the woman. She was watching her intently. Automatically, Lindsey looked around at Daisy—she too had her eyes locked on her. By the time she reached the short corridor leading to the toilets, her face was glossy with perspiration. With shaky hands, she pushed open the door and sank onto the pedestal with a long whoosh. She waited a minute before exiting the cubicle. Relieved to find the woman was nowhere in the room, she washed her hands, tidied her hair and hurried outside.

Black fabric was the first thing to catch the corner of her eye as she stepped into the corridor. Lindsey turned her head to see the woman against the wall, her arms casually crossed. Now that she was standing, it was evident her slinky cocktail dress was designed to accent her willowy figure. She looked cool and elegant, attributes that did nothing to allay Lindsey's anxiety. She moistened her lips and managed a sultry smile. "Hello," she murmured.

"Hi there," said the woman. She moved away from the wall, stepping closer. "I'm Marian Carmichael."

"Lindsey…um …Ford."

"I couldn't help noticing you and your friend."

"Daisy's my PA."

"Would you like to have a drink with me at the bar?" asked Marian with a brilliant smile.

"I'd love to."

"Great. I trust your assistant won't mind."

"No, she'll be fine with it. We were only planning to have a couple of drinks. She has another engagement shortly."

"Lovely."

Lindsey allowed herself to be led through the crowd. After they ordered, Marian surveyed her with half-closed eyes. "You look like you know how to enjoy yourself, Lindsey. Why haven't I seen you here before?"

"To tell the truth, I didn't know this place existed. My PA suggested it," Lindsey tilted her head and flicked a blond strand away from her eye, "and I'm so glad she did."

"You're from here?"

"Yes. I have an office in the city though I travel a lot."

"I'm an investment banker, but let's not talk shop tonight." She lowered her hand to Lindsey's knee. "What does a woman like you do for recreation?"

"Oh…this and that. I'm flexible. What about you?"

"Ah…I'm not an outdoorsy type. More passive sports interest me."

Lindsey pulled at her earlobe. "Me too."

A lilting laugh purred into her ear and the fingers began to draw circles on her thigh. "How about we get out of here? My apartment is only a block away and I've a bottle of champagne on ice."

Another more desperate tug on the ear—where the hell was Daisy? Lindsey tried not to flinch away, but she struggled to maintain a friendly calm. "*Hold it together*," she admonished herself, but the panic was now just below her skin. If it burst free, she would be powerless to stop it. Then to her immense relief, her phone rang. With an apologetic shrug, she dug out the phone from her purse and pretended to read the caller ID. "Forgive me, but I have to take this."

After a few curt yeses and nos, she tapped it off. "Damn... I'm so sorry, Marian. There's an emergency at home, nothing major but I do have to go. I'd like a rain check on that drink."

"What a shame," exclaimed Marian, her face scrunched up with disappointment. She handed over a card from her pocket. "Here's my phone number. Call me."

Lindsey tucked the card carefully in a slot in her wallet and slid off the stool. "I'll be in touch," she said, then after a slight hesitation, craned forward and pecked Marian on the cheek. "Sorry again," she called out as she hurried off to the front door where Daisy waited.

Without a word, Lindsey brushed past and ran down the stairs. Only when she reached the bottom did the panic attack subside. It left a feeling of complete inadequacy, a black hole that had swallowed every ounce of self-worth. She was pathetic, a total social misfit. With deep long breaths, she waited until Daisy walked up beside her before turning to face her. "I apologise," she said. "I had a bit of a moment there and just had to get out."

"Hey," said Daisy cheerfully. "There's nothing to apologise about. This was only your first outing. You were fantastic."

"There you go patronizing me again."

"Lindsey, believe me when I say you were great."

"Don't you get it? I nearly had a meltdown in there."

"But you didn't. You played your part to perfection."

"That's all very well to say that, but I barely went the distance," whined Lindsey, wishing she could stamp her foot like a child. Daisy was being deliberately blockheaded about this. A little empathy wouldn't hurt.

"That's because you're only up to step one. The next tutorial teaches you how to communicate verbally once you've established contact."

"Then why did you let me go so far?" Lindsey asked incredulously.

"I admit I shouldn't have, but the bet *was* a spur-of-the-moment thing. To be quite honest, you exceeded all my expectations. You're a natural," said Daisy. "Anyhow, the phone call worked, didn't it?"

"Took you long enough to make it. Besides, I didn't enjoy leading that woman on. She was nice," snapped Lindsey. "And do you always have to be so damn jolly? It gets a bit wearing."

"I'll try to be more serious in the future if it makes you happier," said Daisy with an eye roll. "Come on. Let's get something to eat."

"You want to go to a *restaurant* now?"

"Well, I'm starving…I don't know about you."

"Restaurants are a minefield for the socially inept," said Lindsey bitterly.

"No need to worry. We're not going anywhere fancy. There's an Irish pub in the next street that serves great meals," said Daisy, waving in the general direction. "No one will even give you a second glance because they have a great band Saturday night. It's always a hoot."

Even though she was miffed, Lindsey noticed how the glow of the streetlight caught the highlights in Daisy's auburn hair and accentuated the smoky grey of her eyes. She really was a fetching woman, she mused. It was odd how quickly she had seeped under her defences. Normally someone so bubbly would send her anxiety skyrocketing, but Daisy seemed to have the opposite effect. Lindsey was also beginning to look forward to their sparring and banter, though from the stubborn look on Daisy's face it would be pointless to argue about dinner. There was no winning this one. "Okay, I guess I could do with something to eat," Lindsey acquiesced.

CHAPTER FOURTEEN

The Bally Bog was one of Daisy's favourite haunts, a cosy Irish pub with good hearty food and brimming with camaraderie. As usual on a Saturday night, the bar was cluttered with people and buzzed with noise. A waiter, dressed in a garish green leprechaun suit, led them to a dining table far enough away from the rowdy drinkers to enjoy their meal in peace. To her delight, Sean O'Malley appeared at their table as soon as they sat down. He was the proprietor of the pub, a barrel of a man with a florid face, a bent nose courtesy of his days in the boxing ring, and a mess of greying sandy hair. He was also one of the nicest people she had ever met and one of Marigold's first clients.

With his wife and two teenage children, he had immigrated to Australia from Ireland to find work after the global financial crisis hit. Three years later his wife died from breast cancer, and when his son and daughter eventually left home to pursue their own careers, he had been left desperately lonely. Daisy introduced him to Maureen, a pleasant unassuming woman in her mid-forties, equally as lonely. They made the perfect match.

When Daisy leapt up and hugged him, he gave her a smacking kiss on the cheek. "Daisy luv, how are you?"

"Very well, Sean. This is my friend Lindsey."

"'Tis grand to meet you, Lindsey." His huge hand swallowed hers before he turned back to Daisy with lowered brows. "You've become a bit of a stranger. Maureen would love to see you sometime."

"I know. It has been work, work, lately. I promise I'll give her a ring."

"You've too much life in you to hide away at home. It's good to see you out on the town tonight. So, would you be wanting a pint of Guinness?"

"You know I don't like stout," said Daisy with a laugh. "But I'll have a glass of the Kilkenny draught. What about you, Lindsey?"

"The same, thanks."

"Put away your money, luv. It's on the house. The two of you have a good time now."

With a bemused expression, Lindsey watched him walk off to the bar. "How do you know him, Daisy? He obviously thinks a lot of you."

"Believe it or not, he was one of our first customers."

"Really? I'd never have picked him for that. Did you find him a wife?"

"I did. Maureen, a lovely woman who looked after her ailing mother for years. After her mum passed away, she came to us convinced she was on the shelf. It was a match made in heaven. They are remarkably happy."

Lindsey eyed her thoughtfully. "That's something I've been meaning to ask. Are most of your matches between your clients?"

"No, not many. We don't have the volume of the big Internet dating sites. Ours is an exclusive service—we limit the number of clients. Occasionally I find two people on the books compatible, but mostly if a client doesn't already have someone in mind, then it's my job to find that special person."

"Is it difficult?"

"Not really," answered Daisy. "I've a broad network in the social scene. After the grooming sessions, I introduce a client to people that suit their background and age. Once they've had the pertinent introductions, they generally take it from there. It's not always quite that simple as you can appreciate, but that's roughly how I work."

"And that's all your involvement?"

"Good heavens no. I continue to monitor their dating from further afield. I'm their safeguard. You'd be surprised how many predators are out there to take advantage of the lonely."

"And you have a good success rate," asked Lindsey.

"An excellent one. Only a couple have been with us long term, very nit-picky, but I'm confident I'll match them up in the end. I've only had five I couldn't help."

"Why not?"

Daisy's lips automatically thinned as she remembered. "Four turned out to be sleazebags, so I told them to go."

"And the last?"

"He," Daisy shifted uncomfortably in her seat, "...well...he became fixated on me. It was a very nasty experience, one I don't wish to repeat."

Though Lindsey's eyes radiated empathy, she replied with a hard edge to her voice. "I'm sorry someone put you through that. Nobody deserves to be dragged through hell just because they're pretty...or plain."

About to pass it off with a noncommittal remark, it suddenly dawned on Daisy that Lindsey was truly upset. She'd mentioned her mother called her plain, but Daisy hadn't understood the depth of her hurt. Evidently, she harboured a lot of resentment. When she looked at Lindsey again, the vulnerable look had dropped away to be replaced by something distant and guarded. Then the waiter arrived to take their orders, which effectively closed the subject.

Their stew was so tasty that they polished off their large, full bowls. They were on dessert when the floorshow began, so they angled their chairs around for a better view of the stage. The quick throb of music took over. A piano accordion, flute, fiddle, and tin whistle formed the lively band. The singer had a lilting low-pitched voice and sang his way through most of the traditional Irish songs plus a few modern tunes. As the night progressed, and drink flowed freely, patrons enthusiastically belted out the words with him. Daisy felt a tug of envy. Every Irish man and woman seemed to have been born musical. To her surprise, Lindsey hummed along with the old-time favourites.

"You obviously like music," Daisy remarked.

"I love it," said Lindsey, her eyes sparkling as her foot tapped to the tune.

Daisy felt a twitch of relief. She should enjoy the musical she had planned. "Would you like to see *My Fair Lady*? I've tickets."

"That sounds wonderful."

"You wouldn't be nervous amongst the crowd?"

"I don't think so. I was anxious at the cocktail bar but I feel calm here. Probably because no one's looking at me. Either that or your confidence is rubbing off on me," Lindsey said wryly.

"Self-esteem will come. That's only what you're lacking. You have everything else."

Lindsey didn't say anything more, and as time passed, they sidled closer together. Not touching, but Daisy knew it was a giant step for her to sit so close for an extended period. It wasn't until after eleven that Lindsey called Joe to pick them up.

Half an hour later, they made their way out to the street to find their ride parked nearby. The clouds of the morning were only a memory under the clear night sky and the air had a chilly bite. Lindsey pulled the collar of her coat up to her ears, her eyes filmed by moisture. Daisy didn't know if it was from the cool night breeze or from emotion, but she had no doubt the convivial atmosphere of the pub had affected the reserved woman. Wordlessly they climbed into the backseat to go home.

Aware they had found a real connection to each other, they were both reluctant to chance breaking it with idle conversation. It was too fragile yet. Daisy snuggled back into the leather upholstery with her eyes half-closed, while Lindsey stared silently out the window as they drove through the high-rises to the northern suburbs. The long streams of Saturday night traffic had been left far behind by the time they reached the turnoff into the estate. After the driver drove down the lane to the cottage to drop Daisy off, to her surprise, Lindsey walked her to the front door.

She shuffled from one foot to the other while Daisy fitted the key in the lock. When the door clicked open, Lindsey jammed her hands in her pockets and said in a low voice, "Thanks for the night, Daisy. I don't know when I've had so much fun." Then added after a pause, "Not for a very long time anyhow."

"You're welcome. I'm glad you enjoyed yourself. I'd like to be your friend as well as your mentor."

Lindsey raised her chin, her eyes glittering. "I'd like that too. Goodnight."

Daisy didn't go in immediately, instead thoughtfully watched the taillights disappear into the night. Lindsey intrigued her more and more. Strong one moment, fractured the next. There were dozens of questions she wanted to ask her but it was essential to go slowly. Though they had taken a big step in their relationship tonight, she knew if she pushed Lindsey it could drive her away.

And Daisy needed some distance to be objective. It wouldn't do to be too invested in Lindsey's emotional welfare. She was technically only an employee. A specialised one granted, but she was still there because she was paid to do a job. Ultimately, Lindsey would take control of her own life, make her own decisions and go her own way with whomever she chose to share her life.

She felt a quick ripple of unease. As she had watched Lindsey at the Hazy Grape doing the I-want-you-to-be-interested routine, Daisy's libido had unexpectedly sprung to life. Although her mind was firmly centred on business, her body had answered the mating call.

CHAPTER FIFTEEN

"Good morning. It's not like you to sleep in," Bernice remarked as Lindsey wandered into the kitchen.

"We didn't get in 'til after midnight."

"Oh?"

"Daisy and I had a night out. It was very pleasant."

Bernice stared at her. "Good grief. You went out on the town?"

Lindsey ignored the question and silently filled her coffee cup. Everything was too new, too private to share yet. She sipped as her mind drifted. She tried not to dwell on the near meltdown at the Hazy Grape. Cringe worthy. God knows what would have happened if she hadn't managed to escape in time. An involuntary shudder rolled through her body. It had been close, gross humiliation avoided by a whisker.

The memories of the Bally Bog brought a smile. The pub had a quaint charm that resonated far more with her than the expensive restaurants she had frequented with her parents. It had been so much fun, like back in the days with Kirsty, before the accident, before everything went awry. Strangely, as they grew to know each other more, Daisy seemed to make her feel less awkward and flustered. Maybe it was because she had nothing to prove to her. She knew exactly what a social klutz Lindsey was and it didn't seem to faze her.

She sank back in the chair as a wave of apprehension struck. What would Daisy think of her when she knew how damaged she really was? She closed her eyes, willing herself not to go there. But she couldn't keep it a secret forever. She would probably have to come clean before the actual dating and intimacy began.

She heard Bernice huffing as she flipped the eggs onto a plate and Lindsey prepared for her cross-examination. Her housekeeper hated to be left out of the loop. The sound of the bell saved her. With a bound, she escaped to answer the door. Clutching her briefcase, Daisy stood on the doorstep, dressed casually in faded jeans and a blue T-shirt embossed with the words *Chocolate Understands*. She looked like a Cadbury wrapper.

With a friendly nod, she met Lindsey's eyes. "Hi there. Ready to start?"

"Sorry. I slept in. I'm still having breakfast. Would you like some?"

"I had some cereal earlier. A cup of coffee would be nice though."

A delightful floral fragrance wafted after Daisy as she strolled up the hallway to the kitchen. Bernice greeted her enthusiastically, immediately dishing out another meal, accepted after a half-hearted protest. Lindsey sat back and listened to their prattle, impressed how Daisy shrewdly sidestepped the probing about the previous night. She had promised discretion and was proving true to her word. After the plates were taken away, Lindsey procrastinated over the coming lesson by dawdling over her coffee.

Finally, it was Daisy who glanced at her watch and exclaimed, "Oh my. Look at the time. We'd better make a start."

Lindsey pursed her lips. "Let's adjourn to the study."

Daisy headed for the velvet chairs again, leaving her no choice but to follow. All the built-up goodwill dissolved as reams of papers were produced from the briefcase. "I thought this would only take us an hour at the max," Lindsey said curtly.

"Whatever gave you that idea? This is a carefully tailored tutorial which will take us a while to get through."

"Fire away then. By the way, what did you decide about my proposal?"

"I could manage it," Daisy replied with a smile. "But I shall have to fit the work in when I can. Have you a timeline?"

Lindsey met her eyes, mirroring her smile. "Not really. Building the robots is ongoing. Just make sure you document your hours. I'll get the finance department to write up a remuneration contract."

"Okay. I'll read up on what you've done so far and try to make a start while I'm at the cottage. We can discuss it when we have time."

"Good to have you aboard. Perhaps after we finish here I can show you my notes."

Daisy shook her head. "Not today. As soon as we're finished here I'm taking you for a drive to the beach."

"We're going out?"

"Yep…our second date. We'll have fish and chips for lunch beside the sea and then we'll drive through the hinterland on the way home."

Lindsey squirmed in her seat. She had unwittingly boarded an express train that was gathering momentum every minute. Her quiet orderly station was being left far behind. Better try to step on the brake. She rested both hands on the arms of her chair and said in a firm voice. "My driver is having the day off."

"No worries," said Daisy airily. "I intended to take my car."

"Oh!" Lindsey sank back, unable to come up with another excuse. She wished she could—the little red car didn't look particularly roadworthy.

"Let's begin shall we." Daisy spread out the papers on the coffee table. "First off, I'll explain the stages of courtship. Though each love story is unique, they all have the same basic guidelines. 'How to attract a prospective partner' we covered. The second is more pronounced: initial conversation, ascertaining what you have in common and generally putting your best foot forward. There shouldn't be much conflict at this stage because you're trying to impress."

"There wasn't any conflict with Marian. She asked me to go home with her."

Daisy narrowed her eyes. "Did she now? She was obviously after a hot night, not a long-term commitment."

"You think? She may have wanted to talk in a quieter place. She did give me her number and seemed genuinely sorry I had to go."

"Then ring her when you're ready for the dating scene," Daisy said brusquely. "Just remember that courtship precedes intimacy. Strength of a relationship is built slowly with patience. It takes time to build a good solid foundation. Once you jump in the sack, you can't go back. Trying to find a life partner is very different from when you're young and ruled by your hormones. Instant gratification is normal at that age."

"Isn't intimacy an important part of a relationship?"

"Naturally it is. I didn't say you couldn't go to bed with whomever you're dating. Just don't do it until you know you're both ready."

"How long will that take?"

Daisy rolled her eyes. "Just use your common sense. Surely..." She stopped and peered at Lindsey who was unsuccessfully trying to hide her amusement. "Okay, so you think this is funny."

"Well, it is a bit. I might have emotional hang-ups, but I've a brain. I know what you're saying and I agree. One problem is, the only real dating experience I've had was with boys and that was years ago."

"You've never actually been on a proper date with a woman?"

"No."

Daisy absently toyed with a curl. "Then we shall have to establish something first. Do you see yourself as the one doing the asking in this process or do you want to be asked?"

"I'm flexible to a point. Take Marian for example. I sensed she wanted to be the boss. Nicolle was different. I think the two of us would be on an equal footing."

"Hmmm…so which one would you prefer?"

"Both were nice but Nicolle probably would suit me much better. Though Marian was a lovely stylish woman, she's used to getting her own way. Too intimidating."

Daisy stared at her. "You got all this from talking to them briefly?"

"I've made an extensive study of different personalities when I began working on artificial intelligence. The way people hold themselves, mannerisms et cetera. I also know a lot about powerful wealthy people. I've listened to them often enough."

"So, what do you want in a wife?"

Lindsey let out an exasperated breath. "I wrote that on the questionnaire. You read it."

"For crying out loud, Lindsey, you want a paragon of virtue who doesn't exist. Where would I find a mature academic woman, who is kind, a homebody, tidy and always on time, and as well only has an occasional drink and never eats fast food? Even the Virgin Mary wouldn't meet those standards."

"Nonsense. There will be lots out there."

"Stepford wives are damn fiction. No self-respecting woman wants to be a doormat," Daisy said testily.

"I only want someone who would fit in with me. Why are you making such an issue out of it?"

Daisy opened her mouth then closed it again. A myriad of emotions flittered across her face and colour suffused her cheeks. She ducked her head. "I'm sorry. Let's get back to today's subject, shall we." With her eyes fixed on the papers, she continued her lecture in a monotone. She poked across printouts every so often as she discussed each aspect of the initial communication phase.

Lindsey listened silently, but with only half an ear. All the joy seemed to have been sucked out of the room. She could think of nothing to break the ice. Daisy had obviously decided to keep her at arm's length. Then an unsettling thought hit. She may have even decided she wasn't worth much effort, period. Lindsey's hand curled into a fist as a tight lump lodged in her stomach. Finally, to relieve the tension she stood up. "How about we take this outside into the garden? Leave the bookwork here and you can give me all your pointers verbally."

Daisy raised her head in surprise. "I think getting some fresh air is a wonderful idea."

Lindsey looked down at her and slowly extended her right hand. Daisy stared at it for a second, her gaze frank and assessing before she clasped it and allowed herself to be pulled up.

The soft warmth of Daisy's hand seeped over Lindsey's palm with a pleasant tingle. For a moment, she wondered if the circuits in her brain had crossed—it was such a delightful sensation she had trouble thinking of anything else. When Daisy gave a squeeze before she let go, Lindsey stepped back awkwardly and said, "I *am* trying to fit in with you, Daisy. You just have to be patient."

"I know. I was interfering too much. It won't happen again."

A ghost of a smile flittered into Lindsey's lips. "Ha, now that I can't believe. You won't be able to help yourself." When a chuckle burst out from Daisy, she laughed too, more from relief than humour. Everything was on an even keel again. As she led the way out to the side patio, she didn't even attempt to analyse why the thought of being abandoned by Daisy had upset her so much.

She tucked her hands in her pockets, proud of her garden as they wandered in between the beds. The spring flowers were in bloom: the asters, chrysanthemums, geraniums, gerberas, and plumbagoes spilled out colour. When they reached a rustic white-cedar bench under a poinciana tree, she stopped. "Let's sit here."

"This is ideal," said Daisy as she sank down and stretched out her legs. "I know you aren't fond of dry tutorials so we'll do something more practical. I'll be the guinea pig. This is the scenario…we've just met at a wedding and are attracted to each other, so after a couple of dances we have slipped away into the garden for a quiet chat. I'm a bit shy, so you lead. And I expect you to charm the pants off me."

Catching a raised eyebrow, Daisy added with a chuckle, "Metaphorically speaking."

"Right, here I go. Umm…are you having a good time?"

"Really Lindsey, you have to do better than that. You're trying to make an impression here."

"Okay, okay. I like your dress."

"Nope. Try again."

"Are you from around here?"

That was received with a pronounced eye roll.

Lindsey sniffed, annoyed with how superior Daisy looked as she lounged back with arms draped over the back of the bench. She could be one irritating woman sometimes. It was a pity her compassion wasn't on the same scale as her looks. She really was very appealing with her creamy fair complexion, expressive eyes, cute dimples, and floating corkscrew curls. And today her hair looked extra pretty. In the sunlight filtering through the leaves of the tree, it had lightened to a cherry colour alive with dappled highlights. Absently, Lindsey reached over to pluck off a red petal that had drifted down from the tree above onto a curl. "Your hair is beautiful," she murmured.

Daisy sat up straighter and shifted toward her.

"They say a woman's hair is her crowning glory," Lindsey continued in a low breathy voice, "but I never knew what that truly meant until now."

Daisy sidled closer, her eyes turned a liquid dusty grey. "It's a nightmare to keep tidy. I thought about getting it straightened."

"Don't do that. It's lovely how it is." Suddenly, a blue butterfly fluttered down from a hanging limb to land on Lindsey's lap. She plucked it up gently with her fingertips and placed it carefully onto Daisy's hand. "For a pretty lady, a nature's gift that can't be bought. Isn't it perfect?"

"It is. So delicate," Daisy whispered and uttered a sighing "O" as it flew off again.

"How do you fit into the wedding, Daisy? Are you a friend of the groom or bride?"

"The bride. Evelyn and I are cousins."

"I'd love to hear about your family. Please."

As soon as she began, Lindsey knew Daisy was telling her about her actual family. Somehow, it seemed natural that they slipped back into their real lives. For her the lines had been blurred from the start. "I have two younger sisters," Daisy began. "Meg is twenty-six, married with a baby and Beth is twenty-three, single, travelling and working in England."

"Your parents are alive?"

"Oh yes. And both grandmothers and one grandfather. Dad's an agricultural scientist and Mum's a real estate agent."

Lindsey watched her closely as she described her life. Daisy's upbringing was far different from hers. They were worlds apart. She had loving parents who supported her. Lindsey felt a wave of envy and a sense of loss so great she had to fight back a sob. When Daisy asked her about her life and dreams, she deftly closed the subject. She would never have been able to keep the vitriol from leaking into her words. "That's enough. How did I do?"

Daisy looked at her blankly. "Sorry?"

"With the scenario…the lesson?"

"Oh, that. You were good…better than good actually. I forgot we were role-playing."

Lindsey smiled to reassure her. "I forgot too. I enjoyed hearing about your family. You obviously love them very much."

"I do. Now, since you passed with flying colours, shall we call it a day and get on the road." When they climbed to their feet, Daisy added with a lopsided grin, "We'll act as though this is our first date, shall we."

CHAPTER SIXTEEN

No matter how many times she visited the beach, the surf always fascinated Daisy. Today the sea was restless, ideal for the board riders and wind surfers who were out in droves. As they strolled along the top of the retaining wall, she watched the long lines of white-topped waves rolling in. They broke in explosions of foam onto the beach, leaving clouds of spray swirling into the air like bursts from aerosol cans. Then when the sea receded, the misty curtains were flagged back in the breeze. She never tired of the sight.

After they slipped off their shoes at the bottom of the flight of wooden steps, she smiled at the pleasure on Lindsey's face as she dug into the powdery sand with her toes. "Come on," Daisy yelled, suddenly carefree. "Let's go for a run."

By the way Lindsey laughed as she kept pace, her past was forgotten for the moment. Once they were far enough away from the marked area designated for swimmers, Daisy gestured to a patch of sand at the edge of a rock pool. "Let's sit there and have our lunch."

Lindsey settled down with legs crossed and twisted the caps off the water bottles. "It must be the exercise and salt air because I'm famished."

"Me too," said Daisy. She unwrapped their fish and chips and squeezed over lemon, content with the way the trip had panned out so far. In the hour and a half journey to the beach, they had talked nonstop without any awkwardness. At first, Lindsey seemed a little reticent, but relaxed by the time the freeway left the heavily built-up areas. She didn't appear self-conscious as they lobbed information back and forth, although Daisy made sure the conversation was light. Dumping sensitive material on the first date was a no-no. Surprisingly, their likes and dislikes were similar, although Lindsey hadn't travelled much.

"Did you come to the beach much when you were young?" Daisy asked.

"Never. My mother dislikes the sea, and my father is indifferent to it. It was never an option for an outing."

"What a pity. It's one of my favourite places." Daisy took a bite of battered fish, groaning in pleasure. "This is wonderful."

"I'll say. What is it?"

"Barramundi. Freshly caught this morning, according to the girl taking the order." She shot Lindsey a glance. "This is one place you can bring a date. Not everyone expects to be wined and dined all the time."

"Ha…no worries on that score. I won't be doing that too much." She stretched back casually with her weight on her elbows, looking more relaxed than Daisy had ever seen her. "This is more my style. There's something about waves that's rather soothing."

"Yes. There is."

"What else did you do in your childhood?"

"All the usual things I guess…movies, swimming, sports. We had a big backyard, large enough for a game of cricket with the kids in the street. We were very competitive. What about you?"

"Nothing like that. You know the old saying…children should be seen and not heard."

Daisy looked at her curiously. "Come on. There must have been some highlights."

Instantly Lindsey's eyes became remote and unfathomable. "I spent most of my life catering to a woman who could never accept me for what I was. There wasn't much fun in our household. My mother expected absolute obedience. Any exuberance would be met with tight-lipped impatience, or worse, a lesson on deportment. You have no idea what that does to a child."

Daisy's eyes moistened. "No, I guess I don't," she whispered. She turned to take another bite, remaining silent to give Lindsey time to compose herself. Not that Daisy had any words of comfort that wouldn't sound clichéd. She couldn't imagine a child's pain when her mother couldn't tolerate her. But after a while, her continuing silence seemed as if she was letting Lindsey down. Struggling to keep her tone casual, she said, "I'm sorry. I didn't mean to pry. Let's get onto a less painful subject."

"You're right. I've got to learn to lighten up."

"Just remember I'm here for you," Daisy murmured, reaching over to give her knee a reassuring pat. "Now…you can pick where we next go on one of our dates. What would you like to do?"

"What have you lined up?"

"The theatre, dinner, the art gallery, and museum, maybe a food fest, a movie, and a bit more sightseeing. But I don't want to drag you along to something you would absolutely hate."

"Okay," Lindsey said with a sidelong glance. "I think you'll enjoy this. Let's have a real adventure and go skydiving."

Daisy's heart gave a lurch. "You mean jump out of a plane?"

"You'll love it."

"Shit no, I wouldn't."

"That's not the spirit. You said I could choose. You have to honour your commitment."

Daisy barely could control her hand tremors as something hard caught in her throat. She hated heights with a passion. Just the thought of leaping into the air thousands of feet above the ground sent her into a cold sweat, but she was trapped. She hoped her heart would be strong enough to take the shock. Resigned, she muttered hoarsely, "Very well."

A chuckle bubbled out of Lindsey. "You should see your face. Did you think I was serious?"

"Ha! That wasn't funny. Act your age."

"Uh-uh. Someone can't take a joke."

Daisy gave a reluctant smile. "You had me there. I loathe heights."

"I don't exactly hate them but parachuting out of a plane is the last thing I want to do. Perhaps we might be able to go sailing though. I think I'd like that."

"That sounds a fun idea. I doubt if we'll fit it in this two weeks but what say we do it in three or four weeks? That'll give us something to look forward to." Daisy rose to her feet, dusted off her pants and gathered the empty paper and bottles into the plastic bag. "Come on. It's a lovely day so let's walk up to the point before going back."

* * *

Groaning, Daisy snapped off the alarm. Not only was she still tired, she was also tender from sunburn. What an idiot for forgetting the sunscreen; she'd ended up looking like a lobster. After a bathroom stop and a trip to her laptop to check her email, she made the usual morning wake-me-up cup of coffee. As she sipped, she thought over the previous day. Lindsey had been great company after she'd relaxed: funny, smart, and seemingly without guile. A great catch for someone. One thing she did work out. Lindsey, while she liked some equality in a relationship, would never play the subservient role.

Daisy picked up her phone—time to check into the office.

After a few rings, Allison's voice came on the line. "Hi, what's up?"

"Have you time to talk?"

"Yes. Noel's taking the girls to school today. They've just left."

"Firstly, are there any problems at work?" Daisy crossed her fingers—the last thing she wanted was to have to go into the city.

"Everything's fine. I've nearly finished our website upgrade. I've sent packages out to the prospective new clients, with a memo telling them you will see them in three weeks. I'm going ahead with their profiles. Oh, and the university wants you as a guest speaker in three months for the anthropology department's annual dinner. That's a bit of a coup. The rest of the odds and ends can wait."

"Great. I'm going to be tied up here. Could you check out places to sail, please?"

"Well, well. You're going on a date. Who is she?"

Daisy chuckled. Allison's voice was laced with curiosity. "It's not that kind of date. I'd like to take Lindsey sailing."

"Really? Things must be progressing well."

"All's going to plan. She's settling into the program just fine now."

"Hmmm…you sound as if the two of you are getting along famously," said Allison.

"We are. We went to the beach yesterday and she's really a bit of a sweetie under that Iron Lady exterior."

"Maybe you could come back earlier to the office."

Daisy felt a stab of annoyance at the thought of having to cut her time here short. The cottage was first-class accommodation and she was looking forward to showing Lindsey around the town. As well, she was keen to start with the robot project. A vacation was well overdue and it was beginning to feel like one. "No, no. I'm staying out here for the full two weeks. When I get back, you should take a break."

"Are you treating this like a holiday? What's with the change of heart? Only days ago, you were moaning she was difficult."

"I was wrong," replied Daisy, struggling to keep her tone casual and brisk. "She's good company."

"She shouldn't need too much to get her into the social scene then. That'll make your job a lot easier."

"She's going to need a lot of support because she's very rusty with dating."

"Just be careful. Remember our rule not to get too involved with a client," Allison said.

Daisy's ears pricked. The motherly tone was backed with a hint of censoring. "I'm quite aware of that, but there's nothing routine about this assignment. The woman is paying us a small fortune to find her a wife so I think it only fair I give her as much help as is needed."

"Okay, point taken. You should know what you're doing. I'll text if anything untoward happens."

"Right. Bye for now." She straightened up, irritated. What was Allison's problem? She wasn't a raw beginner. There was no reason why she couldn't take Lindsey out on a few dates. Sure, it was standard practice with her program only to introduce her clients around once or twice, then if they needed more, she would tell them the places to go or arrange the tickets to a social event. They would take it from there themselves. But Lindsey needed much more help, and experience was the best way to teach. Besides, Daisy was single, solvent, and fancy-free. Who better to guide the woman through pitfalls of the dating scene?

CHAPTER SEVENTEEN

"We're going to discuss understanding human emotional interaction today," Daisy announced in a voice that heralded that her full attention was required.

Curiosity piqued, Lindsey studied her. From the concentration on Daisy's face, this lesson was extra important. "I'm all ears."

"Our first chapters covered meeting someone and the first getting-to-know-you dates. The next step is the crucial one. The point when the couple must decide whether to take their fledgling attraction further. That's when the dating becomes more frequent, when sexual intimacy is raised a notch."

"Why does everything have to be based on sex? I thought a more rational approach to finding someone to share your life would be practical. Wanting the same lifestyle should be a priority."

"If that's the only basis you pick a partner then forget it," replied Daisy. "Rational detachment is a euphemism for lack of emotion. You'd both be miserable after six months."

"You think?"

"Yes, I do. We've moved on from the age of arranged marriages. In this country anyhow. Wives were regarded as property and a lot were very unhappy."

Lindsey could only shake her head. "So why did I have to write down what I wanted in a wife? It was obviously an exercise in futility."

"Not at all," said Daisy. "It got you thinking. But finding the perfect match isn't so black and white. It's wonderful, messy and sometimes it hurts. Sure, liking the same things is very important, but ultimately it won't be why you make your choice. It'll be sexual attraction to begin with, but eventually love will take preference. Then it won't be about your own gratification, it'll be to please her." Daisy pointed at her chest. "You filled out that questionnaire with your brain and not your heart. You thought someone who didn't disturb the status quo in your household would make you happy. You may as well marry your robot."

"Be that as it may," Lindsey answered, affronted. "But I know I won't be happy with someone with half a brain or who expects to be entertained lavishly. That's just not me."

"I know, Lindsey, and that's the reason of all this. I'm here to introduce you to eligible women who would suit you. I know that besides attraction, compatibility is very important too. There's no point in trying to match you with someone not swimming in the same lane."

"Does that mean she has to be wealthy?"

"Of course not, though self-made women would be your equal and I know you'd be happier with someone who would take interest in your work. However, there are many bright ladies out there not rich who would be equally as suitable. But that wasn't what I meant. The answer is in your DNA. We have a better chance of being happy if we're biologically suited."

"So how do I know that?"

Daisy gestured to the wad of papers on the table. "I've explained it all in detail here. It's in our makeup. Attraction may feel natural, but that doesn't mean it's random. It's more than good looks or a witty pickup line. Scientific studies have found love is not coincidental. We have a group of genes called HLA and here's where it gets a bit confusing. While everything else should be compatible, we're attracted to those who have a dissimilar HLA gene. Too close and we don't mesh. It's all about genetic diversity—nature's way of ensuring survival of the species. It's why the Tasmanian devil is dying out—the isolated population is so inbred."

"So how do two people know they're genetically meant for each other?"

"Some say the eyes have it, but there's mounting evidence that we smell out this gene. That body odours are strongly linked to sexual attraction. That's why face-to-face has a far better chance of success than chatting on the Internet."

Lindsey's stomach gave an anxious lurch. She hoped she wouldn't fall for someone's deodorant. Daisy's slant on matchmaking was as complicated as ancient hieroglyphics. "I suppose it would be wiser not to argue and do what I'm told," she muttered.

Daisy beamed. "I'd advise you to. Dating is meant to be easy and fun, so let's go through the basics. Since you're a dominant personality, you'll automatically want to take most of the initiative in the courting process once you get the hang of it."

"Does that mean I have to do all that wine-and-dine rigmarole?" Lindsey asked.

"No. It's about showing you care. Send her flowers, a text to say you enjoyed the date, make her feel valued, things like that. Give her little presents like a book or scarf, but nothing too expensive at first."

"Okay. That I can do. Can I ask you something?"

"Sure, go ahead," replied Daisy breezily.

"Do you date?"

"Of course. It's been a few months though. Work's keeping me too busy." She gave a wry smile. "My family has been nagging me to get back out there."

"How many dates do you go on before you go to bed with someone?"

Daisy's cheeks flushed and her fingernails began to scrape on the arm of the chair. "That's a bit personal."

"I'm not trying to pry," Lindsey said. "I just want to understand what the expectations are with sex nowadays."

"I never go to bed on the first date or the second. Kissing is fine. It depends after that on how much I like them."

Lindsey rocked back in her chair and regarded her thoughtfully. "You're not actively looking for a permanent partner then."

"We're all looking once we're over twenty-five, Lindsey. Like all animals, a human's psyche is programmed to procreate and nurture. It's called the biological clock."

"But you're not practising what you preach. You're having sex and moving on."

Daisy gave an awkward little wriggle. "I'm not a damn nun."

Lindsey chuckled under her breath—by the glare Daisy was giving her, she'd managed to get under her skin. "But what you're saying is rather ambivalent. You're telling me to hold off until I'm comfortable with a relationship, but you jump into bed after a couple of dates."

"For shit sake, you're making me sound like I shag all the time. I'm single and I believe in monogamy. If I like someone and we are going out, then yes, I'll have sex. But I do *not* pick anyone up for a one-night stand."

"So, you haven't met the man of your dreams yet."

Daisy looked as if she wanted to go for her jugular now. "That's enough about me," she said in a no-nonsense tone. "This is about you. If you're worried about sex, then don't be. You'll manage. Tell her you're out of practice and she'll take the lead."

"I hope it's that easy. Perhaps you could show me how to go about initiating a goodnight kiss," said Lindsey. When Daisy's face flushed red, she added hastily, "I didn't mean that you would have to actually kiss me, just…you know…give me a few pointers."

"I'll put that on the agenda," said Daisy with a hint of throatiness. "And tomorrow morning we'll have dance lessons."

"Not necessary. I'm an accomplished ballroom dancer…my mother made sure of that."

"That's not exactly the type I was referring to. More nightclub style—hip swinging and leg and arm movements in time with music. Five or six basic moves should be enough."

Lindsey blanched. "You expect me to dance at nightclubs?"

"Believe it or not, Lindsey, women will be falling over themselves to dance with you. You're wealthy, smart, classy, and the new girl on the block. As well as that, you're mysterious."

Lindsey's heart jumped. The last thing she wanted was to be in the limelight. "Look, I used to go to nightclubs at university. I really don't think I'd like that scene now. I've…I've…" She flopped back in the chair, wishing she could just say it but it wasn't any use. She couldn't bear to see the look of revulsion on Daisy's face.

"Don't worry. I won't let you go there until you're ready. We'll take it slow for a start. There's no hurry…even if it takes a couple of months to get your confidence," crooned Daisy reassuringly.

"You don't understand. I—"

"Yes, I do. We all have our insecurities. I saw a funny video clip on Facebook the other day. An interviewer asked ten gorgeous-looking women if they were happy with how they looked. Not one was. Either their hair was too curly or too straight, their noses too long or too short, their boobs too big or too small et cetera, et cetera. It's a rare woman who is perfectly happy with her appearance."

Lindsey bit her lip, deciding to let it go. Daisy was going to be here a while and, in the meantime, she'd figure out a way to tell her.

"So," said Daisy, "I've some literature that I've put together for you to read. It relates to the dating scene today, for things have moved quickly in the last fifteen years. It tabulates the modern fads, popular music and so on. Even though the bulk of your interaction should be face-to-face or by phone, women will text. Practise it. Be wary of sexting though. Do you know what that is?"

Lindsey looked at her blankly. "Haven't a clue."

"Sending dirty messages and explicit photos of yourself via your mobile."

"People do that?"

"Yep."

"That's gross," said Lindsey, rather scandalized.

"It's a no-no until you're in an established relationship. Then you can do what you like but be careful. Those photos can be used for blackmail or revenge porn."

"You don't have to worry about me on that score. It'll never be my scene. I can't imagine anyone wanting to see my private parts," said Lindsey with a shudder.

"You would have to get yourself a landing strip," said Daisy, a spark of amusement in her eyes.

Lindsey cleared her throat, her body prickling. "I guess I have a lot to learn," she said then continued in a bright artificial voice. "There is one question I've been meaning to ask. What happens if more than one woman asks me out?"

"There's nothing wrong with going out on friendly dates with a variety of women. It's a way of getting to know them. Eventually you will decide whom you want to see more seriously." Daisy gave her an earnest look. "Just remember you don't have to wait to be asked out. If you see someone you like, then you do the inviting."

"Okay…one last question. Is it likely I won't be able to choose between two women?" She cleared her throat, embarrassed. "That is presuming there are two women out there who want me."

"True love of a pair bond is anchored in emotional exclusivity. It is a scientific fact that it is nearly impossible to love more than one person at a time."

"I never knew that," Lindsey said, then added with a shrug. "Not that I've ever had cause to give it much thought."

"Don't worry. All that's about to change." Daisy slipped a USB stick into her laptop. "Now, I've a video clip of disco dancing which we'll practise tomorrow morning."

Lindsey sat back with a resigned sigh as a scene of a crowded club morphed onto the screen. For a few moments she stared silently at the crush of people dancing to fast loud music. Couples squeezed into every available space, gyrating wildly to the thumping beat and flashing lights. Her body started to hum as the memories came. Sneaking off with Kirsty to their favourite bar—vodka cocktails—dancing 'til they dropped. She had loved it.

Then Daisy's voice brought her back with a jolt. "Look at that dude in the leather pants. A deluded idiot, doing the typical mating dance that goes down like a lead balloon."

Lindsey leaned forward for a closer look. The man in question was thrusting his pelvis forward while wriggling his hips and waving arms in the air. "He looks constipated," she commented dryly.

Daisy chuckled. "You nailed it. Okay, now have a look at the bloke with the spiky hair and pink shirt. He has all the moves and the attention of everyone around him. See the difference...his movements are subtle and smooth. Take note of them. Basically, there are only six variations in his repertoire."

"What about slow dances?"

"There're a couple on the clip. Pretty much standard. Some couples dance with grace, while others drape themselves over each other." She stood up. "I'll make a start on the robot profiles and get out of your hair so you can watch this in peace."

"Right. I'll see you in the dining room at noon. You can work in the lounge if you like. The décor should stimulate your creative thoughts."

Lindsey turned in her chair to watch Daisy walk out. Her head was starting to throb. Talk about a frank talk. She'd been out of circulation so long she was like a babe in the woods. It was a confusing dating world out there now. And what on earth was a landing strip?

CHAPTER EIGHTEEN

Daisy woke up to the sun shining on the quilt and a constant beeping. After she switched off the phone alarm, she glanced at the time and date. Had it really been ten days since she moved into the cottage? Time was flying by—it always did when she was enjoying herself. She and Lindsey had settled into an easy friendship. They had a teasing banter going, with a casual intimacy characteristic of those who have grown to like each other's company.

The only hitch—Lindsey was still guarded about being touched. The dance lessons had been a fizzer. Not only had she refused to cooperate, Lindsey had become so upset that Daisy caved in and postponed them to a later date.

As she walked to the bathroom a familiar tapping caught her ear. On the windowsill, a peewee pecked at its reflection in the glass pane. It did it every morning until she shooed it away. She wondered if it would ever realize it wasn't another bird, though she doubted it. It was a territorial thing in the breeding season—it saw a rival in the glass. Most everything in the animal kingdom was deep-seated. And humans were no different. Some clients repeated their mistake as the peewee kept doing, repeatedly choosing the same type of unsuitable partner.

She wandered from the bedroom, stuck a mug under the coffee machine and popped a slice of bread into the toaster. After checking her email, she heaped a spoonful of sugar into the hot drink and slathered jam on the toast before settling down to organize the robot notes from the previous day. Her work had been fruitful—she had made significant inroads into the preliminary profile. She'd named the robot *Stephen*, which Lindsey, having been a fan of Stephen Hawking, thought suited him admirably. Daisy didn't mention she'd called it after her grandad because the robot's gait mirrored his arthritic walk.

She and Lindsey had been on more dates, all low-key: the art gallery, a river cruise, a couple of sight-seeing road trips and yesterday they'd spent the afternoon strolling around a food fest on South Bank. Pleasant no-pressure excursions that Lindsey seemed to enjoy.

At eleven, Daisy was leaving for the city to have lunch with her mother, something she normally loved. But not today. Allison had let slip when her mother rang the office that Daisy was temporarily living on the estate. Sheila had immediately phoned, requesting they meet at noon at their favourite restaurant. Daisy felt out of sorts about the invitation, aware she was going to be quizzed. She didn't want to discuss Lindsey with anyone. It was an invasion of the woman's privacy and she'd promised discretion. But she knew her mother would be hard to fob off. *Crap!*

At ten, she put on a yellow sun frock, applied lip gloss, brushed her hair and slipped on her heels. After a fruitless search for her purse, she realized she'd left it at the main house the night before when she'd stayed for a nightcap. The side door was open when she drove around the corner, so she entered via those stairs. About to turn left to the lounge, she noticed the laboratory door was wide open at the end of the passageway. She chuckled. Typical Lindsey—couldn't take a day off. With a jaunty step, she made a detour to say hello before she left.

The female robot was flat on its back on the long stainless-steel workbench, minus the outside casing over its abdominal area. From where Daisy stood, the exposed mechanical parts seemed a mass of wires, cogs, and wheels. Lindsey was hunched over the table, repairing something under a curved plate that served as the rib cage. Fascinated, she edged closer for a better view. The greeting died in her throat when she slowly comprehended what she was seeing. Lindsey was soldering a cog to a thin piece of metal, holding the pieces together with suture forceps while she worked. But they weren't an ordinary pair.

The forceps were the thumb and forefinger of her left hand.

Daisy let out an involuntary, "What the fff…," and just managed to bite off the last word when Lindsey's head shot up. Her heart gave a huge thud as the flashing violet eyes met hers. She took an automatic step backwards. Lindsey looked horrified. *Oh shit!*

"Hi, Lindsey," she said, trying to sound light and casual. "I saw the door open. Sorry, I should have knocked I guess but…" Her voice trailed away. Best to shut up. She thought about a hasty retreat, but that wouldn't solve a thing.

"Get out, Daisy, and leave me alone." The initial angry shock had faded out of Lindsey's face. She slumped onto a chair beside the table and dropped her left arm out of sight.

"No…I'm not going. We need to discuss this."

"Why? So you can see what a freak I really am?" Lindsey's gaze dropped fixedly onto the floor.

"What are you talking about? Having a prosthetic arm doesn't make you a freak. Lots of people have artificial limbs."

"You know all about it, do you?" The bitter words were spat out.

Daisy's heart went out to her. God, how crap was this! "Our neighbour, Mr Beazley, lost his leg in Vietnam. It's obviously not the same but it doesn't seem to worry him."

"Why is it that you always have an answer for everything? Maybe you have one for this. How on earth do I tell a woman I have only one arm when she asks me to dance, let alone when she wants to go to bed with me?" Lindsey turned her head away and gulped. "I was a fool to think this would work."

With a few strides, Daisy rounded the table to kneel in front of her. "I don't know who gave you the idea that good women are so shallow, but whoever told you that needs a swift kick up the backside. Many people have disabilities and live happy lives with understanding partners. My aunt had a breast off and my mother's friend lost all her hair at fifty. One pads her bra and the other wears a wig. Both husbands are very supportive." She gently took Lindsey's right hand. "What I'm trying to say here, sweetie, is that it won't be a major obstacle."

Visibly shaken, Lindsey was silent for a long moment before she muttered, "You don't understand. There is no way I'll be able to tell someone without having a meltdown. I've been seeing a therapist for years and I still go into a sweat just thinking about it."

"Right," said Daisy, getting to her feet, her mind ticking over. "Then we must devise a way to let everyone know *before* we start going out to find a wife. And in a way that you're going to be admired for it rather than pitied."

"How on earth are you going to do that?"

"Don't know yet, but I'll think of a way," said Daisy then continued with an encouraging smile. "Come on. Aren't you going to tell me all about it?"

"You're not going to let up until I do, are you?"

"Nope."

Lindsey gave a half-hearted shrug. "Why not. Here's the abridged version. I was involved in a motorbike accident when I was twenty-one. We hit a truck and my left arm was completely crushed and almost severed. As well, I suffered two broken legs, a bleeding kidney, multiple abrasions and cuts. I was nearly two years in and out of hospitals having reconstruction surgery, skin grafts, and rehabilitation therapy."

"You poor thing," whispered Daisy. "Was that why you decided to form your own company and go into this business?"

"Yes, though it was a two-fold decision. I soon learnt there was an urgent need to bring prosthetics into the digital age and a real need to make them better cosmetically."

"May I see your arm?"

Lindsey hesitated a moment before she thrust it toward her without a word. Daisy ran her hand lightly up to the elbow in awe of the artisanship. "Gosh, it's superb. If I didn't know better, I'd think it was real." She studied the hand curiously. "How do you get these prongs back?"

Lindsey reached across and twisted the two knuckles. The two extensions retracted into her thumb and index finger, leaving no trace on the taut outer skin. "I thought I'd add them to save time and energy when working with delicate parts."

"Very clever. Is it a full prosthesis?"

"Yes, the whole arm," said Lindsey. "The ball at the end fits into the socket joint of my shoulder. The ball is fitted with a receiver that is electronically joined to a small computer with electrodes embedded in the motor and sensory lobes of my brain. It works a lot like a cochlea implant, though far more complex."

As Lindsey continued, Daisy felt her own tension slide away. She was pleased to see Lindsey was becoming more relaxed as her explanation became more convoluted. Daisy didn't interrupt, though her eyes were beginning to glaze over with all the technical jargon. Finally, there was silence and Lindsey said sheepishly, "Sorry. I got carried away. I hope I wasn't boring you."

"No...no, of course not. It was absolutely fascinating. I am totally blown away. You're bloody brilliant and I love how passionate you are about your work. I can see why you're so highly regarded in your field. Maybe another day you might tell me more, but unfortunately I do have to go." Regretfully, she pushed off the floor and dusted her knees. "Sorry, I wish I could stay but I'm going to be dreadfully late if I don't leave immediately."

Lindsey swept her eyes over her. "You look very nice. Big date?"

"Ha...I wish. I'm having lunch with my mother."

"Oh, have a good time then."

Something in the way the words were spoken made Daisy's ears prick. Lindsey sounded disappointed she hadn't been invited. She wished she could have brought her along, but that would have courted disaster. Her mother would have immediately presumed she was her genuine date and given her the third degree. Lindsey's sexual orientation would have been out of the bag in two seconds. She'd toyed with the idea of letting Lindsey know, but she'd made a policy never to discuss her private life with clients. From their perspective, she should only be viewed as a means to an end. Or at the most, a friend.

"I will. She always eats at the same restaurant and the food is incredible. Now I'd better collect my things and be on my way."

She turned towards the door, then swung back around and pecked Lindsey on the cheek. "Thanks for showing me," she whispered.

All the way to town, Daisy berated herself. She'd been as thick as a brick. She should have twigged long ago. All the signs were there: Lindsey's aversion to touch, her refusal to dance, her fear of intimacy, and Bernice's words "the loss of." But the most obvious, her company made the damn things.

There had to be something more to Lindsey's story though. Surely losing a limb shouldn't stay so traumatic after all those years. She would have thought people learnt to adapt, especially Lindsey who wore state-of-the-art technology. But then again, she had never been in that position so it would be wrong to trivialize the effect of such an injury. If she could hazard a guess, she would say something else was a barrier to the healing process and it was likely to have something to do with the mother. Then Lindsey had said *we hit the truck*, which meant there was someone else with her on the bike. Unfortunately, unless Lindsey chose to tell her she couldn't pry.

Daisy pulled into the parking lot and hurried to the front door of the Chelsea. She knew what was imperative to do first. After she finished her lunch, she'd have to work out a way to announce Lindsey's prosthesis to the world.

CHAPTER NINETEEN

As usual, the charming dining room was crowded. Daisy spotted her mother's table.

"Sorry I'm late, Mum," she murmured. After giving her a peck on the cheek, without preamble she picked up the menu. "I guess you're waiting to order."

"Held up with something important?" asked Sheila.

Daisy studied the menu, taking her time to answer. "Nothing world shattering. Just some odds and ends I couldn't leave for tomorrow."

"Hmm…I think I'll have the calamari salad. What about you?"

"I'll have the Thai prawns and peppers."

A waiter immediately appeared, took the order and disappeared.

"So," said Sheila, toying casually with the cutlery. "Allison told me you're living for a couple of weeks on the Jamieson-Ford estate."

Daisy nearly rolled her eyes. She would have to speak with Allison about what she told her mother. She was fishing already. There was no doubt she would have found out how important Lindsey was. "Yes, for two weeks. Would you like a glass of water?"

"Please. They say Lindsey is quite a mystery woman."

"Who says?"

"Oh…everyone," said Sheila with a vague wave of her fingers. "Nobody seems to know a thing about her."

"Really? How odd," Daisy murmured, feigning surprise.

"What is she like?"

"Nice. Intelligent. A regular person."

Sheila peered at her, clearly annoyed. "You're not going to tell me, are you?"

"Come on, Mum. I'm renting her cottage. That's all."

"If it's just that, why are you being so close-lipped about her?"

"Because the woman deserves her privacy. I've no intention of gossiping when she was kind enough to let me rent."

"What on earth are you doing to require accommodation way out that way?" asked Sheila, clearly not ready to let it go.

"I've a client nearby," Daisy replied, tempering irritation as she rattled off her bogus explanation. When her mother raised an eyebrow, she added, "She's disabled."

"Oh."

Thankfully, the waiter appeared with their meals, which gave Daisy an excuse to change the subject. "How is Aunt Di after her op?"

It did the trick. On another tangent now, her mother began a detailed description of her sister's gall bladder operation. Daisy tuned out and peered around the room. A fair-haired woman sitting at a table in the corner with two men in suits caught her eye. Dressed casually in cargo pants and an army military green shirt, the woman looked completely out of place. Though from the easy way she was waving her fork to make a point, she looked like she didn't care what people thought. Daisy smiled. She knew her well—what you saw was what you got with Mackenzie Griffith. When she caught her eye, she acknowledged the reporter with a nod. Mac smiled back with a little wave.

Daisy reached for her glass, her mind racing as an idea crystallised. The best way to tell the world about Lindsey's arm would be through a press article. Publicity was a touchy thing though. Any noteworthy news caused a flood of social media, which invariably included a few downright nasty ones. Lindsey's state of mind was far too fragile to cope with some idiot slagging her. No, the article had to be watertight, with no room for trolling. And who better to write it than Mac, a respected one-time war correspondent and one of the top journalists in Australia. She would jump at the chance to get the prized interview, a huge coup considering Lindsey had shunned the press for so long. Pleased now she had a plan, Daisy shifted her attention back to her mother.

Sheila was gazing at her with a frown. "I swear you didn't hear a word I said."

"I was thinking about something."

"Why are you so preoccupied? You turn up late without an explanation and drift off into fairyland. Care to share?"

"I can't," said Daisy with a noncommittal shrug. "Client confidentiality."

"Whatever it is, it doesn't seem to have affected your health. You look glowing."

"Huh! Is that a polite way of saying I'm putting on weight?"

Sheila gave a soft laugh. "No, it's not. It means you look happy." She peered closely at Daisy. "Have you met someone?"

"Noooo," she answered and bit into a prawn as Lindsey's image popped into her head without warning. Heat touched her cheeks. The slight flush was not lost on her mother who had an inbuilt maternal radar when it involved her daughters.

"There *is* someone," she said triumphantly. "I knew it."

"There isn't, Mum. Believe me, I'd tell you if I was romantically involved. She's just a friend I've been taking sightseeing."

"And you wish there could be more?" Her mother studied her intently.

Flustered, Daisy dropped her eyes and fiddled with the corner of her serviette. She couldn't consider her that way but when Lindsey had become upset this morning, Daisy had felt such a surge of protectiveness that she'd even called her sweetie. She hoped that Lindsey hadn't noticed that slip-up. "It's not like that...she's not available...but...well...we like the same things and have the same sense of humour. I've found in my line of business that it's not common to get on so well in such a short time."

"That's a pity, dear. Maybe she has a sister."

Daisy chuckled. Her mother was always the optimist. "That's enough about my love life or the lack of it. Do you want dessert?"

"Why not. Let's share a piece of that lovely lime cheesecake we had last time."

Daisy pushed back her chair. "You order. I want a quick word with Mackenzie Griffith over there. Won't be a sec."

Determined to go forward with her idea, Daisy wound her way through the room until she reached the table. The trio stopped talking and looked up at her as she approached. She cleared her throat. "Sorry for interrupting but I was wondering if I could have a quick word with you, Mac."

Without hesitation, the reporter rose with a smile. "Excuse me please, gentleman. Hi Daisy, how can I help you? Do you want to go somewhere private?"

"No, no. This will only take a moment. I won't hold you up. I was wondering if you and I could get together soon. I've a proposition for you that I'm sure you will really like."

"That's sound intriguing. Would later this afternoon suit?"

"Super. I'm free after lunch."

"Then how about we meet at the Coffee Club down on the corner at three?"

"Perfect. I'll see you there," said Daisy and with a spring in her step, wove her way back to her mother.

"Planning an article about your agency, dear?"

"It's for a friend," Daisy replied without elaborating.

Sheila pursed her lips. "You're full of yourself today, missy. That is a secret too I presume."

"Yes, Mum, it is. When I can tell you, I shall."

"Well I'll say this for you," said Sheila with a twinkle in her eye. "You're far more discreet than Meg."

Daisy snorted, having been the topic of her sister's babbling and sometimes nasty tongue often enough. "Meg's a conduit for gossip—it runs in and it flows straight out. You don't have to even flick a switch."

"How true. But the trouble is," murmured Sheila, "she doesn't do anything remotely as interesting as you. Ah—here's our dessert. It looks divine."

* * *

Mac was already waiting on the footpath outside the Coffee Club when Daisy arrived a few minutes before three. They shared a quick hug before walking through the entrance. The pleasant aroma of ground coffee beans drifted past the woman behind the counter as she took their orders. On the way, Daisy had debated whether she should refer to Lindsey as an acquaintance, colleague, or friend. Unable to divulge their real association but not wanting trivialise their relationship, she decided on friend.

Once they had settled into a quiet corner booth, Mac looked at her expectantly. "Now what's this all about?"

"I want your advice," Daisy began. "Well, more than advice really. It's about Lindsey Jamieson-Ford."

"The head of LJF Robotics. You know her?"

"She's a friend."

Mac gave her an appraising glance. "Really? Nobody has been able to get near that woman for years. She's ignored all overtures from the press, and believe me, we've all tried. I hope you're going to say she wants to give an interview?"

"She does. Are you interested?" The twinge of guilt was ignored. She would work out later how she was going to break it to Lindsey.

"My oath I am, I'd jump at the chance."

"Good," said Daisy, relaxing now the first hurdle was over. "But there are certain requirements for this article. She wants you to write a piece about her work, not her personal life." When Mac looked puzzled, she plunged on. "The thing is, Lindsey has a problem and she's touchy about it. I'll let her explain…it's not my place to break her confidence. She's agreed to the article because she's sick of being a hermit and wants more of a life. To go places and meet people."

Mac tapped her pen on the table, silent for a long moment before she focused back on Daisy. "Now I'm really curious."

"All will be revealed when you talk to her. I can only say I think the world of her and she's a brilliant scientist. Her company is launching new products soon. What she needs is exposure."

"Hmm. I think I can give her that without too much trouble but I'm at a loss to understand why she needs it. She's widely regarded in her field. She would have to be wealthy. Do you know if she does anything for charity?"

"Plenty. She has a program set up for kids who have lost limbs because of land mines. You'll be fascinated by her research."

"So," said Mac, leaning forward with interest. "You've obviously seen her work. Do you think she'll show me?"

Daisy shook her head. "I doubt it. Scientists are paranoid about their research."

"How did you meet her if I may ask?"

Daisy paused, not having planned a reply for this particular question. She should have, of course, but overcome with her brilliant idea, had rushed into things. "Oh…she's a friend of a friend of my cousin. She introduced us at…um…at her office in town. They're work colleagues," she answered vaguely. "Lindsey's interested in anthropology. We became friends."

"Right. Tell me about her."

"Well, she lives on an estate in a large two-storey house with—"

Mac waved her hand impatiently. "No, Daisy. I want to know about the real woman."

"The real Lindsey…yes, well, okay," she mumbled, feeling like a Judas. "The first time I met her, she looked like one of those dragon bosses. You know what I mean…damn scary…made of ice except when she's breathing fire. That couldn't be further from the truth. But it's all a front…she's incredibly shy. Mind you, she doesn't abide fools, but then again," she twiddled her eyebrows, "nor do you."

The reporter chuckled. "I don't. Rachel says it's my worse fault. How does being wealthy affect her interaction with people?"

"She has a big house, a housekeeper-cook that she's known all her life, and a chauffeur-cum-handy man but that's all. She doesn't seem to care much about money, more interested in her research. She's an entirely different person in her lab. I suspect she probably doesn't even know how much she's personally worth. She doesn't splash it around that's for sure."

"You obviously like her," said Mac, watching her closely as she took a sip.

"We get along really well," said Daisy and added to explain the unlikely friendship, "I'm doing a bit of work for her, but that's confidential."

"Naturally."

"When can you set up a meeting?"

"I'll let you know. Sooner the better though."

"I'm at your disposal."

"I'm aware you're freelancing now. What would be the best platform for your article: a paper, magazine or TV?"

"TVs out. Too intrusive. Online is also out—it's too open to trolling," Mac said with a reassuring smile. "If you want the target market to be women, a magazine would be ideal. The *Woman's Weekly* is the top selling women's magazine in Australia but it's a monthly publication. I presume you want to get onto it immediately?"

"As soon as possible."

"*Woman's Day* comes out weekly so we may have to go with that one. There's also *Time Australia*, *The Monthly*, or one of the financial or science magazines considering her business reputation."

"What do you suggest?"

"A woman's magazine—for the sympathy factor. *Cosmos*, the popular science magazine, would without a doubt be the right place for the article but it wouldn't have the readers you want. Maybe we could put it in both. I could tailor the text to suit each production."

"Right," said Daisy with authority, "let's do it."

"Then that's settled. You give the time and place for the interview and I'll make sure I fit it into my schedule."

"Will do," said Daisy, pushing aside the feeling she may have bitten off more than she could chew. Persuading Lindsey mightn't be quite this easy.

"Sorry, I have to run in a minute," said Mac, glancing at her watch. "We're having a dinner party at the end of next month if you'd like to come. I know that's six weeks away but I was going to get on to you. Bring a friend."

"I'd love to, though it'll be only me."

"Then make sure you do. We've a couple of very nice unattached ladies coming."

CHAPTER TWENTY

It took a while for Lindsey to settle down after Daisy disappeared out the door. And as always when agitated about her arm, the memories flew in like black crows on the wind.

* * *

2004

Lindsey opened her eyes to an empty room. A moment of blind panic until she worked out where she was. She swallowed with difficulty. Her tongue felt bloated and her mouth tasted foul, but it was a relief to find the artificial airway had been replaced with an oxygen mask. She tentatively pressed her chin down to look at her body. Wires and tubes were running everywhere like a busy city intersection—an intravenous drip ran into a cannula in the back of her right hand and the monitor was attached by a string of wires to her chest. Pain shot through her body when she attempted to move, so she lay still and croaked, "Hello?"

A stocky woman in a blue uniform immediately bustled in. "Good, you're awake, Lindsey," she said in a low clipped voice and fiddled with the IV before she continued. "The button for your pain medication is near your fingers so you can self-administer when you need relief from now on. Don't worry… you can't give yourself too much."

As she was edged up onto the pillow, Lindsey felt a strange sensation. Her body seemed lopsided. Now that her head was elevated, she could see both her legs from the upper thighs downward were swathed in bandages. A sharp pain suddenly sliced through her left shoulder as she craned forward for a better view. She dropped her head back with a gasp.

When the medication finally kicked in, the agonizing spasm receded enough for her to rotate her head. For a moment, she barely comprehended what she was seeing. When it sank through the narcotic fog that the arm was no longer there, that it had been amputated, a fierce wave of nausea hit her stomach like a jackhammer. She silently screamed. It was a ghastly nightmare—a free pass to hell. She blinked out two tears, too exhausted for more.

The next time she woke, she had arrived in hell. Her mother stood at the foot of the bed staring down at her with an expression she knew only too well. Intense disapproval mixed with distaste.

"Well, you've really done it this time, my girl. Are there no depths to your stupidity? What possessed you to ride on a motorbike and more to the point, with a common girl like Amy Cross?"

"How is Amy?" Lindsey whispered urgently. It was all coming back. Leaving the party on the bike—on the beach with the wonderful girl—meeting the truck on the corner. She squeezed her eyes closed, forcing the memories away.

"She's gone." The words were spat out.

Lindsey opened her eyes to stare at her mother. Amy… lovely Amy was dead. She began to sob. "Tell Kirsty I need to see her."

"That friendship is finished. I sent her on her way and she won't be back. As you well know she's Amy's cousin."

"She's my best friend," Lindsey said, attempting to sit up. A film of perspiration formed on her lip and she gulped wildly. "You can't stop her coming to see me."

Her mother curled her lip. "I can and I will. You only have your family now and we're saddled with you. No self-respecting man would touch you after you went off with a filthy lesbian. And who'd want you anyhow. You only have one arm."

* * *

2006

For the last time in the private hospital rehab unit, Lindsey picked up her coat on the way out and meticulously folded it over her arm. Two years after a very taxing regimen, she had finally been pronounced fit. It had seemed to take forever. Her arm had been ripped off and the end of her shoulder crushed to almost nothing, with little skin remaining—just raw, meaty pulp. She would have been finished much earlier except for the three skin grafts. They had dragged on the need for exercise therapy, and delayed the healing of the shoulder.

Though she was now physically fit, she understood well enough that it was only her body cured not her mind. Nightmares plagued her sleep. Controlling anxiety was a constant battle and she'd developed a crushing social phobia. Her sessions with the psychologist would have to continue for God knows how long. What she wanted, and intended to have, was a calm orderly life and she was about to take the first step to achieve that.

Her father was waiting for her in the nearby park. She gave him a peck on the cheek before she took a seat beside him on the bench. "Thanks for coming, Dad."

"What's so important that you couldn't wait until you got home?"

"I'm not going home. I've taken a lease on a flat in the city."

He went still, then put his hand on her knee and gave it a squeeze. "Good for you, kiddo. The only peace you're ever going to get is to break free of your mother's control. I'll help as much as I can. What do you need?"

Lindsey gazed at him in surprise as her stomach unknotted with relief. "I can't live with her anymore, Dad. She constantly puts me down and she never lets me forget I'm a disappointment."

"I know, Lindsey," he said, his eyes moist. "I've let her bully you over the years for the sake of peace, but enough is enough. What do you want to do?"

"I'm going to start my own company," she said and with a wry smile held up the plain plastic limb, "and design something much better than this. I'm already well on the way…I've started drawing. It was something to do."

"You'll be needing money. Your trust fund is quite substantial. Buy yourself a house, and your company can be incorporated with the firm until it's established. You can build a lab in that empty warehouse down by the river for a start."

Lindsey stared at him in surprise. "You sound like you've been planning it for a while."

"I knew this day would come…I've been preparing for it since you reached your teens. Bernice can organize getting your belongings transferred to your apartment. Would you like her to stay with you?"

"I'd love her to, but Mother would hardly allow that."

He stood up and looked down at her. "Leave your mother to me, Lindsey. Now go and make yourself a life."

* * *

Lindsey pressed a fist against her mouth, willing the memories gone. This time they didn't linger. Daisy's ready acceptance of her disability was like a balm—she was filled with more hope than she'd felt after years of counselling. There was no denying that if anyone could help her, Daisy could with her ceaseless cheery optimism.

Instead of returning to work, Lindsey sat staring into space with her thoughts still centred on the events of the week. It was a long time since she felt such a strong connection with anyone. She was simply not good at establishing contact with people anymore. But this feeling for Daisy went beyond anything she'd felt for Kirsty. That had been a close friendship, someone to have fun with, to confide in, a steady presence in her young life. But with Daisy, she felt invigorated, albeit a little confused. When she had called her sweetie, Lindsey's breath had hitched in her throat though she knew the endearment was simply compassion. The urge to pull her close had been so overwhelming it had rendered her speechless. Then when Lindsey managed to say something, all she could do was babble on about having a meltdown.

She forced herself to begin work again, but the momentum had gone. A home truth crept in. She needed to face reality. Her life as a lab rat obsessively chained to her experiments and neglecting her personal life had to end. It was no way to live— the outings of the past two weeks had shown that. A big wide world was out there with places to go and things to do. Daisy would find a partner for her. She prayed so because she was sick of living without love, fed up with no one to share her life. To make it worse, her body now seemed to be going through some hormonal transformation. She constantly simmered with a mixture of frustration and unaccustomed longing.

Out of nowhere, an image of Daisy naked on her bed popped into her mind. She pushed it firmly aside and replaced it with a mature voluptuous woman in a flimsy nightgown kneeling at her feet. As the siren kissed her way up a leg to her inner thigh, Lindsey reached down to fondle the silky straight hair. As she fanned the strands through her fingers, the blond hair began to morph into auburn curls.

Bringgg…bringgg…bringgg.

The call shattered the illusion and it dissolved like a summer's mist. Smouldering with arousal, she growled into the phone. "Lindsey Jamieson-Ford speaking."

"I've been held up at my sister's and won't make it back by dinnertime, Lindsey. There's a meal in the freezer you can microwave."

"No problem, Bernie. Enjoy yourself. I'll see you at breakfast."

Feeling completely abandoned, and after only a cursory glance at the robot on the table she headed for her study. It could wait until tomorrow. She'd had enough. Dispirited, she prowled over her notes on her desk, picked up one at random then tossed it back down. Boring! Boring! With a grunt, she left the desk and dropped onto the couch to brood.

She spent the rest of the afternoon mooching around doing nothing. Still miserable, she made her way to the kitchen for an early meal and was about to reach into the freezer when the phone in her pocket sprang to life. Her eyes widened at the sight of Daisy's ID on the screen and she hurriedly pressed answer.

"Hello."

"Hi, Lindsey. Would you like to come over to the cottage for dinner? I picked up some Thai takeaway on the way home and I've a bottle of wine in the fridge."

Lindsey bit her lip to stop the laugh of delight tumbling out and somehow managed to keep her tone casual. "I'll be over in twenty minutes."

"Great. See you then."

The depression of the afternoon completely forgotten, Lindsey ran upstairs to her bedroom with a bounce in her step. After a quick shower, she rummaged through her new wardrobe with a discerning eye—tonight she wanted to look especially nice. It was the first time that Daisy had invited her to the cottage.

CHAPTER TWENTY-ONE

Before she answered the doorbell, Daisy straightened her top and smoothed down her recalcitrant hair with the palm of her hand. When she opened the door, she sucked in a quick breath as a tingle shot straight down her body to the very tips of her toes. Dressed in black skinny jeans, a tailored dark green silk shirt and black ankle boots, Lindsey looked stunning.

"Hi. Thanks for asking me over," Lindsey said earnestly, clearly aware of the scrutiny by the way she was shuffling her feet.

Daisy averted her eyes and awkwardly waved her inside. "Come on in."

As they moved into the house, she went slowly to study Lindsey more discreetly. Her body was angular and strong, tapering down from well-defined shoulders, to slim hips and a tight behind, to long shapely legs. About five ten, she walked with poise and had a commanding air to her movements, an intrinsic quality that couldn't be bought. She was the quintessential power lesbian. Once she gained confidence, Daisy had no doubt Lindsey would slide into that role as easy as slipping on a glove.

She gave a nod of approval. For all her image that she'd cultivated as a friendly I-am-in-charge modern woman, Daisy was attracted to intelligent masterful women who took the lead. And Lindsey fitted all those criteria. She probably would be an incredibly thoughtful lover once she got the hang of it.

"Go into the lounge and I'll get us a drink," she said.

After Lindsey disappeared, she popped the cork. Champagne could be relied upon to set a good mood and lower the defences, so after a glass or two, she'd bring up the proposed article. When she returned with the drinks, Lindsey was relaxed with legs crossed in an armchair. Daisy handed over the bubbling flute, put the ice bucket beside her chair and sank down on the long sofa opposite.

The cottage was anything but spartan. She loved its cosiness but thought the loungeroom especially charming. The walls were a light cream, the floor polished wood partially covered by a thick red Turkish rug, and a butter-soft brown leather lounge was arranged in a semi-circle in front of a high-tech entertainment unit. Clever ambient lighting created an intimate mood, while the glass door leading out to a vine-draped pergola let in a stream of sunlight during the day. A faint scent of honeysuckle tinted the air.

"So," said Lindsey. "Did you have a nice lunch with your mother?"

Daisy cocked her head in surprise at the wistful tone. "Tasty food as always at the Chelsea. Maybe we could go there one day."

"I'd like that."

"Then what say we do that and catch a movie on Saturday?"

"That would be really great. I haven't been to a cinema in years." Lindsey gave a small cough. "Not since the accident."

"It's a date then." She studied Lindsey's face. In a way, she was an anthropologist's dream. The woman hadn't moved socially forward from the past, since she was twenty-one, and had little knowledge of a society that had evolved without her. It was so much fun showing her how things were today, reinventing her was like having a blank slate. And the new Lindsey seemed to be enjoying herself. Things couldn't be going better. "What kinds of movies do you like?" she asked.

"I don't watch TV much. I'll let you pick the film."

"What do you do at night then? And don't tell me you work."

Lindsey took a sip and twirled the stem of the glass absently. "I read and play championship chess online," then she added with a hint of pride, "and I designed a video game last year."

"Oh. My. God. Lindsey, you're a total geek!"

She ignored the statement and said stiffly, "The game is to be kept a secret. I designed it under an alias."

A peal of laughter tinkled out of Daisy. "Really? What is it? Robogirl?"

"Very funny."

"So, what books do you read?" Daisy asked then held up a finger. "Aha…don't tell me. Let me guess. Either technical or science fiction…or maybe both."

Lindsey shrugged. "Mainly romance. It's the way I chill out."

Daisy blinked. Well that was a surprise. "What like Jane Austen? I can't see you reading chit lit."

"You wouldn't be interested in what I read."

"Try me."

"Okay. Lesbian romances."

Daisy sucked in a surprised breath then began coughing. Immediately Lindsey was beside her on the sofa, her face bent close to hers. "You okay?"

"I'm all right," she hissed, but when Lindsey began to rub her back she forgot even to breathe. The touch sent her body begging for more. Eventually, she reluctantly straightened and moved away.

"I'll get you a glass of water," offered Lindsey.

"No, no, I'm fine. Let's have another champagne before we eat. I have something to discuss with you." Before there was a protest, she refilled the glasses and handed one to Lindsey who moved back to her seat.

"That sounds intriguing. Am I going to like it?"

"I hope so. I've worked out how to let everyone know about your arm before you hit the dating scene," Daisy began.

"Oh?"

"Well…um…I know this journalist, Mackenzie Griffith, who writes freelance." Daisy tapped her fingers against the side of the glass, trying to ignore the intensity of Lindsey's gaze and plunged on. "So, I just happened to see her today and well…I had the idea that she could interview you. I didn't say anything about your arm—that's for you to tell her—I only mentioned you might be amenable to do an article for some exposure prior to launching your new technology."

Suddenly Lindsey's eyes narrowed. "You talked to her without asking me?"

Oh, shit! From the look on her face, Lindsey wasn't taking the idea as well as she had hoped. Daisy fervently wished now she hadn't been so hasty and given it more thought. It had seemed such a good idea at the time but— "I only tested the waters. She'll do the interview just the way we want it done. She's one of the best journalists in the city."

"No."

"You're saying no just like that? Without even discussing it?"

"Yes I am."

Okay—maybe not such a good idea to hit her with it so quickly. "That's being a bit small-minded, isn't it? You haven't even thought about it."

Her face screwed up in disapproval, Lindsey said in a low clipped voice. "Do you know how many times I've been pestered for an interview since I was named on that damn Forbes' list of scientists? Hundreds, Daisy, hundreds. Phone calls, emails, texts, letters…you name it. I just want to be left alone."

They stared at each other warily for a long moment before Daisy tossed up her hands. "Okay. It's your prerogative and it's not worth arguing over. I'll let her know you're not interested. You'll just have to break the fact of your arm to your dates yourself. Drink up and I'll serve out on the dining room table."

She moved off to the kitchen without saying another word, leaving Lindsey to stew. She hoped after half an hour she'd come around to her way of thinking. As they worked their way through the Thai takeaway, Daisy kept up a stream of inconsequential chatter until Lindsey suddenly threw her fork onto the plate and scowled. "Okay. Enough. Who exactly is this Mackenzie person?"

Daisy exhaled a sigh of relief. "She used to be a war correspondent and has been in practically every war zone in the world. She's very highly regarded both by her peers and the public. Noted for her integrity. She's won several Walkley Awards and is about as good a journalist as you can get. But not only that, she's a really nice person and a very good friend."

"How did you become friends. She's not another former client of your agency?"

"No," said Daisy. "Her partner, Rachel, is a detective and an old friend of mine. They met when Mac's twin sister was murdered. It turned out she was another victim of that serial killer who terrorised the city in 2015."

"How awful! That must have been horrific for Mac."

"It was. But something good did come out of all the trauma— she met Rachel. They're getting married next year."

"She's marrying a woman?"

"That she is."

"So," said Lindsey thoughtfully. "How come you know so much about the lesbian community if I'm your first client? You seem to know plenty about them and where they hang out."

Daisy froze. Damn, she'd walked straight into this without a thought. She pursed her lips, thinking. There was no point keeping her sexual orientation quiet now, it could create a rift further down the track if she didn't come clean. She couldn't hide it anyway, for when she took Lindsey to the Beauvoir Club, Carmen would make sure of that. "I'm a lesbian, so naturally I know where they socialize," she said with a casual shrug.

"You're one and you didn't tell me?" The words were barked out.

Daisy winced. Lindsey looked completely pissed off. "Well, it's not my policy to discuss my personal life with clients. I'm here to help you find a wife so you should be regarding me as merely a means to an end."

"What rubbish. Of course, it was pertinent in my case. It would have made me feel a lot better about the whole business. I was extremely embarrassed having to ask you to find me a wife."

"Yes…well…I wanted to tell you but you must understand my position. When I started the business, Marigold wouldn't have been so successful if I'd come out professionally. I expected all my clients to be straight so I made the conscious decision not to mention I wasn't. There was no point in complicating things. It's really not relevant." She gave Lindsey an imploring look. "I am sorry but I had no choice."

"We all have choices, Daisy. You chose to go down that path because it was the one of least resistance. You want people to like you. It's your nature and you thrive on it. But remember that sins of omission are just as hurtful as other offences."

For once Daisy could think of nothing to say. In her heart, she knew the rebuke was deserved. Even if she still chose to remain closeted professionally, she should have acted more compassionately towards Lindsey—from the start the vibes had been there that she suffered from anxiety. Daisy had not only been blasé about her lack of romantic experience, she had thought Lindsey naïve. It couldn't have been further from the truth. Lindsey was a highly intelligent woman at the top of her field, who suffered from PTSD and was making a concerted effort to improve her life.

As much as she tried to think, no answer came. Lindsey had been right in her analysis. She did want to be liked. And the need was fuelled by continuous barbs from her sister Meg about her sexual orientation and choice of career. She knew the rest of the family didn't care, but it still rankled. Now having produced the first grandchild, Meg was doubly infuriating. Her perception that Daisy was her mother's favourite had caused the rift, which was getting wider as they got older. One day soon, they would have to have it out. It was upsetting their family's stability.

Fighting the unexpected urge to cry, Daisy picked up her fork and forced the rest of her food down. When Lindsey cleared her throat, she looked up from her plate. To her horror, she felt a tear escape over a lid and slide down her cheek. Oh hell, now Lindsey was going to think she was a wimp who couldn't take criticism. She quickly averted her eyes, brushed it off and asked, "Would you like coffee or hot chocolate? We can have it back in the lounge."

"Daisy, look at me." Lindsey leaned over the table and said softly, "I didn't mean to upset you."

"You didn't," Daisy said, slumping back in the seat. "You just gave me a wakeup call. Everything you said was quite true. I'm getting to be a self-centred twat and I haven't treated you with the dignity you deserve. If you don't want to do the interview, then don't. I was wrong to push you. We'll work out something else." She hesitated for a few seconds before she added, "That is if you still want me as your matchmaker."

"Hey. You're blowing what I said way out of proportion. Of course I want to continue with you." Lindsey studied her watch. "What about you ring Mackenzie now to see if ten tomorrow morning out here will suit? It's only eight so she'll still be up. If she can't make it then, find out what time she would prefer. Tell her the gate will be unlocked."

"You're sure?"

"I'll see what she has to say before I commit myself."

Daisy pushed back her chair with a smile. "Okay, I'll do it now."

"I'll make us hot chocolate while you're on the phone."

Much to her relief, the phone was answered on the second ring. Clearly pleased to have scored the interview, Mac assured her she would the meet with Lindsey the next morning at the proposed time. Daisy texted through the directions, pointing out the turnoff wasn't on the GPS so not to waste her time.

Everything done and dusted, she joined Lindsey waiting in the lounge with the mugs. The rest of the evening went pleasantly enough, though she was careful not to touch on any subject that could be contentious. Lindsey seemed equally as wary and at nine thirty, she rose to go.

Frustrated, Daisy rose to walk her to the door. Now the easy comradeship between them was gone, she had no idea how to get it back. Lindsey must have been feeling as disheartened because she turned abruptly at the door and gazed at her solemnly. "We're all right aren't we, Daisy?"

She gave a helpless twitch of her shoulders. "I hope so. Are we?"

Then Lindsey did something that completely startled her. She stepped forward and gathered Daisy into a tight hug. It was so out of character that for a second Daisy went still, but then on its own volition, her body melted into the embrace. As their curves melded, the initial surprised pleasure shimmered into something deeper, something very sensual. She pressed close, revelling in Lindsey's essence. She smelt glorious: vanilla and woodsy musk tinged with a hint of polish. Her senses swam as her body responded to the scent. Her heart began to pound and her nipples strained against her bra. She began to tremble. When Lindsey stepped away after a last squeeze, Daisy was left aching with want.

Then Lindsey abruptly turned with a "Thanks for dinner," and quickly walked down the garden path.

Daisy leant against the doorframe, watching her disappear through the gate. Shaken, she whispered, "Wow!" and continued to stare blankly into the night.

CHAPTER TWENTY-TWO

Lindsey eyed the journalist warily as she took a seat across the desk. She didn't care much for reporters—to her mind they were intrusive busybodies. She missed having Daisy with her, but she knew the interview was hers to do alone. Mackenzie Griffith wasn't quite what she expected though. There wasn't the hint of the arrogance that seemed to be built into television interviewers.

She looked, in fact, nothing like the stereotype. She was slim and tanned, her wheat-coloured hair tossed casually in a shaggy short cut. Her otherwise attractive face was marred by a thin scar running down her left cheek, which she had made no effort to hide with makeup. And judging by her T-shirt and army cargo pants, she wasn't out to impress.

Mackenzie leaned over the table, her hand extended. "I'm Mac Griffith."

"Call me Lindsey, Mac," Lindsey said as she dipped forward to shake it. "Did Daisy explain about the interview?"

"She did. Perhaps you would like to tell me in your own words what you want out of this article."

Lindsey drummed her fingers on the table wondering how to phrase her reply. Griffith obviously wasn't a fool, so candour was probably the best option. "Since my early twenties, I've only mixed socially with my work colleagues and professional peers. This directly stems from a motorbike accident."

"I presume then that it was a bad crash?"

"I lost my left arm as well as other multiple injuries, some severe."

Mac gasped. "Christ…that's bloody terrible." She cast a glance at Lindsey's left hand. "I had no idea. I imagine you experienced serious PTSD as well. How's that going?"

Lindsey didn't even try to deny it. By her sympathetic tone, Mac seemed to know what she was going through. "It has taken a long time to get under control."

"Yes. People think it goes away but it doesn't fully." She stroked her scar. "I refused plastic surgery to remove this. I left it there to remind me how short and fragile life truly is."

"What happened if I may ask?"

"I was in a hotel wine cellar in Bosnia with some press buddies when the town was bombed. The ceiling collapsed on us. It was a couple of days before they dug us out."

Appalled, Lindsey stared at her. "How dreadful for you."

"It was bloody awful," Mac said flatly. "I suffered PTSD and a lot of guilt because I was saved by those on top of me. They didn't make it. A dear friend showed me it wasn't my fault and Rachel, my partner, helps me manage the nightmares. Time does heal."

"You were lucky to have someone," Lindsey said unable to suppress the bitterness in her voice.

"You didn't have support?"

"Hardly. My mother said I brought it on myself. Blamed me for going off on the bike and leaving my guests."

As Mac looked at her thoughtfully, Lindsey couldn't help squirming under the probing gaze. "Do you blame yourself?" she asked.

Lindsey almost couldn't get the words out. "Amy…she died in the accident. I lived."

"You know you have to let it go."

"How can I," she whispered in a trembling voice. "I can still see the truck hurtling around the corner. It haunts my dreams."

"You said yourself it was an accident. It wasn't your fault."

For the first time in her life, Lindsey felt a strong urge to confide in someone. She finally needed to tell the whole truth, needed to get it off her chest or she'd never be able to move on. "But it was. I had been drinking champagne at my birthday party and was a little drunk. When the truck suddenly appeared in front of us, I panicked and yanked Amy's arm. The bike wobbled and the next second, we clipped a headlight. The bike shot into the air. I tumbled off and my arm was squashed under the back wheel of the truck. I can't remember what happened next, but the driver said my dress caught on something and I was dragged along the bitumen until it stopped. Amy was thrown over the handlebars."

"You were lucky to be alive."

"I guess," Lindsey said morosely. "But it doesn't alter the fact that because I did something stupid, Amy died."

"You probably would have done the same cold sober. We can't be responsible for our reactions under stress. I learnt that often enough in war zones."

"Maybe so. But then I did the unforgivable. When the police interviewed me in hospital when I could finally speak coherently, I denied having anything to do with the accident. I told them I couldn't remember what happened. How callous is that?"

"Nobody would judge you for that, Lindsey."

"It wouldn't matter. I do a good enough job of that myself."

"And you've hidden away ever since, holed up in this house with your guilt. Is that what you're telling me?"

Lindsey looked at her in bewilderment and struggled to collect her thoughts. "I was too self-conscious to go out in society, but I didn't hide away only because of guilt. When I lost my arm, I was devastated. I was a scientist, I invented things…

the loss of my arm was huge. The prosthetic one the hospital gave me was so basic that it was demoralizing to have to wear it. It was next to useless, and it hurt. I decided then what I was going to do with my life. Give proper mobility and pride back to amputees. I set up a company to bring prosthetics into the future. High-tech stuff. I hired five of the best young minds fresh out of the universities, and with my father's help set up an R&D lab."

"Then why are you just coming out in public now?"

Lindsey gave a long sigh. "Because I'm lonely. I want someone to love and friends to confide in. I took a hard look at myself and realized I was turning into a crusty, bitter relic."

"You're hardly that, Lindsey. Don't be so hard on yourself," Mac said with a shake of her head. "Now I take it you're worried about your arm?"

"I'm paranoid about it. I know a friend would accept it unconditionally, but I can't see how a lover would."

"It'd be a hard man who didn't."

"Woman."

"Ah," said Mac with a smile. "I thought you could be but wasn't quite sure. Let me rephrase that statement. Any woman who shunned you because of your disability wouldn't be worth knowing."

"That's what Daisy says, but over the years, I've been brainwashed into believing nobody would want me. When you hear something often enough, it's hard not to believe it." When Mac raised an eyebrow, Lindsey added dolefully, "My mother."

"Shit, she must be some kind of ogre."

"She is," Lindsey replied, resisting a strange urge to giggle. "She insists on perfection. Abhors anything flawed."

"Well, bully for her. I hoped you told her to get nicked. Did she scream at you?"

Lindsey felt a fresh burst of humiliation. "Our family doesn't *do* loud emotional bursts. She's subtler than that. I left eventually, but I had to listen to her recriminations for two years while I went through my rehabilitation because I needed support. As soon as I was pronounced fit, I moved into my own place."

"Good for you," Mac said with a nod. "Do you see her much now?"

"I haven't seen her since I left twelve years ago." She looked at Mac anxiously. "I don't want anything about my mother in the article."

"Understood. This discussion is off the record—it's to help me to understand where you're coming from. Now tell me about your work and your charities."

After the unwanted rush of emotion evoked by the conversation, Lindsey suddenly felt free. She was over the worst, coming out of the dark forest of her tangled memories. Her spirits rose as she began to talk about her life's work. The pain gradually vanished, replaced by a feeling of self-worth tinged with a little euphoria. At the end of her monologue, she had to pull herself out of the zone to focus on her audience. Relaxed back in the chair, Mac had stopped taking notes and was simply listening.

"Sorry," Lindsey mumbled, feeling awkward. "I made this more of an exposition than a simple explanation. You must have been bored."

Mac chuckled. "I can't say I understood all of it, but I got the general gist. Enough for the article to make me sound a science buff."

"Where will we go from here?"

"If you agree to a published article, I'll do a write up for *Woman's Day*. It'll target women. I'd also like to do one for *Cosmos*, though that will be more technical. I'll need your help with that one. I'll have you review everything before I submit it anywhere." She reached into her bag and produced a camera. "Would you agree to a few photos? Most reporters use professional photographers but I prefer to take my own."

Lindsey's heart fluttered. Photographs sounded so final. "What do you want them of?"

"You in your office and lab. After we take some here, I'd like a few of you working on an artificial arm and the mobility suit."

"Sorry, I don't allow anyone into my laboratory, but wait here and I'll fetch the suit and an arm. Maybe we might take a stroll in the garden afterwards. That might interest readers," Lindsey said hopefully.

"Okay. Get someone to take some photos in the lab and send them to me for *Cosmos*." Mac flashed a smile. "Your garden gives me an idea. Maybe I could also do a smaller article as well for *House and Garden*. It has a huge circulation."

Lindsey exhaled slowly as her unease subsided. "I'll leave all that in your hands. We'll have morning tea before we start."

The photo shoot wasn't as simple as Lindsey had envisaged. Mac fussed around with the lighting, taking numerous shots in various positions. Then she did the same in the garden. After what seemed an interminable session, she eventually announced that she was satisfied.

When Lindsey ushered her out to the door, she felt completely drained. And bruised. It had been confronting, but as she watched the car ease off down the driveway, she also felt somewhat liberated as well.

Her life was now on a new path. Whether she liked it or not, the wheels were in motion.

CHAPTER TWENTY-THREE

"Hmmm… hold it more firmly. Yes, that's good…just like that," Lindsey murmured.

Daisy's brows creased in concentration as she squeezed the nipple between her fingers. The dusty coral-pink nub felt incredible, so taut yet silky to the touch. "It's perfect," she whispered.

"Stretch it out a bit more and hold it very still."

Daisy gently wriggled it out further, watching as Lindsey soldered the underneath wires to the centre of the brown slightly puckered areola on top of the robot's breast. "Gosh, it's so life-like. A work of art."

Lindsey smiled, though she didn't look up until everything was firmly attached. "She's just about finished. What shall we call her?"

"Oh, I don't know. Let's sleep on it."

"Okay. We'd better call it a morning and get ready for our luncheon date."

"I'll see you in an hour then." The melodious humming of "I Could Have Danced All Night" followed her out the door. Whatever she had discussed with Mac had certainly put Lindsey into a better frame of mind. She had been cheerfully affable the rest of the week, a side of the diffident scientist she'd not yet seen.

Outside, the bright sunlight and gentle breeze mirrored Daisy's mood. Everything was going so well. The only blot on the horizon was that her time out here was nearly over. It had been a relaxed four days post-interview, with the theatre date the highlight. After some dragging of feet at the door of the Entertainment Centre, once the first act began Lindsey seemed to relax. The play was an evergreen favourite, and it was with obvious emotion that she said goodnight at the cottage door.

Once the tuition was wrapped up, it seemed only natural that Daisy would continue to help in the lab when needed. They worked well together, their silence as comfortable as their conversation. Her initial superficial interest in the science of robotics deepened into one of fascination. Lindsey was the cleverest woman she had ever met, generously sharing her knowledge. Daisy only hoped her profiling would be acceptable—the bar was set very high though it was a challenge in which she was revelling. It was a long time since she'd had to use her anthropology so specifically, and she hadn't realized how much she missed the work.

At the cottage gate, she checked her watch. Half an hour to get ready. Normally there was no need to book for lunch with so many good dining places in the city, but the Chelsea was always popular, especially on a Saturday. After she dived through the shower, she donned her floral dress with the sweetheart neckline and took a little more care than usual applying her makeup. When the toot of a horn echoed outside, she slipped on her sandals and stepped out the door.

The sight of Lindsey immaculately dressed in navy slacks, striped shirt, and three-quarter sleeved, fitted white coat sent a warm tingle through her belly. Strangely, she felt a bit tongue-tied as she sank into the plush upholstery. This Lindsey was far more daunting than the one she'd just left in a stained lab coat. Quashing down her flutter of attraction, she gave an approving nod. "I love that outfit."

"It's comfortable. You look very nice. Pretty dress."

"It's a Kate Spade." She held up the matching floral handbag. "Isn't this delightful? Don't you think her creations are divine?"

"Um…yes."

Daisy chuckled. Lindsey might be a science star but she didn't know the first thing about fashion. "Tell the truth. You don't know who she is, do you?"

"Haven't a clue," Lindsey replied with a gleam in her eye. "But then again, it doesn't really matter. You don't have to wear designer clothes to look attractive."

"Why, Lindsey, I do believe you're mastering the art of flirting."

This brought a smile. "I do believe I am."

Relaxed now, they chattered about their work until the Mercedes purred to a stop. Daisy looked around in surprise. "We're here already?"

"Yes, ladies," said Joe.

Alighting onto the footpath, she was pleased to see Lindsey immediately walk to the door. She didn't hang back when the waiter showed them to their table, displaying no nervousness in the crowded room. Once seated, she discreetly studied Lindsey reading the menu. She did look very smart.

A smile touched Lindsey's lips when she caught her staring. "What?"

"Oh nothing. I was just thinking you looked rather nifty."

Lindsey placed her hand over her heart with a chuckle. "Flattery, Daisy, will get you everywhere. Now tell me what you recommend on the menu."

"The calamari are delicious, but then so are all the dishes. Their chef is fantastic. Pick anything and it'll be a treat."

For the next hour they concentrated on their meal, happy to keep the conversation light. It was an unspoken agreement that emotional topics were off the table on this date. There had been enough of those the past two weeks.

After the dessert plates were cleared away, Daisy sat back with a contented sigh. "That was yummy."

"It was superb," agreed Lindsey. "I'll make sure this place is on the agenda when I start dating. Maybe Nicolle would like to have dinner here."

"She should love it," said Daisy, scrunching up her nose at the thought, but quickly forced a smile when she met Lindsey's eyes. "The movie doesn't start for another hour. Shall we have coffee?"

"Good idea." She signalled for service.

As she idly watched the waiter manoeuvre through the tables with their order, Daisy noticed a woman across the room staring at them. When their gazes met, the woman looked away quickly. Daisy lingered on her face trying to place her but couldn't. She concluded she'd never seen her before. When the coffee arrived, she poured in milk, stirring it around until a tiny whirlpool formed in the centre. Then casually, she raised the cup to her lips and shot the woman another glance. Again, she was looking directly their way.

"Lindsey," she said quietly, "I think there's someone here who knows you...or thinks she does. She's been staring at us."

"Unless it's someone from work, which is highly unlikely, it wouldn't be me. It'll be you."

"I haven't a clue who she is. Besides, if she knew me she would have acknowledged me."

"Where is she?" asked Lindsey, now showing interest.

"At a table against the back wall with five other women. You'll have to turn to the left to see her."

"Tell me what she looks like so I'll know who I'm looking for."

"She's wearing a sleeveless light blue dress and, at a guess, I'd say she's in her early- to mid-thirties though it's a bit hard to tell from here. She's very attractive...wavy golden-blond hair and a heart-shaped face."

"Tall or short?"

"She's sitting down, but I'd say not too tall."

After she turned slowly to look, Lindsey expelled a hiss.

"Do you know her?" asked Daisy, but she knew it was a rhetorical question. Lindsey's face had drained of colour, her knuckles white clutching the cup. She was intently focused on the woman who had risen from her chair to walk over. Trembling visibly, Lindsey placed the cup on the table before she slowly rose to greet her.

Daisy waited silently for the scene to play out. The stranger was much the same height as herself, dressed in a stylish frock that hugged her slim body in all the right places. Daisy felt a spurt of envy—she was downright gorgeous.

"Hi, Lin," she said in a low quavering voice.

The muscles in Lindsey's face tensed. "Hello, Kirsty," she whispered back.

"Oh, come here and give me a hug," the woman exclaimed. And they were in each other's arms, rocking gently as they clasped each other tightly.

Lindsey was the first to break the connection. Taking a step back, she reached up to touch her hair. "You look wonderful. I've missed you so much."

Kirsty let out a small sob. "I missed you too. You look so good."

"You do too. You're even prettier now. Come…sit down."

"I'm with friends for a birthday celebration, so I only can stay for a minute. Will you come to lunch tomorrow?"

"I'd love to. Jot down your details." Lindsey tugged Daisy to her feet. "This is a friend of mine, Daisy Parker. Meet a dear childhood friend, Kirsty…" she glanced down at the left hand where a huge diamond ring glittered on her finger. "What is your married name?"

"Hickman. I married Martin, Lin."

Daisy watched the emotions play over Lindsey's face as she absorbed the information. She looked first surprised then intrigued. "Did you really? I didn't even know you liked him."

"I always thought he was nice when he was taking you out. Truth be known, I envied you. Then after your accident, we comforted each other when your mother was being such a bitch. Four years later, we met again in London and started dating."

She dropped her eyes to the table. "You must think I'm the shittiest friend."

"You envied *me*?" said Lindsey incredulously.

"Well, just a bit," said Kirsty with a little toss of her head. "You were always so complete: articulate, rich, and clever. You never had to worry about failing subjects like me. And you had Martin. But then my family weren't exactly in your parents' class."

She turned to Daisy who was watching the exchange, fascinated. "It's nice to meet you, Daisy. Have you a pen?" Kirsty wrote down her address and number, and placed the slip of paper on the table. "Now I must get back. I'll see you tomorrow, Lin."

Lindsey watched her make her way across the room before she sank down onto her chair. She raised the coffee cup to her lips, her fingers tense on the handle. Gradually they relaxed, one by one. She met Daisy's gaze, her voice breathless as she said, "That was a surprise."

"She's quite lovely," said Daisy.

"Yes, she is. She was my best friend."

"What happened, Lindsey?"

"My mother wouldn't let her see me after the accident." Her voice hitched. "I guess she gave up trying."

"I wonder why she didn't try to contact you at some stage later. Do you think it was because she married your boyfriend?"

"No. She knew I wasn't keen on him."

Daisy swallowed then asked the question that had been puzzling her since viewing their reunion, "Why haven't you tried to contact her? You were obviously very close."

Lindsey went still. "Probably the same reason she didn't want to see me. Amy."

"Oh?"

"That's all I'm going to say. I didn't realize just how much I've missed her until I saw her walking toward me. We'll sort things out tomorrow. I want her back in my life."

"I'm happy for you, Lindsey. Now if we don't hurry, we'll miss the start of the movie."

"Let's go. And since this is our last date, we'll make a night of it. I've lined up a surprise for you."

* * *

"I'll walk home, Joe. It's a pleasant night for a stroll," Lindsey called over the seat as the car eased to a stop outside the cottage.

"Very well, Lindsey," he replied. After opening their doors, he slid back into the driver's seat.

"Thanks, Joe," Daisy called out and watched the car disappear into the darkness before she walked to the front door. After she fitted the key in the lock, she said with a warm smile, "I had a really fun date. And thank you once again for the joyride in the company helicopter, Lindsey. It was awesome."

"I'm glad I could give you something you'd never done before."

"Coming in for coffee?"

"No thanks. It's after ten and I'm a little tired."

"Oh," murmured Daisy, taken aback. She had hoped they wouldn't end the date yet. Tomorrow she was going back to her own apartment in town. She looked around wistfully. She was going to miss all this.

As she leaned forward to open the door, she was suddenly conscious how close they were standing. Near enough to inhale the spicy perfume.

Then Lindsey did the unexpected. She bent until their eyes and mouths were level and leaned in slowly, an inch, then another, until their mouths touched. Her lips tasted of the chocolates and the brandy nightcap they'd had in the car on the way home. The kiss was soft and fleeting like sisters saying goodbye, but to Daisy the effect wasn't sisterly. Her every nerve ending sparked. She sidled closer, itching to roam her fingers through Lindsey's silky hair and tug the head closer to devour the mouth. With a concerted effort, she managed to keep her hands to her side.

She was so glad she did, for Lindsey stepped back and said lightly, "How was that? Before you went, I wanted to practise initiating a kiss. I hope I didn't take too much of a liberty."

Daisy's whole body sagged in relief. Fuck, she'd nearly made a complete fool of herself. "You're a natural. No more practice required in that department," she replied with a burst of enthusiasm she didn't feel. Then reluctant to end the connection, she hovered on the doorstep. "I guess this is goodbye. I'll be gone by the time you get back from Kirsty's tomorrow. I'll ring you during the week."

Lindsey suddenly looked sombre. "Thank you for being here for me, Daisy. Perhaps we can get together again next week. I'm going to miss our outings."

"Me too."

"What happens next with the dating business?"

"Mac said the article will be published in about two weeks. You might like to have that drink with Nicolle then, or lunch, whatever. I'll organize a night out at the Beauvoir Club on Saturday night in three weeks. It's an exclusive women's club with some lesbian and bi members."

"Are you a member?" asked Lindsey.

"God no. Out of my league!"

Lindsey's eyes ran over her like a radar scanner. "Then how can you get me in. They wouldn't just let anyone through the door."

There was a tiny beat of silence. "I know a member," replied Daisy innocently.

"I'm not surprised. I've never come across anyone who knows so many people." Lindsey scuffed the toe of her shoe on the wooden boards. "So…I guess I'd better be off."

Daisy stepped forward before she had a chance to step off the porch and clasped her around the waist. "Goodnight," she murmured. "Have a lovely day tomorrow."

This time Lindsey didn't pull away immediately. They both lingered a little before they broke apart. Lindsey turned quickly, saying in a quick breath, "Goodbye," and hurried down the garden path.

After a dry swallow, Daisy managed to say goodnight but Lindsey had already vanished down the road.

CHAPTER TWENTY-FOUR

Lindsey looked around admiringly as she made her way up the paved path to the front door. The impressive two-storey house occupied a quarter-acre block on a hill in an expensive inner suburb, with a splendid city view. Martin's law career must be thriving to afford something so grand, she mused. Not that she found it surprising. He had always been obsessed with money, one of the reasons she hadn't cared much for him.

Kirsty and a small girl greeted her at the door. The child's face was framed by blond curls, her eyes were wide and wondering. It wasn't hard to tell she was Kirsty's daughter; she was a miniature version of her mother. Lindsey ducked until she was at eye level and said softly, "My, aren't you a cutie."

Giggling, the girl slipped in between her mother's legs and looked at her shyly. Kirsty put her hands on her shoulders. "This is my daughter, Isabelle."

"Hi, Isabelle," she said, captivated.

Isabelle cast an anxious gaze at her mother who nodded. "Hello. Mum said Lin was comin'. Are you Lin?"

"Yes I am."

"Oh. You must be nice 'cause Mum says I can only to talk to nice people."

Lindsey straightened up and smiled at Kirsty. "Then I must be."

With a chuckle, Kirsty waved her into the house. "Come on in. We'll sit out on the terrace for a chat before lunch." She turned to her daughter. "Go back to Play School, honey, while we have a talk."

"Okay." Isabella wandered off to the TV without a backward glance.

"Three-year-olds," murmured Kirsty, "have the attention span of a gnat."

"She's gorgeous," said Lindsey, feeling a touch of emotion. Isabella wasn't much younger than Kirsty had been when they first met. And now her childhood friend had a child of her own. It was hard to believe.

"She has her father wrapped around her little finger. Now come on through. We've just finished renovating and knocked out a few walls to let in more light. The old place was rather dark with too many pokey rooms."

Lindsey could see the refurbishment had style and flair, the whites and soft greys contrasting nicely with the polished timber floors. The lounge-dining-living area had been converted into one room in an open-air plan, with modern furniture and impressive artworks. The kitchen had stone bench tops, with a timber cabinetry bench separating the room from the living area. They walked out onto the deck where a lush garden surrounded a pool and barbeque arbour.

She sank into one of the chairs. "You have a lovely home, Kirsty."

"Thank you. We're proud of it. Now tell me how your life has been after the accident. From all accounts, you've achieved extraordinary things." She looked pensive. "I knew you would, you know. With your talent and brains, you were destined to rise above the ordinary."

"I'm proud of what I've accomplished, but it hasn't been easy."

"Why is that? You're only in your mid-thirties and already one of Australia's leading scientists."

Lindsey gazed at her curiously. "Did my mother ever tell you about my injuries?"

"Are you kidding me? Nobody was told a thing. I came every day to that damn ward for two weeks, only to be turned away at the door. Then one day I found you'd been discharged. Since your mother informed me in no uncertain terms that I wasn't welcome at your home, I had to give up."

"I was taken to a private hospital. It took two years before I was pronounced completely fit."

Kirsty stared at her blankly. "Everyone thought you'd had a swift recovery. How bad was it?"

"I was lucky to survive. Compound fractures of both legs, multiple contusions, a damaged kidney and," Lindsey cleared her throat, "I lost my left arm." She held it up. "This is an artificial limb."

"Oh my God!" Kirsty clapped her hand over her mouth and stared at her in horror. "What an awful friend you must have thought me." She began to cry.

"I prayed you'd look me up after I went out on my own, but you never did," said Lindsey, blinking away her own tears. "Why didn't you?"

Kirsty tugged a tissue from her pocket and wiped her face. "I couldn't. Your mother said if any of my family came near you, she'd sue Amy for taking you on her bike. And I always thought that if you were interested, you'd find me."

"What do you mean sue Amy?" whispered Lindsey.

"Just what I said. Because she was driving, according to your mother she was liable for your injuries. Martin said later that Amy would have had grounds to fight that allegation, but her parents aren't wealthy so we kept away."

Lindsey stared at her, struggling for composure. "Kirsty... listen to me. I thought Amy died in the crash?"

"No, she didn't," Kirsty replied with a frown. "She was pretty knocked around, but just broke her collarbone. Her family took her home the next day. Wherever did you hear that she was dead?" Then her eyes widened as the truth struck home. "Your mother. What did she say?"

Lindsey sprang to her feet, needing the distance, desperate to stop the helpless rage building inside her. "When I asked her what happened to Amy, she said she was gone."

"Did she say anything more?"

"She never mentioned her again—ever. She knew perfectly well I thought she meant she'd died in the crash."

"What a bitch."

Lindsey wanted to break something, to smash it into little pieces. With her hands clutching the railing, she said bitterly, "That's why I never looked you up all these years. I thought you wouldn't forgive me going off with Amy and getting her killed. Where is she now?"

"At the moment in Afghanistan trying to catch a shot of the Hindu Kush snow leopard for a wildlife magazine. She's a photographer. She always was adventurous and has travelled all over the world."

"Good for her. I really liked her."

"Geez, Lin, what your mother did was so nasty. Do you ever see her?"

"No. I walked out when I was twenty-three and I've never been back. Bernice came with me, which must have really infuriated her. Dad often comes in to see me at my town lab but we have an agreement never to mention her." Lindsey closed her eyes, caught up in the past. "I'm her daughter. It always terrified me that I could become like her."

"Are you crazy? You couldn't have been less like your mother. You were poles apart. She cared about nobody but herself. You cared about everyone *but* yourself." Kirsty searched her face. "How have you *really* been? I tried to follow your career, but apart from an occasional snippet about some invention, there was nothing about your private life. And I couldn't find you on social media."

"I don't have much of a private life," Lindsey replied, calmer now. With a sigh, she eased back into the chair. "I had problems with post-traumatic stress and found it too hard to socialize. It was easier to stay at home."

Moisture swam back into Kirsty's eyes. "You've been living like that all this time?"

"Yes." When Kirsty's tears began to spill over, Lindsey managed a reassuring smile. "Stop blubbering. It isn't all that bad. My work is fulfilling. It's amazing how much can be achieved if there are no distractions."

"I'm not blubbering. So…what happened? It's plain to see you're not hiding away now. You're looking good. Very avant-garde."

"Thanks. Daisy's the reason for that."

"The woman you introduced yesterday?"

"Yes. She's been doing some computer work for me."

"Good for her." Kirsty gazed at her with amused regard. "Just a friend?"

"What's that supposed to mean?"

"Well, Amy is my cousin you know."

Heat flushed across Lindsey's cheeks. "She told you?"

Kirsty's eyes sparked with curiosity. "I was your best friend for years and never once suspected. Just think all the times we compared notes about boys. Was it always me who initiated the heart-to-hearts?"

"Yes. I usually sat back and listened."

"That sounds like I was a self-absorbed princess. How come you never told me you liked girls?"

Even now at the thought of her mother's reaction to that revelation, a frisson of fear crept up Lindsey's spine. She shivered. "It was a survival thing. It would have been suicide to bring *that* news home. I barely acknowledged it to myself. I wanted to tell you so many times, but I dreaded it getting out. As well, I couldn't afford to lose you." She felt fingers twine with hers and sighed. "We were happy, best friends. Why would I have jeopardized that for feelings I didn't know how to handle? Telling you wasn't an option."

Kirsty's grip tightened and she shook her head. "We were so naïve and full of hope. Remember our dreams. You were going to invent something fantastic and I was going to go on the stage and be a young Judi Dench."

"Yes, I remember only too well. That bike ride changed everything. We're different people than we were fourteen years ago. So…tell me about you. Did you ever get any stage work?"

"After I graduated, I went to London to study for two years at the Mountview Academy of Theatre Arts. It was a wonderful experience but led to nothing. Only a few bit parts, so I had to support myself by working in pubs. Martin was there to pick up the pieces when I finally realized I didn't have the talent to make it."

Lindsey sat quietly, studying Kirsty as she talked. The wisp of humour was gone, replaced by a melancholy in her friend's face. Along the way, her dreams had been shattered too. What a mess they'd made of their friendship. They should have been there to support each other. "Are you happy now?" she asked quietly. The transition from stage-star hopeful with starry-eyed dreams to housewife in the 'burbs must have been challenging.

The slim shoulders shrugged. "Anyone would envy my life."

If they hadn't been such close friends, Lindsey wouldn't have caught the edge to the words. It was ever so subtle, but it was there. It suddenly dawned on her that perhaps there was trouble in paradise. "Yes," she said blandly, "you do have everything. But that's not what I asked you."

"You always could read me like a book, Lin." She patted her stomach. "I'm pregnant again. Sixteen weeks. Don't get me wrong, I'm very happy about it and Isabelle needs a sibling. It's just that I'm never going to be anything but a housewife now. I spend my time between playgroups and luncheons, which doesn't do much for any ambition I might have. Martin has his work and doesn't understand. We're going through a rough patch at the moment."

"You'd like to work?"

"I'd love to, but every time I suggest something, he gives some reason why I can't."

Lindsey regarded her thoughtfully as an idea formed. It would be a great way to rekindle their friendship as well as assisting them both. "Perhaps I can help. You were always an expert social organizer. Would you like to work for us as an event coordinator? We have a few new products almost ready to launch and we've been asked to run seminars on our work in robotics. I've always shied away from the public arena, but my designers are becoming insistent that we make a better effort with our marketing. If I don't let them get more of an international profile, I may lose them. It would be a part-time position and you can do most of the organization from home."

"Are you serious?" asked Kirsty, the flush on her cheeks showing her interest and excitement.

"Yes I am. You'd be doing me a big favour. I'm too anxious with strangers, so you can handle all our social business. As well, I trust you. I allow very few people in. Too many trade secrets—industrial espionage is rife."

"It all sounds so cloak-and-daggerish," Kirsty said with an amused glint in her eye.

"You'd be surprised," said Lindsey with an answering gleam. "So…would you be interested?"

"Very much so."

"Good. Come out next week to my home and I'll show you my work. We'll put a plan in place then."

Kirsty rose from the chair with a bounce in her step. "I'd better get lunch and that little girl away from the TV. Come on through."

As Lindsey walked with her inside, Kirsty poked her in the ribs. "Did you ever fancy me?"

"Behave!"

CHAPTER TWENTY-FIVE

When Lindsey reached home that evening, the sunset had changed the grounds to mauve and gold like the painted sets of an old Hollywood film. It suited her mood. She was energized in a way she hadn't been for years. The revelation that Amy hadn't died in the crash had freed something inside, her initial anger replaced by enormous relief and irrepressible elation. For the first time since the accident, she felt her life had turned for the better.

Bernice hadn't returned from the weekend with her sister, so she popped a frozen meal into the microwave. Then armed with a flat white from the coffee machine, she sank into one of the tubular chairs in the loungeroom and propped her feet up to reflect quietly on the events of the day. On the way home in the car, her mind had been a jumble of thoughts, but in the tranquillity of this special space, everything fell into an orderly pattern. It was her calming room, designed specifically to control her PTSD. An idea she had worked on after studying autistic children—soothing visual aids were most effective in the treatment of their anxiety.

Kirsty and she had talked all afternoon, reliving old times. They'd pored over old photo albums that went right back to their first day in primary school when they had bonded in the playground. Kirsty's family weren't exactly top-of-the-tree. Nevertheless, Lindsey's mother had accepted her as a suitable playmate for her well-heeled daughter. Her many stiff little parties and carefully organized outings became a standing joke between them when they were older.

Although Kirsty was back in her life, Lindsey knew their friendship would never be quite the same. Too many years had passed and they had pursued their own lives. Today though, had been a step in the right direction with Kirsty agreeing to be the company event manager. Not only would it go a long way to repairing their bond, Lindsey knew it would be the perfect job for her very social friend.

A sharp ding from microwave scattered her thoughts. She was dying to discuss the day with Daisy, but didn't want to appear needy. The meal finished, she ignored her embarrassment as she dialled.

"Hi, Lindsey," came the familiar voice almost immediately. "I was hoping you would call. How did the day go with your friend?"

Lindsey stretched back in the chair, feeling a little breathless. Daisy had wanted her to call. *Wow!* "I hope you don't mind me ringing. I know this might seem an imposition, but I just needed to talk to someone." She gave a small cough. "Well, not just anyone...I wanted to tell *you* what happened."

"And I'm dying to know. Tell me everything."

For half an hour, she chatted about Kirsty's house, Isabelle, the next pregnancy, and her job offer, while Daisy threw in a question or remark now and then. Finally, when Lindsey reluctantly said, "I guess I'd better let you go," there was silence at the end of the line. "Are you still there?" she asked.

"Come on, Lindsey. You left out the important bits."

"I don't know what you mean."

"Yes, you do. I'd take a punt from the tone of your voice that you ironed out some of your personal problems. Am I right?"

"Yes."

"What happened between the two of you to cause the rift? Was it about Amy? Who was she?"

Lindsey felt all the old hurt and humiliation build up inside her again, rising like steam inside a pipe until the pressure was unbearable. She heard herself spitting out the entire painful story of the accident and the aftermath.

"And how do you feel about learning it was all a lie and that Amy had survived," asked Daisy, her voice filled with concern.

"Very happy. Relieved. Furious with my mother," she replied gruffly. "Disappointed in myself. I didn't even try to contact Kirsty all those years."

"But she didn't either. It wouldn't have been hard to find you."

"I know. In her defence, she did spend years in London," Lindsey said. "But I suppose when it comes down to it, we both should have tried harder."

"Never mind. It's in the past so no use beating yourself over the head with it. Time to move forward. You're back in each other's lives again and you should be able to pick up where you left off."

She took a long breath. Why did Daisy make everything sound so simple? "I hope we can."

"You will. Now, I was meaning to ask you yesterday. Would you like to go to the symphony on Wednesday night? They're playing a selection of Mozart. Allison gave me tickets."

A wave of pleasure coursed through Lindsey. She had become used to their outings and she adored Mozart. "I'd love to."

"Great. I'll ring you tomorrow night with the time. Bye."

With a little satisfied smile, Lindsey clicked off.

* * *

On Tuesday morning of the following week, Lindsey woke on tenterhooks. The article was due out today. She hadn't dwelt on it—the last ten days had been too full. She and Daisy had slipped into the routine of talking on the phone each night, and it had only seemed natural after the concert to spend more time together. The weekend was filled with a day at the New Age Science expo, dinner at Daisy's flat Saturday night, then a leisurely stroll through the Art Gallery on Sunday afternoon to see the French Impressionist exhibition. The epiphany had struck Lindsey between a Matisse nude and a Degas ballerina—for the first time in her adult life, she was completely happy. And she wasn't lonely anymore.

Nothing could pierce her happy glow over the next few days. She wafted around the house on a cloud, with Bernice's questioning looks and comments bouncing off her like bubbles. But when she crawled out of bed this morning, reality set in. Crunch time. Today the whole world was going to know her secret.

At breakfast Bernice, eyeing her half-hearted attempts at eating, asked testily, "Whatever's the matter with you, Lindsey?"

Lindsey lifted her head up from her plate and replied after a pause, "There's an article about me today in this week's *Woman's Day*. I'm rather nervous."

"What do you mean an article? You hate the press. When did you agree to an interview?"

"A couple of weeks ago."

"Why didn't you tell me? Not that I'm surprised…you've been acting very oddly lately. When did you start keeping important things from me?"

"I didn't want to bother you," Lindsey mumbled.

"I thought you trusted me, but apparently you don't as it turns out."

Lindsey winced. The usually placid Bernice sounded very annoyed. Not that either one of them would ever raise their voices at each other. Even though their relationship was far more than employer and employee, they still practised a certain level of decorum. It was ingrained.

"Okay, here's the truth so settle down. I didn't tell you because it was a decision only I could make for myself." She cleared her throat, which had suddenly become hoarse, before continuing. "I'm sick of living like this. I want a relationship…

someone to share my life. I needed the loss of my arm to be common knowledge to save any embarrassment when I ask someone out, hence the press article."

"What about poor Daisy?" asked Bernice sharply. "You've been thick as thieves this last month. And don't think I don't know you talk to her every night on the phone. I'm disappointed in you, playing with her affections like that. She's a lovely girl and doesn't deserve that treatment."

Lindsey pursed her lips. Things were getting far too complicated. Better to come right out with an explanation before it accelerates. "Our friendship is not what it seems. She's employed to be my personal social assistant for a while. It's strictly business."

Bernice's eyes widened. "Business?"

"Um…yes."

"Well that explains the new hairstyle and clothes and why the two of you have been gadding about," Bernice stated flatly. "But not why you've been mooning about the house."

"Don't be absurd. I haven't been mooning. I've had a lot on my mind. And the outings were Daisy's idea to ease me into the social scene."

"Then all your dates were purely business?"

Lindsey placed her fork onto her plate with a calm deliberate movement. "Yes. Daisy is simply my employee. Now let that be the end of the inquisition."

"I don't—"

To Lindsey's relief, the phone ringing cut off the next probing question. When Daisy's number appeared, she walked out into the hallway to take the call. "Hi. Is it out yet?"

"Yes. I'm at your gate with a copy. I'll see you in a couple of minutes."

"I didn't expect you to bring it out. I was going down to the local news agency after breakfast."

A chuckle burbled into her ear. "I want to be there when you read it."

"Is it any good?"

"You'll see. Bye."

Although she had deteriorated into a bundle of nerves, Lindsey couldn't help feeling a thrill that Daisy was bringing it out all this way herself. It would be nice to have support when she read it. By the time she pulled open the front door, the red Nissan was already nosing to a stop in the courtyard. When Daisy stepped out of the car, Lindsey's stomach flip-flopped. Casually dressed in faded jeans with an unadorned white sleeveless shirt, two emerald studs winking at her ears and curly hair blowing in the breeze, she looked more appealing than she had ever seen her.

Suddenly tongue-tied, she gestured her in with a wave. With a bound Daisy was beside her at the door, bringing the warm spring air with her. Instinctively, Lindsey wrapped her arms tightly around her until she realized what she was doing and quickly let her go.

"Sorry. That was a bit too enthusiastic," she muttered. "I'm just glad to see you."

Daisy grinned. "Hey, no probs. I love hugs." She waved the magazine in the air with a whoop. "Just wait 'til you read this, you celebrity you."

Consumed with curiosity, Lindsey followed her into the house. Daisy certainly seemed more than happy with the article. Trying to curb her impatience, she put on her reading glasses and sat ready at the dining room table while she waited for Daisy to greet Bernice in the kitchen. Then when the magazine was handed over with a theatrical flourish, she could only stare in astonishment at the cover. The picture of her was astounding. She stood with arms crossed in front of her desk, radiating power and poise. Though the photograph was incredible, the caption above it captured her attention more. "Australia's Own Wonder Woman."

Impatiently, Lindsey flipped to the article on page four and studied the series of photos. Mac certainly knew her stuff. They were excellent. Daisy slid her chair closer and draped an arm over the back of Lindsey's as she read. Mac had portrayed her as a woman who had overcome adversity by sheer talent and determination to become both a scientific leader and a humanitarian. In so doing, she had subtly made her artificial arm a badge of honour rather than an impediment.

By the time she finished the three-page spread, Daisy had moved even closer until their shoulders brushed. "Well?" she asked. "What do you think?"

Lindsey felt her cheeks flush with embarrassment. "It's way over the top."

"But it's great, isn't it? Come on…admit it. You love it."

"Okay. I do and I'm very flattered."

Daisy chuckled, looking smug. "I told you she was good. This should set you up very nicely to start socializing. Have you told Bernice yet?"

"At breakfast."

"What did she say?"

"She was upset I hadn't discussed it with her." She cast Daisy a sideways glance. "I told her I'd hired you as a personal social assistant. She doesn't know you're a matchmaker."

"And she won't hear it from me. Shall we call her in to read it?"

Bernice was quick to appear at the door as soon as she was called. When she took a seat opposite them, Lindsey pushed over the magazine. As she read, it seemed natural that she and Daisy remain side by side. When a myriad of emotions flitted across her old friend's face and her eyes filled with tears, Lindsey wriggled even closer to Daisy until their thighs pressed together. The feel of the warm leg sent goose bumps tingling over Lindsey's skin. Without thinking, she began to stroke Daisy's knuckles with her thumb.

It was only when Bernice lifted her head and stared at their hands, did Lindsey realize what she was doing. Hastily, she straightened up and shifted away. Her body protested the loss of the contact though she managed to ignore it. "What do you think?" she asked.

Bernice pressed her hand to her chest, her voice quavering. "It's wonderful."

"A little unrealistic," murmured Lindsey.

"No, it's not. It's about time you are recognized for your achievements. I'm so proud of you."

"Here, here," piped in Daisy. She gave Bernice a wink. "What say we celebrate with a cuppa?"

"I'll go and put the jug on."

After she disappeared out the door, Daisy tilted her head to study Lindsey. "I guess it's time to move on to the next phase of the program."

"Dating?"

"Yes. You might like to ask Nicolle out for that drink if you still want to. I'll ring my friend about a night out at the Beauvoir Club and we'll take it from there."

Lindsey digested this in silence. "Okay," she said after a moment. "I'll give Nicolle a ring tonight and see if she would like to have lunch at the Chelsea on Saturday."

Something flashed in Daisy's eyes, but she couldn't tell if it was annoyance or just the reflection of the fluorescent light. "I'm sure she'll be happy to hear from you."

"I hope so. Shall we adjourn to the kitchen for that cuppa?"

Daisy didn't stay long, pleading work commitments for her quick departure. When Lindsey returned to the kitchen after seeing her off, Bernice didn't look up but by the tight set of her shoulders, Lindsey knew she was in for a grilling.

"Well, I guess I'd better get back to the office," she said cheerily.

Bernice put the tea-towel on the rack then turned to face her. "I thought you said you had only a professional relationship with Daisy."

Lindsey bit back a sigh. The old girl wasn't going to let it go. "Yes, but we have become friends. I value her advice."

"From the way you were touching her, it looked like you wanted more than advice."

Lindsey felt an uncomfortable prickling across her skin. Maybe she was getting too familiar with Daisy. Hadn't she had complained that one of her clients had become obsessed with her and given her a hard time. Was she doing the exact same thing? Perhaps it was time to pull back. She would definitely call Nicolle today. "I like Daisy. Okay? She's fun and non-judgemental. We get on well and she's easy to be with because that's her job," she said gruffly.

"She's also a desirable young woman. Watching you together today, I realized I was wrong. I was worried that you were playing with her affections, but you're the one becoming attached. Just be careful, dear. You're very vulnerable at the moment. What you see in the friendship mightn't be what she does. You could get hurt."

The flood of guilt dissolved into annoyance. "I'm thirty-five, for God sake, not an adolescent with a crush."

"If you say so."

"Yes, I do," said Lindsey, rising to go. "Now let that be the end of it," she added sternly.

At the door, she cast a backward glance. A foolish woman might've thought she'd won the argument, but from the sceptical look on Bernice's face, she clearly hadn't.

CHAPTER TWENTY-SIX

Lindsey looked appreciatively at Nicolle as she entered the hotel foyer, with the confident smooth rhythm of a dancer. Dressed in a mauve suit meticulously cut in a deceptively simple style, she looked all class. When she saw Lindsey, she paused confidently and kissed her on the cheek.

"Hi, Lindsey. Thank you so much for inviting me. It was a lovely surprise. The restaurant has a top reputation and I've always planned to come here one day."

"I'm glad you could join me. I came here a few weeks ago with Daisy. The food is superb."

"Wonderful. Good food is one of my greatest loves," Nicolle said with a smile. "Or vices."

"Shall we go in then?" murmured Lindsey, any lingering anxiety vanishing when Nicolle gave her right hand a quick squeeze.

Aware that she'd have to expect some recognition after the article, Lindsey tried to ignore the curious glances and nods of acknowledgment directed her way as they were shown to their table. Fortunately, after their initial interest most people had the good manners to give them privacy.

"So," said Nicolle, her blue eyes sparkling. "You're quite the celebrity."

Lindsey rolled her eyes. "I hope fame is fleeting, as the saying goes. Being in the public eye doesn't sit well with me. I'm a very private person."

"What possessed you to give that interview then?"

Lindsey forced herself to control the tension creeping back as she rattled off the prepared white lie. "My company is doing well, but we need more exposure globally. We have some new products ready to launch. The interview was the first step. I've recently hired a friend as an event coordinator."

"For what it's worth, I think you're an extraordinary person and very brave. Now I'm sure you want to get off that subject so shall we order? What do you suggest?"

Not knowing what to expect with the date, it went far better than she had anticipated. Nicolle was engaging—the conversation didn't lag or fall into uncomfortable silences, so when they rose to go, Lindsey was genuinely sorry it was over.

"That was lovely," said Nicolle as they reached the glass doors leading out of the foyer. "Would you like to come to dinner with me next week? There's a nice little Greek restaurant I'm sure you'd enjoy."

"Um…that would be great," Lindsey replied with a cautious smile. "I'm not quite sure if I'm free on the weekend though."

"Perhaps Thursday night?"

"Thursday will be fine."

"Good. It's a date then. I'll ring you on Wednesday with the time. I have a showing at three so it won't be early," Nicolle said. "Now I'd better ring for a taxi."

"Can I drop you somewhere? My driver's parked outside."

"Thank you. I'd appreciate that." The reply was simple and gracious. The dress designer was not one to gush, which Lindsey liked.

Lindsey studied her companion as they moved through the city. She really was a charming woman: bright, successful, and seemingly completely in control of her life. She imagined that if Nicolle wanted something, she would find a way to get it. If she was aware she was being examined she gave no indication.

They drove in companionable silence with only an occasional comment and presently stopped in front of an attractive apartment building overlooking the river. Nicolle turned to look at Lindsey with a distinct gleam in her eye. "It's nice to meet someone who is so easy to be with and on the same wavelength. I think we're going to get on famously."

Then Nicolle did something so unexpected it caught her completely off guard. She leaned over and kissed her. As softly, slowly, her mouth roamed over hers, Lindsey remained planted on the seat and didn't pull away. After teasing her bottom lip with her tongue, and with infinite care, Nicolle pulled back, her warm breath caressing Lindsey's cheeks as she withdrew.

She slid over to the door with a long cool look. "I'll see you on Thursday. Be safe." Then she stepped out of the vehicle in a fluid movement and Joe closed the door before Lindsey could reply.

Lindsey touched her fingers to her lips as the car nosed back into the traffic. The kiss had been soft like a benediction, and a definite declaration of Nicolle's intentions. But though sweet, it hadn't stirred her blood or sent tingles through her body. Maybe that would come later, for it was clear that Nicolle intended there to be a later. Anyone would be lucky to have her as a lover. She was warm, considerate and articulate—also wealthy in her own right. They were well suited.

With eyes closed Lindsey sank back into the seat, revelling in the solitude. Even though the date had been very pleasant, it had been a little draining. She felt confused. Why couldn't she push Daisy out of her mind when Nicolle was a perfect candidate for a relationship? That very brief kiss she had given Daisy outside the cottage had affected her far more than this one. It had sent her body throbbing for more, why she couldn't fathom. They were so different in lots of ways even though they got on well. She was a woman who liked order and detail while Daisy thrived in disorder and was inclined to trivialize minutiae.

When Joe dropped her off, she changed into her old work clothes. Gardening was her therapeutic way to relax, the physical work always soothing. She worked steadily until the light had completely faded before trudging upstairs to shower for dinner. At least she would have peace and quiet while she ate.

She and Bernice had reached an impasse since their words when the article came out. Lindsey didn't discuss her new social life and Bernice ignored the fact that she had one. The meal was a subdued affair: Lindsey was cranky because her back ached from weeding and Bernice surly because she couldn't ask where she went for lunch. So as soon as she swallowed the last mouthful, Lindsey disappeared into the lounge to watch TV. Tomorrow she'd mend the bridges—they had been too close over the years. Tonight, though, she just wanted to chill out.

Even though the movie was good, Lindsey couldn't concentrate. She missed Daisy's nightly call. They hadn't spoken since she delivered the magazine and the two times Lindsey had rung, the call had gone to voice mail. She was beginning to think that she had been right. Daisy wanted space from her, that she thought Lindsey was getting too familiar. With a weary sigh, she switched off the television and was about to climb the stairs when her phone jangled. When Daisy's voice came on the line, her heart skipped a beat.

"Hey, Lindsey. Umm…I know it's rather late, but I was wondering how you got on today."

Lindsey slipped back into the chair with a broad smile. "Hello there. I haven't heard from you since Tuesday. What's been happening?"

"I've been pretty busy with work, and Mum had the flu so I've been helping out with meals at night."

"Oh. Is she all right?"

"Much better now. So…how did your date with Nicolle go? You did ask her, didn't you?"

"I did. We had lunch at the Chelsea today and it went very well. Extremely well in fact. She was charming and we got on like a house on fire. She's so easy to be with…I had no anxiety at all."

There was silence at the end of the phone for a moment then Daisy said, "Really? Then you clicked?"

"We have a lot in common."

"Are you going to see her again?"

"She's asked me to dinner on Thursday night," Lindsey replied. "A Greek restaurant."

"That sounds nice. I've organized a night out at the Beauvoir Club on Saturday, so you'll have a busy week. Apparently, it's their monthly party night. Carmen said it's always a hoot."

"Carmen?"

"She's one of Australia's top models. I've been out with her before," Daisy murmured.

Lindsey glowered into the phone. It would seem Daisy had a love life after all. "What's her last name, if I may ask?"

"Carmen Zambini. She's a bit of a fashionista but fun."

"I can't wait to meet her." *As if.*

"Good, because she's dying to meet you."

"Uh-huh," said Lindsey with an eye roll. "What do I wear to this party?"

"Carmen says it's not too dressy, though she always looks a million dollars. Go for something good but not too formal."

Lindsey felt a twinge of dismay. Great. Just what she needed. A beauty queen as an escort. "She sounds interesting." *Or not.*

"She'll make sure you have a good time."

"You will be coming too, won't you?" Lindsey asked in alarm.

"Oh yes. Carmen insisted."

"Good. I'm looking forward to it," Lindsey muttered, resisting the urge to ask Daisy if she always did what Carmen wanted. She was beginning to dislike the model.

"I'll give you a ring Friday to sort out the finer details."

"Okay. I'll be able to tell you how my date with Nicolle went."

"Oh, right," replied Daisy brusquely.

"She made it plain she's interested." Lindsey lowered her voice into a whisper. "She kissed me in the car."

"I don't expect all the intimate details. That's between you two," Daisy snapped.

"Sorry. I thought you did. You being the *Minority Report* guru an' all. I'd better let you go then. Bye for now." Lindsey clicked off the phone with a satisfied smile. The smugness didn't last long. What she had done was petty. She'd mentioned Nicolle simply because she resented Carmen liking Daisy.

Unable to help herself, she hurried to her study to google *Carmen Zambini model*. When the image popped up her stomach lurched. The woman was gorgeous. No way could she compete with someone who looked like that.

CHAPTER TWENTY-SEVEN

Daisy tossed the phone onto the bedside table then burrowed under the covers.

"Goddamn it," she snarled into the pillow. Nicolle certainly hadn't wasted much time with Lindsey. If she were honest, the dress designer was very eligible and would suit Lindsey admirably. But she hadn't been thinking with her head when Lindsey told her about her great luncheon date. Instead of being an encouraging matchmaker, as she had been hired to be, she'd raved on about how fucking great Carmen was.

Then when Lindsey announced Nicolle had kissed her, a pang of indignation shot right through her. She vowed to be more vigilant about her feelings in the future. Not that she hadn't tried. She had already decided to give Lindsey more space. She knew she had to stop monopolizing her now she was ready to look for a wife. Daisy had to fade into the background—Lindsey was her client not her girlfriend. However, all it had succeeded in doing was to make her life miserable. She'd even let Lindsey's calls go to voice mail which had really stung.

With a sigh, she snuggled deeper into the bed. Maybe ringing every second night wouldn't hurt, she thought as she drifted off to sleep.

* * *

"Whatever is the matter with you?" Allison asked as Daisy pushed aside her half-eaten donut. "You moped around all day yesterday and you're no better this morning."

"Nothing's the matter. I just feel out of sorts."

"Go on home if you're not well. I can handle things."

"I'm not sick," replied Daisy testily. "Give me a break. I can't be cheery all the time."

Allison looked at her in surprise. "Well, something's got your knickers in a knot. Out with it…what's wrong?"

"I don't know. I'm just down in the dumps."

"Ah," said Allison, her attention fully caught. "You've been extra happy lately. At a guess, I'd say you've met someone and you've had an argument."

"What! No!"

"Sounds like it to me. Who is she?"

Daisy stiffened. Was she that obvious? *Damn.* She took a swig of her coffee and said nonchalantly. "When have I had time to date or even meet someone for that matter?"

"You could have met her on the Internet."

"I did—" Daisy stopped. Why not make up a girlfriend? Allison would hardly approve of her crushing on one of her clients. She took a deep breath and said, "Okay…you're very perceptive. An old girlfriend got in touch and we reconnected. But that's all I'm saying on the subject. I don't want to jinx it."

Allison's eyes widened. "Now you've got me curious. When you're ready, I'd love to meet her."

"Not for a while," Daisy answered with a firm shake of her head. She needed to get out of the office immediately, for by the look on Allison's face there were more questions on the tip of her tongue. "Now I've errands to run. I'll head home afterwards and see you tomorrow. Fresh air should buck me up."

She quickly collected her bag and laptop, quashing the pangs of conscience as she slipped out the door. She hated lying to her friend. Outside, the air was warm with a barmy breeze blowing which did boost her spirits. As she drove out of her parking space, she was in two minds what to do.

She intended to work on the robot profile at home—her agency work had taken up all her time since she'd returned to town. It was becoming urgent to submit part of the first draft. The thought of working in her cramped study in her apartment didn't appeal as much as Lindsey's futuristic lounge. Ideas seemed to flow in that sci-fi setting.

She paused at the exit sign in the carpark. Could she just casually drop in? She shrugged. *Why not?* Without further hesitation, she swung the car north. When she reached Lindsey's steel gate, nostalgia swept over her. She hadn't stayed there long, but the estate inside looked warm and inviting like an old friend. Once the password was punched in, the gate swung open with a small click and she drove through with a smile.

A minute passed after she pressed the doorbell before she heard footsteps. Bernice opened the door, blinking in the bright sunlight. "Daisy, I didn't know you were coming."

"A last-moment decision. I hope I'm not intruding, but I thought I'd continue with my robot profile at the desk in the loungeroom. Lindsey said I could use it anytime."

"Come on through. She went into the town lab early this morning."

"When will she be back?"

"Sorry, dear, she didn't say. She usually makes a day of it if she travels all the way in."

Disappointed, Daisy followed her into the lounge. When Bernice disappeared upstairs, she settled down at the desk and opened her laptop. After typing a few sentences, she stopped to watch Stephen dusting the furniture. With the identity nearly finished, she had begun to think of the robot as *him* not *it*. Usually when she was in the room, he was turned off. She had never been shown how to reactivate him, which she suspected was deliberate on Lindsey's part. She was very secretive about the robots.

Though he resembled a human, there was no mistaking that he wasn't. His skin was a little too waxy and his face too symmetrical. As well, his movements were a tad jerky and stiff. She knew Lindsey was working on making them smoother. She had also mentioned that she had developed a new algorithm to enable the robot to react to a variety of falls—from a gentle nudge, to a rolling motion to break a high-speed tumble.

Curious, Daisy walked to the centre of the room and said slowly and distinctly, "Hello. I'm Daisy."

The head swivelled around with a tiny whirring sound. "Hello Day-see. How are you?" The voice was slightly distorted, slightly plastic, and very digital, but for all that, he sounded fine.

Fascinated, she studied him closely. He was obviously programmed with a set of autonomous functions like cleaning and dusting, but how much more could he do? Lindsey had said he would obey commands. Okay, she'd give it a go. She waved. "Do this, Stephen."

Though not as fluid as her, he waved an arm with surprising agility. She moved a leg in the air. He did the same.

Excited now, she sidled closer. Maybe she could teach him a simple dance. "I want you to do what I do now."

She leaned forward and back, then leaned to the right and to the left. She put both hands out front, sweeping from side to side. She raised her arms over her head, pivoted and clapped. "Now do that, Stephen."

Unhesitatingly, he performed the sequence without a hitch. Delighted, she repeated the movements, which he copied again perfectly.

"Okay. We're going to do it together."

"Yes, Day-see."

Daisy blue-toothed her phone into the sound system, then clicked on her favourite feel-good songs, beginning with "The Days." Once she was facing the robot again, she began to dance. "Follow me," she called out.

The robot was the perfect partner. For over ten minutes, she danced enthusiastically while Stephen followed in perfect sync. Caught up in the music, she failed to hear the footsteps approach from the hall until she heard, "What the hell do you think you're doing?"

Panting, she whipped her head towards the sound. Lindsey was standing in the doorway with hands on hips, her face like thunder. The next second, Stephen lurched sideways when he jerked his head around to follow Daisy's lead. He teetered for a moment on the edge of toppling. Before she could react, he had deftly swung his body back into an upright position.

"Stand down X32," Lindsey shouted.

The robot stopped in his tracks. Then he turned, slowly walked across to a small compartment in the corner and backed in. His eyes dimmed slightly.

Daisy hurriedly turned off the music, then waited nervously. Lindsey took her time, locking in the robot securely before she turned to face her. "Do you have any idea what that robot is worth?" she growled out.

Daisy remained silent.

"Over four million dollars. He is not a toy. What on earth were you thinking? He could have been damaged. Or worse, you could have been seriously hurt if he had accidently hit you."

"Sorry. I just wanted to see what he could do."

A hiss escaped from Lindsey. "Then you should have asked me, not gone off on your own tangent."

"I guess I wasn't thinking. I couldn't resist."

"Really, you'd try a saint's patience, Daisy. Why didn't you start with something simpler?"

"What's the fun in that? He's a great dancer by the way."

Lindsey shook her head in disbelief, but then her face softened, her lips curling into a twitch of a smile. "That he is. I've never pushed him to do anything so complicated. Did he take much to teach?"

"Got it first time."

"Good, the updated program must be working well." Lindsey smiled over at the robot. "I've been hesitant to push him too far. I did a very complicated manoeuvre with one of the dogs and froze its hard drive." She focused back on Daisy. "What are you doing here today? I didn't know you were coming."

"Last-minute decision. I wanted to work on Stephen's profile. It's easier to get into the swing of things here. You'll be pleased to know his family tree and childhood memories are complete. I've started on his school years…teachers, friends and so forth." She peeped at Lindsey slyly. "Since everything's set up, why don't we have that dancing lesson? It's the last thing left in the book."

Lindsey shot her an incredulous look. "Now?"

"Yep."

"I know perfectly well how to disco. I've been to nightclubs in my younger days."

"Good. Then I'll put on the music and you can show me your moves. Unless, of course, you've something more urgent to attend to," said Daisy, shooting a challenging look.

Lindsey seemed like she was going to refuse, but then threw up her hands. "All right…why not. You won't stop nagging until I have that damn lesson. I'll give you half an hour and that's the end of it. Agreed?"

"Yes." Before she could change her mind, Daisy hunted through her phone. "Ah, here's the playlist I wanted. There are some good ones on this. We'll start with 'We are Family.'" She hiked up the volume and swayed up to Lindsey. "Come on. See if you can keep up with me," she said, letting herself embrace the pulsing music.

The tune wrapped her in the beat, throbbed through her veins until she was consumed with the dance. She swung her hips, bobbed and weaved, with her arms flying, feet stamping. It was pure pleasure. When Lindsey joined in, Daisy laughed delightedly. The woman had rhythm. Energy flowed between them as the songs rolled on, and by the third, their movements became more intricate and sexy. Daisy was just about to call a halt, when the end of "Dancing Queen" changed into a gentle love song.

They stopped, looked at each other, then very slowly, very tentatively, Daisy moved in close. Her body gave a quick little jolt when Lindsey slid her right arm around her until they were pressed together, and carefully took her hand with the left. On impulse, Daisy pulled the artificial hand to her mouth and kissed it. Lindsey smiled and with a sure practised movement, began to waltz. Daisy had never danced like it before—she was floating. As they dipped and spun, gradually the friendly, light mood changed. It darkened, deepened, lengthened. The rhythm became as seductive as jungle drums.

Their movements slowed to a shuffle, they melted together. Lindsey's fingers began to cruise lazily up and down Daisy's back until her skin shivered. She slid her arms around Lindsey's neck, pressing her breasts against her shirt. Her pulse raced as the hand on her back began to skim lower. Soon the touch became firmer, bolder. Daisy gave a throaty moan as the heat built. She wandered her lips over Lindsey's chin and trailed down to the tender hollow in her neck. She smelt so good. Peaked nipples poked into Daisy's chest and her fingers itched to undo her buttons. She flicked the top one open.

Then abruptly the tune changed. Heavy metal blasted through the room in a loud aggressive cacophony, thick wailing music that shattered the intimacy into a thousand shards. Daisy sprang back in alarm. "Oh shit! I'm sorry, I don't know..." her voice tailed off feebly at the expression on Lindsey's face. She looked mortified.

"I'm the one who should apologise. I don't know what came over me pawing at you like that." She jerked her fingers through her hair. A blond strand flopped over her forehead.

She looked so adorable that Daisy had to bite back the urge to sweep it off her eyes. Her body still reverberating with arousal, she gave her a reassuring smile. "Hey, I was there too. We just got carried away in the moment."

"That's putting it mildly don't you think?"

"I guess it was a bit more," Daisy replied ruefully. When she continued, the words took more effort. "We could ignore what happened, but that would leave it simmering in the background. We would be too self-conscious with each other. I think we should talk about it."

"I suppose so," Lindsey whispered.

More in control of her emotions now, Daisy gestured towards the lounge chairs. "Let's sit down first. I'm dying to get off my feet."

Lindsey didn't argue, immediately walking quickly over to a chair without a word. When seated, she looked at her expectantly. "Go ahead."

Daisy clasped her hands tightly on her lap and tried to relax. "Okay. I admit…I am attracted to you." She took a big breath —it was taking a great deal of effort to keep her voice calm. "You're extremely…um…appealing. And I don't just mean your looks. We get on well and we're comfortable together. You're great to be with. But no matter how much I like you, there is no way I can let it go any further. That's presuming you want to take it further of course. It would be most unprofessional. You hired me to do a job in good faith."

"If we both like each other, why would it be so unprofessional to explore the attraction and see where it goes? We're both single."

"Lindsey, you've been out of the dating scene for years and you're looking for someone to love. It's only natural that you're going to latch on to the first presentable female who comes along and shows interest. I've seen this so many times before with lonely clients."

Lindsey looked affronted. "I've never been frivolous with my emotions."

"I didn't mean it as an insult. I meant you really must do the dating scene for a while. Go out and meet a variety of women."

"Huh! What exactly are you suggesting I do? Flit from one woman to another."

"I'm saying you need to explore your options."

"Oh?" Lindsey replied sarcastically. "I'm to go out and date some eligible ladies but you're not available. Is that what you're saying?"

"In a way. Yes."

"Why aren't you in a relationship, Daisy? You're bright, good-looking, successful, and nearly thirty. And don't give me that crap about not having time."

"My love life has nothing to do with this."

"It has everything to do with it." Her dark eyes flashing, Lindsey leaned forward and said curtly, "For all your expertise in the human relations, you're a fraud. I think you're frightened to commit to anyone. And don't worry, I won't be touching you again." She abruptly rose from her chair. "Now I'm going upstairs to shower, then I'm doing some gardening. I need some fresh air. Text me the time you want to be picked up on Saturday night. Bernice will show you out."

Stunned, Daisy watched her stalk out of the room. *Well, that went fucking well.*

If only Lindsey knew the truth. She wasn't afraid of commitment, she just hadn't met a woman who lit up her heart. Dating was never casual to her, she constantly searched for that deeper connection. But it was always the same—no fireworks, no ache of longing. She wanted everything that she'd seen lucky couples have: passion, romance, true love. She wasn't prepared to take less.

Unfortunately, there was nothing casual about how she felt about Lindsey. Her mere touch sparked her libido. It wasn't all about the physical either, as they seemed to have a strong emotional connection. But how could she possibly act on it? It would be unethical as her matchmaker to claim one of the most eligible women in the city before giving anyone a chance to meet her.

After a few months it wouldn't matter. But then again, it wasn't likely that she'd have the opportunity again. She'd burnt that bridge.

CHAPTER TWENTY-EIGHT

Lindsey stared out the car window, though too preoccupied to take in the scenery as they sped through the city to collect Nicolle. She repeatedly replayed how Daisy had felt in her arms: how her soft body had melted into hers and how her breasts had pressed against her. Wonderful. *Too* wonderful. The throbbing between her legs had sent her nerves jangling. She couldn't remember ever being so aroused. Trisha had never managed to inspire anywhere near that much passion. But then again, had she really expected her to?

She thrashed their conversation around in her head, knowing in her heart that Daisy was right. It would be foolish to rush into a relationship at this stage before she saw the program through. But common sense did nothing to alleviate the hurt of rejection. It had cut to the quick and she had retaliated churlishly. She shuddered at the memory. God, she'd even called her a fraud. She'd be lucky if Daisy even talked to her again.

"We're here," said Joe as he eased the Mercedes into a parking bay outside the apartment block.

Turning her attention back to her date, she looked out the window to see Nicolle threading her way between a group of elderly well-dressed women at the doorway. She gave her a silent tick of approval—she was ready and waiting without any fuss.

"I'll get the door today, Joe," she called out.

"I appreciate you picking me up," Nicolle murmured as Lindsey opened the door and guided her into the backseat.

"My pleasure. It only makes sense to utilize my chauffeur. He has to bring me into the city."

Nicolle winked. "It's good to know neither one of us has to be the designated driver. That outfit looks very nice on you by the way."

"Thanks to the designer," said Lindsey with a smile. "How did your showing go?"

She settled back as they moved off, tilting her head to watch Nicolle as she described her day. As expected, she was a vision of sophistication. The blue frock was understatedly elegant, her fashionable heels complemented the outfit perfectly and her makeup was flawless. Her perfume finished the outfit.

Lindsey idly wondered if she ever got messy or wore chipped nail polish or went without a bra at home. Probably not, she decided. That would be losing a little control—Nicolle seemed to be a woman in complete charge of her life. Strangely, for all her friendliness and warmth, she could visualize her quite happily at her mother's dinner parties, laughing at her jokes. She blinked back the image, annoyed with herself. Nicolle was nothing like her mother. Then the thoughts vanished when they pulled up in front of an unassuming weatherboard building.

"You'll love the food. Constantinou's Kitchen is a family-owned business and very popular. Bookings only," whispered Nicolle as they strolled through the door.

The restaurant looked homely and welcoming. The walls were a rustic white with two rows of tables and chairs set up under low romantic lighting, each setting far enough apart to give the illusion of privacy. Dried flowers trailed down posts and scenes of the Greek Islands were scattered about the walls.

Lindsey could see through the far double doors that there was al fresco dining in a cobblestoned courtyard. A young musician was seated on a stool between the two areas, quietly strumming a bouzouki.

The waiter appeared almost immediately and led them to a table outside where grapevines trailed on a trellis above the diners.

"It's delightful," exclaimed Lindsey.

"It's one of my favourite eating places," Nicolle said with a smile as she handed over the menu. "Would you fancy an assortment of appetizers to start?"

"Sounds lovely. You choose."

Nicolle ordered the platter and then raised her eyebrows at Lindsey. "They have a nice Brown Brothers Sauvignon Blanc. Or would you prefer red?"

"No, no. The white will be fine."

"Excellent."

When the wine arrived, Nicolle took a sip as she watched her keenly. "Tell me. How did you meet Daisy?"

Even though Lindsey was prepared for the question, she was still uneasy. It wasn't likely that Nicolle didn't know what Daisy did and she was clearly fishing. She gave a nonchalant shrug. "She's doing some programming for the company for a couple of months. Since I needed a new wardrobe and because I've been out of circulation for so long, she took me to your showroom."

"And I'm very thankful she did. Are you good friends?"

"We get on well, though I haven't known her long. How do you know her, if I may ask?"

"A friend of mine was keen on her," Nicolle replied though she didn't elaborate.

"Oh?" said Lindsey, trying to keep her face deadpan. She ignored the slight flutter around her heart. "What happened?"

"Nothing. That's always the way with Daisy. She never gets involved long term with anyone."

Lindsey gazed at her, intrigued. Something in her body language suggested she was warning her off Daisy. "Really. That's interesting. I wonder why, because she's lots of fun."

"I've no idea," replied Nicolle with a shrug. She took a bite of a pickled feta and crab canape, and groaned. "Try this. It's divine."

To Lindsey's relief, they drifted off to another subject. Discussing Daisy had been taxing. Nicolle was no fool and she doubted she could have kept her interest from showing much longer.

As the night progressed, Lindsey found she was enjoying herself immensely. The food was superb and Nicolle was the perfect date: well-read, entertaining, and solicitous. But after a while she began noticing little things that made her feel uncomfortable: how often Nicolle's foot brushed against hers and how she always reached over to touch her to get a point across. By the time they rose to go, it was quite clear she expected more than a kiss goodnight.

As they stepped out into the night, Nicolle took her right arm and pulled her closer. The words were quiet, whispered in her ear. "I had a great time, Lindsey. You're a handsome, exciting woman."

Lindsey cleared her throat, feeling the hot blush on her cheeks. "Now you're embarrassing me."

Nicolle chuckled. "You have no idea how refreshing it is to be with someone completely without an agenda."

Lindsey was saved from having to answer when the black car appeared around the corner. "Ah, here's our ride," she said and tugged Nicolle to the kerb.

It was nearly eleven by the time they reached the apartment block. When they pulled to a stop, Lindsey climbed out and walked around to open Nicolle's door. She was rewarded with a blazing smile. Discreetly, Joe moved on to park further down the street. She knew he would wait there until she returned or rang to tell him to go home and pick her up in the morning. She imagined with her new dating regime, he was going to have a lot more driving at night. She'd better give him a raise.

Nicolle immediately claimed her right hand as they strolled up to the door. When she waved her key card over a red light, it flashed to green and the door slid open to reveal an elevator in the small foyer. With no hesitation, Nicolle stepped through, leaving Lindsey no choice but to follow her inside. The door swung shut and locked with a click. For a moment they stood a little apart, waiting for the other to speak. Then Nicolle took a step closer, and slowly reached up to stroke Lindsey's cheek. With infinite care, she pressed her lips against her mouth.

As the kiss deepened, Nicolle's tongue brushed against her inner lips seeking entry to her mouth. Before Lindsey could react, Nicolle's arms were tight around her waist, bringing their bodies flush together. Her hands went lower to cup Lindsey's buttocks, squeezing hard as she pulled her pelvis against her. She edged her back against the wall and slipped a thigh between her legs. Even though Lindsey's body was having a definite physical reaction to the pressure, there was no emotional connection. When Nicolle pressed her leg up harder, all she felt was the first fluttering of panic.

She managed to pull her head back and whisper urgently, "Whoa. Stop. This is going too quickly for me."

Her face flushed, Nicolle dropped her hands and stepped back a fraction. "I'm sorry. I got carried away…I've been wanting to touch you all night. I didn't mean to ravish you in the foyer. We'll continue it upstairs in my bed." She smiled and touched Lindsey's lips with a finger. "I promise to go slower, honey."

Lindsey took a long deep breath as her anxiety faded. She removed the hand gently from her face, fighting to kept her voice steady. "No, Nicolle. I meant what I said. It's way too fast for me. I'm not ready…I can't do this."

Nicolle's eyes widened. "You're serious?"

"Yes, I am. I guess I misunderstood what this date was about."

"But we're mature women, not blushing girls."

"And I'm too old to be playing these games. I'm after much more than sex. I've had very little experience with dating… extremely rusty to be honest…but I know what I want. And that's to find someone to love."

Nicolle's face paled as she stared at her. "What a fool I've been. I…well, I thought you—"

"Casual is not for me. I imagined we'd go slower, get to know each other before we went further. I like you, Nicolle, but I don't *know* you."

"I am so very sorry. You're the most interesting woman I've met in years and I…oh, shit, I've really stuffed it up."

"We both did. Now I'd better be going. Goodnight. Dinner was wonderful and I had a great time," Lindsey said in a rush, just wanting to get out of the place. She quickly walked to the door and punched the exit button, then hurried out into the street without a backward glance.

The cool night air hit in a soothing rush. She paused to collect herself, taking a deep breath before she walked up to where the car was parked. Joe didn't say a word as he opened the back door.

"No, Joe. I'll sit up front with you tonight. I'd appreciate the company."

"Of course. Would you like some music?"

"No, just peace and quiet," she answered. Mortified, she stared out the window and attempted to ignore what had happened. But as much as she tried, she couldn't forget or stop the welling tears. She brushed them away irritably.

"Are you all right, Lindsey?"

She turned to look at him, catching the concern in his voice. "I'm fine. Just tired."

Then she realized that his presence was making her feel much better. He was so normal, one of her most trusted and loyal employees. She always felt completely safe with him— Joe was her protector as well as chauffeur. He was a solid, fit man in his early forties, hair cropped short in a military style and a leathery, lined face. Ex-army, he had been in first wave of Australian SAS soldiers to hit the ground in Afghanistan after September 11.

After the loss of his left hand in a landmine explosion two tours later, he was discharged with a prosthesis and limited employment prospects. He had been one of two hundred people applying for the position of courier-chauffeur when she bought her house. It wasn't the fact he was an amputee that won him the job—it was the way he unapologetically fronted up to the interview knowing he had little chance against more able-bodied applicants.

After hiring him, she sent him to the lab to be fitted with one of their experimental limbs.

Unable to shake the feeling of vulnerability, she eyed him with some disquiet. Was he content in her employment? She'd always presumed he was but had never asked. "You've been with me over ten years, Joe. Are you happy?"

"I am. I like the job and nobody interferes with me. The accommodation is great."

She smiled, knowing he took pride in his flat above the garage. Being a loner, he preferred to look after himself, though she knew Bernice took a dinner plate over to him most nights. "I'm probably going to need you more often for personal trips in the coming months. I'll have my accountant draw up an increase in your salary."

"That won't be necessary. My present wage is generous."

"Nonsense. You've enough to do ferrying things between the two labs, collecting our shopping and attending to the odd jobs around the house without having to go out at night. You'll be bored silly waiting for me. Call it nuisance money."

He flicked her a quick warm look. "It's good to see you going out at last. Your new clothes are very nice."

"Why thank you," said Lindsey, flattered. Joe was not one to voice an opinion. "Daisy persuaded me to upgrade my wardrobe."

"Ah, Daisy. She's a nice girl, that one. Never fails to thank me for a ride."

"She is very friendly and thoughtful."

"Fun too. You should see her do her impersonations. She had Bernice and I in stitches."

Lindsey looked at him in surprise. While Daisy was living in the cottage, she obviously had more interaction with the staff than she realised. Joe seemed as enamoured with her as Bernice was. "I'll have to ask her to show me," she said, a little annoyed she'd been left out of the fun.

"Whoever gets her will be a lucky woman," Joe said quietly.

Lindsey shot him a glance. Was her driver inferring Daisy would be a good catch for her? From the tone of his voice, it certainly sounded like it. "No doubt," she said finally.

She huffed to herself. What was with her staff? First Bernice and now Joe. Interfering busybodies. Then she couldn't help herself, ignoring the fact it wasn't her business. It was his turn. "Have you a girlfriend, Joe?" she asked.

"I'm not one to socialise. It's been hard to adjust back into civilian life."

A wave of guilt hit. Swept up in her own problems, she'd had no idea what he'd been going through. How could she have been so blind? He would have suffered PTSD, though to what degree she didn't know. He had always seemed so in control. "I understand fully," she said compassionately. "But maybe it's time to let things go."

He cleared his throat then said in low voice. "Daisy has a lady she wants me to meet. She lost her husband in a boating accident. I'm taking her out Saturday night after I drop you off at the club."

Lindsey sank back into the leather seat. Trust Daisy to recognize in only a few weeks that Joe was lonely. She hadn't noticed in a decade. "I'm sure you'll find her lovely. Daisy has a knack of matching up couples."

Knowing he wouldn't want any more questions on the subject, she said nothing more and they fell into silence for the rest of the trip.

At last in bed, she had little hope of sleep. Now alone, her mind was firmly on the events of the night. All her old insecurities rushed back. She hadn't wanted to go to bed with Nicolle, but she could have handled it better. Just said no without sermonising. Been more adult about it, instead of rushing off like a frightened rabbit. Maybe she just should have had sex with her. It had been long enough. But at that thought, Daisy's image popped in and she jammed the pillow over her face.

Get out of my head, Daisy!

Giving up, she took a sleeping pill. She closed her eyes, remembering Nicolle's heated kiss and her leg squeezed between her thighs. But as she drifted off, the face shimmered out of focus and it was Daisy kissing her, sliding her fingers under her panties.

CHAPTER TWENTY-NINE

Daisy peered at her reflection in the bathroom mirror as she twitched out a few stray eyebrow hairs. Satisfied, she took a long hot shower, rubbed on her most expensive body lotion and put on a lacy bra and matching knickers. Not that anyone was going to see her underwear, but she couldn't possibly wear her best dress with grannie bloomers and a plain bra. Straightening her hair with the hot wand took a while, but eventually the curls stayed tame. Although she wasn't one for too much makeup, she took more care tonight. Carmen always looked like a walking ad for Estee Lauder.

Finally finished with the preliminaries, she reached into the wardrobe, bypassing her favourite black number for the blue sparkly knee-high dress with the plunging neckline that she reserved for very special occasions. She put on her silver strand necklace with the matching teardrop earrings, a birthday present from her mother, and twirled in front of the mirror. After giving herself the thumbs-up, she grabbed her Gucci evening bag and slipped on the gorgeous slingback sandals that she'd picked up for a song at a sale.

When ten minutes later the doorbell rang, her stomach began to churn. They hadn't spoken since their argument, only texted to confirm the pickup time. Daisy had no idea what the reception from Lindsey was going to be like. Friendly? Cool? Reserved? Sour? A long deep breath settled her nerves as she opened the door. All her fears vanished like butterflies in the wind.

With a shy smile on her face, Lindsey stood in the hallway clutching a bouquet of red roses. Daisy's heart flip-flopped. *Wow!* Dressed in the tuxedo, Lindsey had discarded the bowtie to leave the shirt unbuttoned to the top her cleavage. Her only jewellery was gold studs in her ears to match her cufflinks and the thin gold chain around her neck. She must have revisited the salon, because her hair was newly trimmed and the colour brightened.

"Hey," Lindsey said in a husky voice. "You look beautiful."

"Why thank you, Lindsey. And you look very dapper. That's sweet of you," Daisy murmured as she was handed the roses. "Wait there a minute while I pop these in a vase."

When she came back, Lindsey did something totally unexpected. She stepped forward and hugged her tightly. Daisy sank into the embrace, then wriggled in closer with a little sniff. She smelt so good.

When they broke apart, Lindsey looked bemused. "Sorry for that display," she said. "I'm just glad to see you. I thought you might be angry with me."

A huge surge of relief flooded through Daisy. "I was worried you'd be still annoyed with *me*."

"I had no right to say what I did. I'm sorry."

"You had every right. I shouldn't have been so pedantic." Absently, Daisy brushed the shoulders of the tux and straightened the shirt collar. Suddenly realizing what she was doing, she dropped her hands with an awkward little laugh. "Shall we go."

Joe was already waiting with the car door open.

"Hi, Joe," Daisy said brightly, eyeing his sports coat approvingly. Raylene was really going to like him. She gave him a wink. "You look great."

He merely nodded with a twitch of a smile. She climbed in, and slid over to let Lindsey follow her in.

"So," Lindsey said in a low voice. "Joe told me you've set him up on a date."

Daisy looked at her curiously. "Do you mind?"

"It's entirely his business. But…well…I'd like to thank you. I think he's lonely."

"My client lost her husband five years ago and is very lonely too. I'm hoping they hit it off. She deserves to meet someone nice and she needs a father for her two boys."

"He's a good man."

"I wouldn't have lined up the date if I thought he wasn't," said Daisy, then added after a pause. "Um…how did your date with Nicolle go?"

"Nice restaurant."

"What was it called?"

"Constantinou's Kitchen," Lindsey replied, then shuffled around in the seat.

Daisy looked at her in surprise. As no more information was forthcoming, she presumed the date mustn't have gone well. Though bursting with curiosity, she clamped back further questions. Maybe Lindsey had had a panic attack, but whatever had happened, the subject was closed.

She was searching for something to say when she had an idea. As well as allaying any fears Lindsey may have, it would also give Daisy an excuse not to go home with Carmen. "I was thinking you might like to stay at my place tonight. I've a comfy bed in the spare room and a tracksuit that should fit. We can make an early exit if warranted. We'll take a cab home from here."

Lindsey's eyes widened. "Really, I couldn't—"

"Why not? You don't have to be anywhere early tomorrow, do you?"

"No, but—"

"Good, then that's settled." Daisy sat back, pleased with herself.

When the club came into view ten minutes later, she looked expectantly at Lindsey and flicked her head toward the driver's seat.

After a pause, Lindsey said reluctantly, "I'll be staying in town with Daisy tonight, Joe. Pick me up at ten in the morning."

"Okay, Lindsey. Have a good night," he replied, his voice displaying no surprise.

Carmen was waiting for them in front of the dark-panelled door at the entrance, a gold-sequined cocktail dress sculptured to her model-thin body. Her black hair was piled into an updo style and large hoop earrings glittered in the streetlight. Daisy snorted. So much for *it's not too dressy*. The model looked like she'd just stepped out of *Harper's Bazaar*. From the corner of her eye she could see Lindsey studying the model.

Carmen swayed forward on impossibly high stilettos and planted a lingering kiss on Daisy's cheek. "Hi, babe."

With a wince at the endearment, she hastily introduced the women to each other. She had hoped in her desire to impress her important guest, Carmen would drop the girlfriend act. No such luck. She casually draped her arm over Daisy's shoulders as she led them inside. The foyer, decorated with elaborate tapestries and polished antique furniture, radiated wealth. Thankfully, Carmen dropped her arm as they walked up three marble stairs to a small lounge. There was no doubt that the Beauvoir was soaked in prestige and exclusivity. It was as if the pages of *Vogue* had come to life: all chic in cool greys and neutrals, with subtle feminine undertones. No testosterone within these walls.

Music floated out from somewhere further in but Carmen ushered them over to three plush chairs in the corner. "Let's have a quiet drink before we join the party, shall we."

Immediately after they were seated, a waitress appeared with a tray of cocktails. Daisy was mostly quiet while they chatted, content to watch the two women interact as she sipped a pineapple concoction. She had expected the model to fawn over Lindsey, considering her new star status, but it wasn't the case. She was as pretentious as ever. Really, the woman was insufferable. She tried to imagine sitting at home with her, just the two of them. What would they talk about? Food? Nope. Carmen looked like she survived on salads. Fashion? Nope. She would take over the conversation. What did they have in common? Very little. When that first rush of sex wore off, they would be bored with each other within six months.

Daisy swept her eyes around the room. She knew no one. Most were in the over-fifty age bracket, obviously preferring a quiet drink with friends to partying. Then when she heard Carmen ask in her best hoity-toity voice, "Aren't the furnishings in the foyer superb?" she refocused on the conversation.

Lindsey gave a languid shrug but there was a distinct gleam in her eye. "My mother preferred Chippendale to Louis Quatorze, but it's all the same to me."

Daisy intervened hurriedly. Lindsey looked like she wasn't far off from giving the model a taste of her temper. Not that she would blame her. "Shall we adjourn to the next room?" she said hastily and jumped to her feet ready to take Lindsey's arm. With a deft movement Carmen adroitly slipped in between them, placing a hand on her back. Daisy forced down the surge of anger as she allowed herself to be guided into the next room.

The party was in full swing in a very festive atmosphere. Women of all ages and sizes filled the room and spilled out onto the terrace. The dance floor was crowded, patrons bouncing merrily to the music of an all-female jazz quartet. Carmen ushered them through the crush to one of the last available tables. "I'll get us some drinks."

Daisy hummed happily, tapping her feet to the beat. She nudged Lindsey. "This is super fun. Do you—"

She trailed off when a woman stopped at their table and exclaimed, "Lindsey. I don't believe it. Is that really you?"

Lindsey looked up and sprang to her feet. "Margarette."

The woman gave a delighted laugh. "But this is wonderful. You disappeared for years and now…poof…you appear looking quite marvellous."

Intrigued, Daisy watched them embrace. The woman wasn't young. Her hair was streaked with grey, and beneath the cosmetics life-lines were etched into her face. Lindsey was smiling broadly as she turned to introduce her former mentor, Dr Margarette Bellerose.

When Carmen reappeared with the drinks, they shared a polite hello. "I see you've met my friends," she said. Something in voice suggested she and Dr Bellerose weren't exactly close.

"Lindsey is an old colleague and friend," Margarette answered without elaborating. She turned to Lindsey, pointing to a table across the room. "Could I spirit you away for a little while? My friends would be thrilled to meet you. Your work has been ground-breaking."

"I'd love to." Lindsey picked up her glass, flashing a smile at Daisy. "I'll see you later."

Carmen tucked her arm around Daisy possessively. "Don't worry, I'll look after her," she said smugly.

Frowning, Lindsey glanced down at Carmen's hold, nodded and walked after Margarette.

With a pang, Daisy watched her go. She'd hoped to show her a good time and introduce her around. Judging by the ages of the three women at the table, they were hardly marriage prospects. And now she was left with Carmen. Oh, well. Better make the best of it. She downed the champagne and said brightly, "Wanna dance?"

Carmen arched her eyebrows. "Let's go."

As soon as Daisy hit the floor, she deliberately lost herself in the beat.

Two songs later, Carmen hissed, "Slow down. I'm wearing four-inch heels and a bloody tight dress."

"Oh, lighten up," she said gaily. "Get a drink and have a rest. I'm not ready to sit down yet." When she disappeared to the bar, Daisy continued to dance alone, though not for long. A tall woman with the streamlined body of a long-distance runner took Carmen's place. Daisy laughed delightedly— the woman certainly knew how to move. They jumped about enthusiastically, and when the band began to play "I've Had the Time of My Life," they launched into dirty-dancing mode. When the crowd began to clap, they exaggerated their actions.

Finally, when the band took a break, she waved goodbye and went in search of Lindsey.

She was still talking to Margarette as Daisy approached. "Lost Carmen?" Lindsey asked inscrutably.

"She's about somewhere. Can I get you all a drink?"

"We've a bottle of champagne in the ice bucket. You're welcome to join us. We've a spare glass," replied Margarette, shuffling a chair over.

"Thanks. I'd love one."

"I imagine you would be thirsty after all that dancing," said Margarette with a wink. "Oh, to be young again."

Daisy waggled her eyebrows. "I don't know…you look pretty sprightly to me. I probably wouldn't be able to keep up with you."

This received a chuckle. "You're good for the soul, my dear."

While Daisy found Margarette and her two friends charming, Lindsey barely spared her a glance as they talked. The conversation was stimulating, but she gradually became more uncomfortable. Lindsey's attitude was puzzling and upsetting. When at last she heard Carmen calling her name, she eased out of the chair, relieved. "I guess I'd better go. Do you want to join us for something to eat, Lindsey?"

For the first time since she sat down, Lindsey looked at her directly. Her expression was close to disdain. "No thanks. I'm quite happy here."

Suddenly Daisy felt small and stupid. She forced herself to say pleasantly, "Okay. Let me know when you're ready to go home." Then hurried away to find Carmen.

She was at the buffet, delicately selecting low-kilojoule tidbits.

"Oh, for shit sake," Daisy snapped. "Eat something decent." She grabbed a plate and piled it high. "You won't find food this good at home. Now where do you want to sit?"

"What's got you so upset," asked Carmen after they found a table.

Daisy glowered as she bit into a coconut prawn. "Nothing." When the flavour hit her tongue, she became a little calmer.

It was by far the best prawn she'd ever tasted. By the time she worked through the meal and dessert, her good humour was restored. Stuff Lindsey. What did she care about the uptight woman anyhow? If Daisy's company wasn't good enough for her, then too bad.

"Come on," she said with a burst of enthusiasm. "Let's get some fresh air."

On the way out to the terrace, she caught sight of Lindsey and Margarette at the buffet. When Lindsey glanced over, she quickly slid her arm through Carmen's and strolled towards the open doors. It was a beautiful night, the air on the terrace refreshingly crisp. They joined three women leaning on the railing looking out over the city lights.

When the others went back inside, Carmen whispered in her ear, "Come with me. I know somewhere private." She tugged Daisy's arm. Happy enough to sit down, she allowed herself to be led around the corner to a small secluded alcove with a bench chair. Carmen pulled her close and leaned forward.

Before the kiss landed, Daisy pushed her away irritably. "What are you doing?"

"I wanted to be alone with you. We need to talk about us."

"There is no *us*, Carmen. For heaven's sake, we've only been out once."

"But I've known you for ages. Come on, babe. I like you… you know that. I want you to come home with me tonight."

"Sorry. Lindsey is staying at my place tonight."

Carmen went still, her eyes turned a wintery blue. "What?"

"Her chauffer isn't available tonight so she's coming home with me."

"You know her well enough to give her a bed for the night? I can't imagine why you'd bother…she's so pompous."

"Damn it, Carmen, you don't even know her. How can you be so judgemental?" exclaimed Daisy, indignant.

"I've seen enough. She's arrogant…and that voice. You'd think she was the fucking queen."

Daisy leaned back, scrutinizing the model. Having known her socially for a year before she had agreed to go out on a date, she'd never seen her even remotely this upset. Lindsey had certainly got under her skin. Without a doubt, Carmen was envious. Lindsey had everything she craved—good breeding and old money, or as the French put it, she was *le bon ton*. And now the woman she wanted was taking her home.

Suddenly, Daisy felt a wave of compassion. For a person who seemingly had everything, underneath Carmen was quite insecure. Daisy gently cradled her hand. "Hey. You've got Lindsey completely wrong. She's a nice person who has been through a serious trauma. Now she simply wants to live an ordinary life. And whatever you're imagining is going on between us is not. We're simply friends."

Anger fading from her face, Carmen looked at her in astonishment. "You have no idea, have you?"

"Of what exactly?"

"That she wants to get into your pants."

To her utter consternation, Daisy felt heat flush over her cheeks. *Damn.* She was blushing like a schoolgirl. "That's rubbish and do you have to be so crass?"

"Oh, lighten up, Daisy. Get into the real world. You're so old-fashioned and full of that soulmate crap."

"It is not crap."

"How the hell would you know. You've never let yourself get close enough to anyone to find out."

"Nonsense," Daisy snapped.

Carmen sidled closer. "Then kiss me and tell me you feel nothing."

"Okay," Daisy hissed furiously and smashed her mouth against the bright red lipstick. The lips were as soft as silk and she slowed, taking a moment to savour the experience. But as much as it was wonderful to feel a woman in her arms again, there were no fireworks, no aching longing. Her libido barely felt a twinge.

When she pulled back, Carmen gave a moan of frustration. "Don't stop."

Daisy wriggled out the embrace with a look of apology. "I'm sorry. It was nice…you're nice. And you were great having us as here your guests. I do like you but—"

"But you don't feel anything for me," said Carmen with a long painful sigh. "I guess I knew that but it still hurts. And I should be pragmatic and wish you well but I don't. Come on, let's get back to the party."

Daisy nodded silently. As they made their way back from the terrace, she checked her watch. It was after midnight—time to go home. There was no need to search for Lindsey to ask if she was ready. She was standing stiffly at the doors with her arms crossed.

"Ready," said Daisy brightly, ignoring the scowl.

"Yes."

"Then let's go." And with a twirl, she walked briskly from the room, leaving Lindsey to trail in her wake.

CHAPTER THIRTY

Lindsey waited impatiently while Daisy reached into her bag for her keys. All she wanted was to go to bed without Daisy knowing how upset she was. The ten-minute ride in the cab had been tense, both women maintaining a frosty silence. She clamped down on her anger as Daisy fumbled to fit the key into the lock.

"Hurry up," she snapped.

When the door clicked open and they stepped inside, Daisy whirled round, smouldering anger in her eyes. "What the hell's wrong with you. I have no idea why you're being so rude."

Lindsey struggled for composure. "No idea be damned. First off, you let that pretentious model paw you all night and then you…you make an exhibition of yourself on the dance floor."

"Excuse me. What right have you to criticise my behaviour. You are neither my partner nor my mother."

"No, I'm not, but I thought you would have had more brains than to get romantically attached to someone like Carmen."

"I am *not* attached to her," Daisy said coldly. "On the contrary, we do not suit each other at all. She unfortunately, has a thing for me which I have never reciprocated."

Lindsey moved closer to crowd her against the wall. She wiped her finger down the side of her mouth. "Then what's that lipstick. It's certainly not your shade."

"How dare you touch me. It's none of your business," Daisy ground out. "And what does it matter to you anyhow?"

"It matters."

"Why?"

"Because—" Lindsey's stomach clenched. She was so close to Daisy she could feel her soft breath on her neck. Her skin began to tingle, her leg muscles tightened. Pressure began to build in her groin, her body having a will of its own. She pressed firmly against Daisy and whispered hoarsely into her ear. "Because I want to be the one who gets to touch you…to kiss you. Not her."

With a swift movement, she captured her mouth. When Daisy went still, she deepened the kiss. Then Daisy suddenly sank against her, her arms coming up to circle her neck. Encouraged, Lindsey flicked her tongue into the open mouth, losing herself in the warmth. Their tongues began to duel. She was beyond stopping now. She sucked an earlobe into her mouth, then nibbled her teeth lightly along the line of Daisy's jaw. Dimly, she heard Daisy moan as she kissed down her neck, tasted the light salty skin at the base. She moved up to anchor the body against hers with her prosthetic arm.

She pulled down Daisy's dress top and eased her breast out of the bra. She rolled the nipple in her fingers until it was hard and erect, rewarded with a faint groan from Daisy. Possessively, Lindsey lowered her head and sucked the nipple into her mouth. As she began to lick and suckle it, the supple body arched into her. When Daisy's hands urgently ran through her hair, any lingering restraint vanished. Lindsey's limbs felt white-hot, molten. She was blind with need. Hurriedly, she pushed up Daisy's dress, eased her leg between her thighs and slid her hand down under the lacy underwear. When her fingers slipped into the velvet sex, Lindsey nearly exploded. Daisy was so wet.

When she began to stroke Daisy's clitoris, a voice sliced through her consciousness, "Oh...oh...God, Lindsey."

Awareness rushed through her. What was she doing? She stilled her hand, though didn't remove it.

"Don't damn well stop now," groaned Daisy. "I need you. Please."

Lindsey moaned, her vision blurring as she probed the moisture again until she found the sensitive nub. Trembling, she rubbed herself against Daisy's thigh as she stroked it. Daisy thrust against her, and the pressure between her legs built to a boiling point.

"Inside me, please...oh...so good...please," Daisy gasped.

When Lindsey slid in two fingers, being inside Daisy sent her to a fever pitch. She thrust in and out until the walls began to swell then contract against her fingers. Daisy stiffened and dug into Lindsey's back as the first fluttering of her orgasm began. "Oh fuck," she wailed when it finally overwhelmed her.

Lindsey whimpered as her own climax followed immediately in giant spasms that rippled in a torrent of exquisite pleasure.

They stood slumped against each other, Lindsey's heart hammering against her rib cage. "Are you all right?" she finally asked anxiously. "I'm sorry. I didn't mean...I hadn't planned—"

"Whew. That blew me away," said Daisy. She disentangled from their embrace.

"I swear I never meant to—"

"Shush now," Daisy said, her voice soft and caressing. "Don't apologise. I enjoyed every minute. Now no more talk. Come with me to bed."

Lindsey felt a new wave of arousal flood her thighs as she followed her down the hallway. Daisy already had her dress off by the time they reached the queen-sized bed that was covered by a big fluffy doona. Lindsey licked her lips at the sight of Daisy in her brief lacy underwear bending over to turn back the covers. She was drop-dead gorgeous. Unable to resist, she sidled up behind her and began to massage her bottom.

Daisy turned and swatted her hand away. "No, you don't. It's my turn. Get your clothes off."

Lindsey froze. Could she take off her shirt? As if sensing her agitation, Daisy quickly added, "Undress in the bathroom. Leave your shirt on but get rid of the bra and leave the front open."

Grateful for her understanding, Lindsey disappeared through the door. When she returned, Daisy was naked on the bed. She crooked a finger at her. "Now get in here with me so I can warm you up."

As soon as Lindsey stretched out on the bed, Daisy twisted to face her with a heated expression. With one hand resting on her thigh, she kissed Lindsey firmly on the mouth.

"Hmmm," Daisy murmured. "So soft."

With a last open-mouthed kiss, she moved down to tease her nipples with her teeth and tongue. Lindsey squirmed closer, her body burning as her nipple was consumed by the hot wet mouth. Then when Daisy climbed on top and slid up and over Lindsey's pelvis as she sucked the breast, Lindsey let out a long loud moaning, "Ahhhh!"

Humming, Daisy slipped down further, trailing kisses down Lindsey's abdomen until she reached the curly hair on her mound. Lindsey tensed in anticipation. But Daisy went down to her inner thighs, moving her mouth slowly up the skin. She remained there for a moment before she spread Lindsey's legs wider with her hands. Then she parted the folds exposing the distended clit. When she finally began to flick her tongue over it, Lindsey had to clench her jaw to keep from crying out. All she was conscious of now was the exquisite feeling as the clever tongue lapped her into a rising crescendo of passion.

Lindsey ruffled Daisy's curls urgently. When her orgasm hit it was sudden and with such force that she screamed. As it washed over her, any control shattered. Lindsey fell back into the bed completely spent, shaking with after-tremors.

She opened her eyes to find Daisy looking at her smugly. "You liked that, huh?"

"It was incredible," said Lindsey, her head pressed into the pillow.

Daisy gazed at her curiously. "How much experience have you had with women? How long has it been?"

Lindsey drew a shaky breath. If she hoped to have any relationship with Daisy then she would have to be frank with her, have to let her in. Tonight, when she had seen her with Carmen, she was so consumed with jealousy that she couldn't deny her feelings any longer. She was quietly falling in love with her matchmaker.

She reached over to trail a finger down the side of Daisy's face. "You gave me something very special tonight. Belief in myself. Now I know what real intimacy and emotion feel like. I needed to hear them breathing inside me to believe I could be capable of loving someone."

"You've never been in love?"

Lindsey shook her head. "I always believed love was for people who had something to offer in return, something more than damage and need."

"Then you've never been in a relationship?"

"No. After the accident, I was not only a mess socially but also sexually dysfunctional. My only experience with a girl had ended in disaster, and with only one arm I felt less than a woman. The guilt was compounded by my mother's utter condemnation of my sexuality. I had lost my best friend and had no one. I couldn't bear anyone touching me. You saw what I was like. Well multiply that by a hundred and you have the picture."

"It must have been hell."

"It was. I retreated further into my isolated world until even my work was beginning to suffer. Bernice managed to keep me sane."

"But you have many scientific achievements. How were you able to move on?"

"After battling with my phobias for three years, my psychologist referred me to a sex surrogate. She said I'd never completely control my PTSD until I learnt to be intimate. After some badgering, I agreed to see one in the end. A very expensive woman. Trisha."

Daisy propped herself up on an elbow and looked at her curiously. "I presume a sex surrogate is…ah…hands-on."

Lindsey cleared her throat then nodded. "Yes."

"How long did that therapy take?"

"Three and a half years, though the last year was only monthly sessions." She looked at Daisy anxiously. "Intimacy was nearly impossible in the beginning, but she worked me through it and out the other side. It took twenty sessions before we even went to bed."

Daisy toyed with the edge of the sheet. "Did you ever get… um…attached to her?"

"Are you asking if I fell in love with her?"

"Yes, I guess I am."

"No, I was never in love with her. I was very close to her, probably more than a lot of lovers ever get. But our relationship wasn't about loving sex, it was built on my pain-filled shame. Pain is an intimate emotion that finds places inside even passion doesn't. And it stays longer. No, our time together was more about gaining trust. She gave me hope."

"You haven't seen her since?"

"No. Although we grew to be good friends, she was my therapist. It was understood our relationship had to remain professional, and when the sessions finished I was to move on. One day though, I intend to look her up again but only when I've settled down with someone. I'd like her to know I didn't crawl back under the same rock again."

Daisy smiled. "She would have seen your write-up in the magazine and I'm sure she's been following your career. I like to know how my clients fare after our contract is finished."

"I've often wondered if she ever thought about me again."

"Believe me, she would have." Taking her face in her hands, Daisy kissed her softly. "Thank you for telling me. I'm glad she was there for you."

With a sigh of relief, Lindsey gently settled Daisy against her. "So where do we go from here?"

"What do you mean?"

"Well, we're together now, aren't we? There's no point in me continuing the program."

Daisy snuggled into her curves and mumbled sleepily, "Come on…we've discussed this. I have to be fair to you. You can't rush into anything. Now let's get some sleep."

Lindsey stared down at her not comprehending what she had just heard. When it sank in, she nearly choked with hurt. After the most wonderful sex, she was expected to go out and date other women. Had it just been a pleasant diversion for Daisy? She opened her mouth to protest but Daisy was already asleep.

She stared at the ceiling while an occasional little snore echoed beside her. The feeling of betrayal gradually increased until she could stand it no longer. Careful not to disturb Daisy, she eased out of the bed and then dressed quickly. After she scribbled out a note in the kitchen, she rang for a taxi.

CHAPTER THIRTY-ONE

Sunbeams streaming through the window woke Daisy. She stretched out from under the doona and eyed the bright room. It had to be after eight thirty for the sun to be high enough over the neighbouring tall apartment building to hit her house. When the memories of the night flooded in, she automatically reached behind to feel for the body beside her. Puzzled, she found the bed empty. She hadn't heard Lindsey get up. When she turned to look, there was no dint in the sheet. Lindsey had long since gone. She bounded out of bed, then realizing she was naked, hastily pulled on a tracksuit.

The spare room bed hadn't been slept in. She walked through the lounge to the kitchen to see if she was making breakfast but found it empty. Totally confused, she tried to think—Lindsey would hardly disappear without saying goodbye. Not after last night. It had been wonderful. Never in her wildest dreams had she expected anything so powerful and perfect. Lindsey was all the things Daisy ever wanted in a lover: receptive, strong, and passionate.

About to go out to look on the back balcony, a piece of paper on the dining room table caught her eye. She picked it up nervously. Something told her she wasn't going to like what it said. And she was right. A bad taste flooded her mouth.

I won't be requiring your matchmaking services anymore and will be taking it from here myself. I obviously read something into our lovemaking (or should I say sex) that wasn't there. I imagine last night was the last lesson in your book. I trust I passed the exam with at least a B.

Anguished, Daisy flopped down into the seat. Tears pricked her eyes. What had she done? How could she have been so stupid? She had only tried to be fair to Lindsey, even though she had a major crush on her. So often she'd seen desperate clients fall for the first person who came along. She called it the loneliness-rebound syndrome. If she hadn't been so tired when Lindsey had asked what happened next, they would have discussed it properly. Now Lindsey thought she was some sort of lesbian Don Juan, a heartless bitch who casually seduced women then threw them aside. *Crap!*

The rest of the day Daisy mooched around the house, her face red and blotchy and eyes puffy from crying. Ever so often she sent a text to Lindsey, but after the fifteenth, she gave up hoping for a reply. It was clear the break was final.

The next three weeks weren't the greatest in her life. Nothing went right: one of her more demanding clients broke up with her latest boyfriend, her car engine blew up and the pipe under the sink burst, flooding the kitchen. It was made even less great when Meg sent a postcard from New York, a place Daisy had always wanted to see, saying smugly what a fantastic time they were having.

She missed Lindsey fiercely. She tried to forget about her but couldn't. Her face kept popping up in her head no matter what she was doing. Rachel and Mac's dinner party on Saturday night was the only light on the horizon. They were always fun—it would be an opportunity to forget her troubles.

To stop herself from sinking into complete misery, Daisy had launched into an exercise regimen that she had been meaning to do for years. A brisk run around the block before breakfast, twenty sit-ups before her morning shower and an hour at the gym on her way home. To her delight, when she rushed home from the gym the night of the dinner party, she was able to slip into her usually tight skinny jeans with ease. She could barely breathe when she'd last worn them.

Feeling light and cheery for the first time in weeks, she sailed off. Rachel appeared at the door, dressed in a frilly apron printed with the caption *Trophy Wife*. Daisy chuckled as she gave her a hug—Rachel Anderson was anything but a trophy. The fiery detective wasn't someone to be trifled with.

"Come on in, Daisy. You're the last to arrive." Rachel gave her a nudge with her elbow. "I'm glad you didn't cry off. One of our newest detectives is dying to meet you."

Daisy gave her a half-hearted smile without comment. She wasn't in the mood to play nice to someone, she just wanted to relax and have fun without pressure. When they entered the dining room, the rest of the guests were already sitting around the twelve-seater table. The air buzzed with camaraderie. She had only a second for a friendly wave to the chorus of "Hi, Daisy," before a tall, well-built woman rose and pulled out the empty chair next to hers.

Daisy took the offered seat with a polite nod. "Thank you," she said, sizing her up as she settled into the chair. This presumably was the member of the force Rachel had referred to. In her early to mid-thirties, the detective was an athletic woman with a high forehead, strong jawline, and brown hair cut in a short bob.

"Hello, Daisy. I'm Kerry," she said, her engaging grin deepening the dimples in her cheeks. "Rachel's been telling me about you."

Daisy pursed her lips. Why did all her friends play the matchmaker? "You work with Rachel?"

"Yes. I've just been transferred from the drug squad to homicide. Can I get you something to drink?"

"I'll have a glass of the white wine," Daisy said, reaching over for the bottle. She swept her eyes around the table, acknowledging those she knew with a smile. When she reached the end of the table to her right, she nearly dropped the wine. Lindsey was staring at her, her violet eyes almost black. Despite herself, Daisy flashed an involuntary smile. Lindsey's lips curved in response but then faded and her eyes became intense again.

"I'll pour it for you," said Kerry, taking the bottle out of her hand.

"What? Oh…yes…all right," Daisy muttered, feeling oddly disoriented. For a moment she wondered what Lindsey was doing here, then realized Mac would have invited her after the interview.

Soon Mac and Rachel appeared with big pots of spaghetti. After two more trips into the kitchen, the table was laden with mountains of garlic bread and trays of antipasti as well. "It's Italian night," Rachel said. "So, dig in."

"This is really something," Kerry said over a mouthful of spaghetti.

Daisy heaped her plate full, sniffing in the savoury aromas appreciatively. As she ate, she tried to concentrate on what Kerry was saying and not look Lindsey's way again. That became impossible when everyone joined in a general conversation. The woman in the seat beside Lindsey, introduced as Cecilia, a professor of English Literature, had a lot to say. Too much in Daisy's opinion. She disliked know-alls. She even tried to debate with her a couple of times but was smartly shot down.

But infinitely more annoying, Lindsey seemed riveted on Cecilia's every word.

Resentment prickled. Daisy's attention fully grabbed now, she studied the professor critically. She looked to be around forty, with dark brown hair tied back in a loose ponytail, hazel eyes, and the pallor of someone who spent all their time indoors. Her brown slacks and pale yellow high-collared blouse made her appear colourless. Although she had nice boobs and a slim body, she could do with a makeover. Her hair was the wrong style for the shape of her face and she needed a bit of exercise outdoors to bring some life to her.

Absorbed in her cynical assessment, she lost track of the conversation until she heard Cecilia say, "I always try to be a little early. It's the height of rudeness to be late."

When she realized she was gazing directly at her, Daisy swelled with indignation. Was she meaning her? Not that she cared particularly. The woman was so uptight she probably had a clock in every room.

Then when someone mentioned that the new Asian takeaway chain, Jollibee, was opening an outlet in their street, Cecilia announced fastidiously, "I never eat fast food. Too much fat and sugar."

Kerry leaned over and whispered in her ear, "Just as well she's not a cop. She'd starve."

"She needs to lighten up and get rid of the stick up her arse," Daisy muttered sharply back.

Kerry raised her eyebrows comically and murmured, "Maybe I'll lend her my handcuffs."

Daisy hastily stifled a giggle when she caught Lindsey frowning at her. *Oops!* She smoothed down her hair to compose herself before she turned back to Kerry, who gave her a long glance and asked, "You know Lindsey Jamieson-Ford?"

"I do some part-time programming for her."

"I read her article. She's very talented."

"She's a whizz at robotics. The smartest woman I've ever met," Daisy said proudly, forgetting for the moment that Lindsey despised her. "And a very nice person with it."

"Cecilia seems to think so. She's been flirting with her all night."

"Really?" said Daisy a little too quickly. As if she hadn't damn well noticed. She refilled her glass, taking a healthy swig as she tried to ignore how Cecilia was leaning into Lindsey. Shit, the woman was nearly in her lap.

Rachel appeared with more wine and beers. "How are the drinks going?"

"Not for me," said Cecilia. "I rarely have more than the prescribed two standard drinks, but I'm sure Daisy won't say no. Her second bottle is nearly empty."

Daisy glared at her, insulted. Was the damn woman inferring she was drinking too much? If she was going to count, then she should do it properly. Couldn't she see the woman across the table was sharing the bottle? With a defiant glare, she emptied her glass in one gulp. The drink went down the wrong way. All eleven women turned to stare at her as she spluttered and gasped. To her horror, her eyes wouldn't stop streaming. Smarting with humiliation, she rummaged in her bag for a tissue.

"Are you okay," asked Kerry, who slapped her vigorously on the back. "Here…have some water."

Gratefully, Daisy wiped her eyes and took a sip. "Thanks. I don't know what I've done to upset Professor Uptight."

"Don't worry about her. She resents you."

"Why on earth would she?"

"Because you have far more personality and Lindsey hasn't stopped looking at you."

A warm glow shot through Daisy. Perhaps Lindsey wasn't too annoyed with her after all. She pulled a face as another scenario popped in. Maybe she was going to make a voodoo doll of her and was planning where to stick the pins.

From then on, she made a point of ignoring the prissy professor, though she just drank water for a while. The last thing she wanted to do was get sozzled. Kerry turned out to be good company with a clever sense of humour. They were chuckling at a joke from the solicitor across the table about her stay-at-home ex-girlfriend who only went out when the Wi-Fi died, when Cecilia piped up, "There's nothing wrong with being a homebody. I prefer a quiet orderly life."

Daisy was about to say something flippant when the remark sank in.

Oh fuck! No. No. No. This was a bad dream.

She met Lindsey's eyes in dismay and a silent communication passed between them. Lindsey gave a twitch of her lips, daring her to deny it. She couldn't. Cecilia fitted all the criteria of

Lindsey's ideal wife, straight from the page of that blasted questionnaire. There was such a woman out there after all. And what crappy luck she'd turned up here.

Defeated, Daisy gave a shrug of surrender and slumped back into the chair. She willed the stone in her stomach to dissolve but not even the fabulous desserts had appeal anymore. She would have burst into hysterical laughter if it wasn't so utterly devastating. She just wanted to go home and have some comfort ice cream in front of the telly. It took every muscle in her face to fix on a smile as she lifted her head to look at Kerry.

To her surprise, the detective gave her a wink with a wicked let's-shit-stir expression. "Watch this," she whispered and called out, "What do you do for kicks, Cecilia, if you stay home all the time."

Cecilia fixed her hazel eyes on her with distaste. "I'm on the organizing committee of the university press which keeps me busy. I'm also in a book club and play bridge."

"I actually wasn't referring to those extra-curricular activities, however exciting they sound. I mean what gets you going. Erotic books...Internet sex?"

The room fell into silence.

Daisy felt a sudden giggle rise inside her. The professor didn't look amused. "Don't judge everyone on yourself," she snapped.

"No need," replied Kerry, wagging her eyebrows. "Women love a girl with a badge."

Spots of pink mushroomed into Cecilia's cheeks. She looked ready to rip off Kerry's head, but surprisingly it was Lindsey who defused the situation. She hadn't said a word all night, so when she asked in her best-cultured voice, "Do people actually have Internet sex? How bizarre," there was a startled silence before laughter rippled around the table.

Her eyes twinkling, Daisy quirked an eyebrow at Lindsey and received an answering gleam. Cecilia deflated like a leaky balloon and began to shuffle her knife and fork around on her plate.

Then suddenly out of the blue, Lindsey called out, "Do you like girls with badges, Daisy?"

Daisy caught her breath, her nerves twitched. Aware that Kerry, as well as everybody else around the table, waited for her answer, she sat paralysed. The room was silent. She was under no illusion what the question meant. Lindsey was giving her a final chance. Well damnit, she wasn't going to deny her again. Critics would have to wear it. "No. I'm more partial to girls with robots," she replied shyly.

"Good. That's all I wanted to hear," Lindsey said and rose to her feet. "Now if you ladies will excuse us, Daisy and I have unfinished business to discuss."

Daisy didn't argue. She patted Kerry's hand and said, "Thanks for your company. I had fun." Ignoring the surprised stares, she rose and entwined her hand in Lindsey's. Mac gave her a tiny way-to-go smile as Rachel accompanied them to the door.

"Well, well. You two are a surprise," said Rachel. "That darn Mac never said a word. I would have sat you together had I known. Do you want me to order a cab?"

"I've texted my driver. He'll be here shortly," said Lindsey. "Thank you for the lovely evening. My company is planning a Christmas function and I hope you'll both come."

"We'd love to. Take care now."

When the door closed behind them, they walked down the steps into the front garden. Daisy's nervousness flooded back. Finally, this was it. Lindsey was officially hers. Her heart began to pound and she felt the blood beating in her ears as they looked at each other in the semi-darkness. She put a hand on Lindsey's cheek then covered her mouth with hers. Lindsey pulled her against her, the kiss raged to a searing one that made her head buzz. They were still locked together when headlights shone through the shrubbery. After the car pulled into the footpath, they separated reluctantly.

"My place or yours," Lindsey whispered throatily.

"Yours."

"I was hoping you'd say that."

CHAPTER THIRTY-TWO

The security lights winked on as they climbed the steps to the front door. Home had never seemed more welcoming to Lindsey: the slate-clad walls seemed to glow with warmth and the ivy above the door looked like Christmas decoration.

"I've missed you, Daisy," she said, not able to keep the hitch out of her voice. "This place isn't the same without you. I didn't really know what a dull world I lived in until you came bouncing in. I can't go back to that. The house has been like a mausoleum these last weeks."

"I had the most miserable time too. I didn't realize what I had until you left. I felt like tipping my drink over Cecilia tonight. You seemed to hang on her every word."

"You don't honestly think I was attracted to her?" said Lindsey, amused.

"I was so jealous. She was practically sitting on your lap."

"You're exaggerating now. Just let's say she didn't impress me much."

"But she was your ideal wife," said Daisy, giving her a dig in the ribs.

"Yes, well…I was completely wrong. You were right…are you satisfied?"

A peal of laughter echoed. "That's why I'm the matchmaker."

"Huh! You were very friendly with Kerry though," Lindsey said. Instinctively she reached for Daisy's hand for reassurance.

"Actually, she was really nice. And fun. I may have been interested at one time but not now. My heart's taken," said Daisy with a reassuring squeeze. "I'll keep her in mind, though, if I get more lesbian clients. She'll make someone an excellent wife."

With a smile Lindsey closed her eyes. How she had missed this. Every day was going to be an adventure. And how wonderful to be a part of a solid whole at long last.

When she'd left Daisy's apartment, she was like a rudderless ship cast into a bleak sea. She would never have believed that love could hurt so much. After stewing all day, she deleted Daisy's texts and removed her number from the phone. But by the next day, her righteous indignation had dissolved into abject misery. No longer angry with Daisy, her fury turned against herself. There was no one else to blame for her emotional heartburn. She hadn't even tried to understand Daisy's point of view, even though it had some logic. As a matchmaker, she genuinely thought she had to do the right thing.

As the days went by, Lindsey wondered where Daisy was, how she was doing, what she was feeling. It was like poking a bruise. When she finally decided to put her pride aside and phone, she found the number she'd deleted had been a private one. Her courage failed her at the thought of contacting the office and having Allison answer. She'd probably give her a tongue lashing for upsetting her friend.

She didn't have a clue what to do. Bernice had turned cool and though nothing was said, it was obvious she blamed her for Daisy's absence. Joe was more silent than usual, answering in monosyllables. When Mac emailed the invitation, she'd accepted eagerly. It was a chance to get out of the house and she was sure to have Daisy's number.

"Do you want a drink?" she asked, suddenly feeling shy.

"Hmmm-mm…" said Daisy nuzzling her face into the curve of her neck. "I don't think so."

"Then I'd better get you to bed," she said with a helpless sigh.

As they swayed toward the stairs, Daisy aroused her unbearably with long sweet kisses. When Lindsey felt the soft body shiver against hers, desperate needy sounds squeezed out of her throat. The simple act of climbing the steps became nearly impossible as Daisy's mouth ran down her neck to her cleavage. When she slid her hand into Lindsey's bra, she barely made it to the top without slipping.

"The bedroom better be close," Daisy said, busily unbuttoning Lindsey's shirt.

"It's here," she said in a strained voice.

Daisy gave little murmurs of approval as the king-sized bed came into view. "It's huge."

"I like plenty of room."

Fire flashed in Daisy's eyes, all lightheartedness gone. She was smouldering with want. "Then we'd better use every bit of it."

"Lie down," said Lindsey. She gently pushed her down onto the bedspread.

"I—"

"Shush. Let me," Lindsey whispered. She pulled off Daisy's blouse, then moved her hands up and down her sides, her thumbs just brushing the nipples.

"Hmmm, hurry sweetie. I need you."

"There's plenty of time, so relax. I intend to enjoy this to the fullest. I want all of you." She unclipped Daisy's bra, traced a finger over the swell of her breasts and flicked the nipples. They hardened into little bullets. Desire curled in Lindsey's stomach. "You're so beautiful," she said reverently, then dipped her head to take a nipple into her mouth.

As she sucked and massaged her breasts, Daisy pressed closer. "You're making me crazy," she whispered.

"I want to." She caught her wrists, holding them above her head with her prosthetic hand while she worried the nipples lightly with her teeth. She worked open the jeans and slid them down as far as she could with her other hand. Then she continued a slow tormenting journey over her abdomen with teasing fingers until she slid under the pants into the warm slippery flesh beneath. Pleas tumbled off Daisy's tongue as she writhed on the bed, "Yes…please…oh…please."

Her fingers very sure now as she stroked, Lindsey was blind and deaf to everything but the desire to please. When Daisy finally climaxed, crying out in ecstasy, Lindsey had never felt stronger. Now she knew what Daisy had meant when she said that to love someone would be more about her partner's pleasure than her own.

With Daisy's warm body curled into her side, Lindsey lay back staring at the ceiling trying to find ways to express how she felt. In the end, she said simply, "I love you."

Daisy propped herself up on an elbow and placed a finger on her lips. "Oh, Lindsey, it's early days for us yet. Let's enjoy each other's company and get to know each other before making a commitment."

Lindsey bit back the disappointment. She'd wanted to hear that kind of admission from her—had waited to hear it. Her mind swam—she felt suddenly vulnerable. Making an effort to be upbeat, she drew the finger into her mouth, nipped it lightly and said archly, "Is that the next step in your courtship manual?"

"It is. You've made your choice, so no more dating other women."

"You won't either?"

"Of course not. We're officially exclusive."

"So…you like me a lot then?"

"What do you think," said Daisy, her eyes hooded. "Perhaps I'd better show you how much."

She slid half over Lindsey, then trailed her mouth over to the left collarbone. "Do you trust me enough to remove your shirt?"

Lindsey went rigid. Then she slowly relaxed—Daisy would never hurt her and she couldn't hide forever. Without a word, she wriggled free of her shirt and bra to expose the top of her body fully. As well as her arm, her shoulder had been half-torn away in the accident. It had taken a series of operations to repair and build an artificial socket into the scapular to fit in the end of the artificial arm. Though the surgeries were successful, she was left scarred. After three skin grafts, another had been advised against, the disfigured skin too thin on the shoulder to repair successfully. Lindsey hadn't insisted, sick and tired of the pain and misery.

She watched as Daisy ran her finger gently over the shoulder and leaned over to lightly kiss the scar tissue. "This makes you all the more special to me," she said. She lingered there to reassure her before she shifted to her breasts. She kissed them thoroughly, stretching out the nipples until they were firmly peaked. She slipped lower, swirling her tongue around the small swell of her belly.

All thoughts, all reason skittered away when Lindsey felt her slacks and underwear pulled off and the heat between her thighs cupped. Her hips arched to meet Daisy's mouth when she lowered her head. This time she inserted two fingers, moving in and out while her mouth and tongue teased. Lindsey whimpered out her pleasure, her hands digging desperately into the bedclothes.

When her orgasm came, it shattered into a kaleidoscope of fractured lights and whirling colours behind her eyes. She heard herself cry out as the pleasure overwhelmed her. When she opened her eyes after the last waves subsided, Lindsey was surprised to see tears on Daisy's eyelashes. Instinctively, she drew her into a cuddle to soothe her. Daisy sank into the embrace and said in a sniffly voice, "Do you mind holding me until I go to sleep?"

"There's nothing I'd like better."

Lindsey opened an eye to peer at the clock on the wall. Eight fifteen. She couldn't remember when she'd last slept this late. Daisy was sound asleep, her bare legs tangled with hers. Lindsey wriggled out very carefully and padded to the toilet. After quickly brushing her teeth she eased back into the bed, reluctant to slip back into her ordinary life just yet. To wake up beside her lover was an experience she wanted to savour. She traced a fingertip over the sprinkling of freckles. "Fairy dust," she murmured.

Daisy's nose twitched, her eyes opened.

As they focused on her, Lindsey brushed the hair away from Daisy's face. "Hi," she said, feeling possessive.

With a grin, Daisy linked her arms around her neck. "Hi yourself." When Lindsey leaned forward to kiss her, she exclaimed, "Hold that thought. I have to go to the loo and I need to clean my teeth."

"There's a new toothbrush in the cabinet on the wall."

"Thanks." She disappeared into the bathroom. A few minutes later she was back. "Now, where were we?"

"I believe I was going to tell you I had a wonderful time last night. That you're glorious."

Daisy tilted her head upwards to touch her lips to hers. "Hmmm…glorious. No one's ever called me that before."

"You're cute too. Annoying sometimes but cute," Lindsey said with a chuckle, letting her fingers toy with the mass of curls. She couldn't get enough of the pretty auburn hair. "You don't have anywhere to go today, do you?"

"No, I can stay all day. When is Bernice due back?"

"This afternoon. I'd like to tell her about us. She's very important to me. Is that all right with you?" asked Lindsey a little anxiously. She didn't want to presume anything after the last argument.

"We'll tell her as soon as she gets in. She's important to me too."

"What shall we do today?"

"We'll figure that out later. Now I'm going to make you scream out my name again."

Lindsey felt her heart stutter, which was the only way she could describe the sensation. "Daisy—"

"Hush now," Daisy said, cutting her off. "I need to show you how much I want you. You rock my world."

Her head reeling, Lindsey opened her arms to embrace her.

It was unheard of in her structured orderly life, but for the second time in the same day, Lindsey opened her eyes to look at the time. She blinked in disbelief as she read the digital clock on the bedside table. *Good Grief! Two thirty in the afternoon.* Aware she should get up to prepare something to eat, she snuggled back into the warm, very naked body beside her. The round of love-making had been followed by another, and then more in the shower until exhausted, they'd flopped back into bed.

Unable to resist, she cupped one of Daisy's breasts in her hand and squeezed lightly. A groan echoed from under the covers. The covers were flipped aside as the soft warm body launched on top of her. Her laugh of delight was cut short abruptly by a knock on the door.

"Are you there, Lindsey?"

Daisy quickly rolled off and whispered, "Shit, it's Bernice."

"Get under the covers," Lindsey ordered in a low urgent voice, then called out loudly. "I'll be down in a min—"

All too late. The door opened. With a worried look on her face, Bernice hurried into the room. "Are you sick?"

"No. Just resting," Lindsey said, with the sheet up to her neck. This was totally mortifying. She couldn't even get up because she was stark naked.

Bernice stared at her in bewilderment. "But you never sleep during the day."

"Late night," growled out Lindsey, then caught her breath when a snuffling giggle echoed from under the covers.

Bernice's eyes widened as they zeroed in on the lump beside her in the bed. She gaped and stuttered, "Sorry…err…I didn't realize there someone in bed with you."

"Um…well…um," breathed out Lindsey, avoiding her gaze.

The curly head poked out. "It's only me, Bernie."

"Oh, it's you Daisy."

"We'll be down in a minute," answered Daisy airily as if it were perfectly normal to be in Lindsey's bed.

"Have you had lunch?"

"Not yet."

"I'll get you something then," Bernice replied. Her sunny disposition restored, she bustled out.

Lindsey stared in disbelief as the door closed behind her. Was she losing her senses? Bernice and Daisy had discussed lunch as if nothing untoward had happened.

Daisy let out a chuckle. "Now she knows. And she didn't seem surprised either. She must have guessed how we felt about each other. Probably before we did."

"She likes you."

"I think she's a treasure. Oh, well," Daisy said, stretching her body like a cat, "I suppose we'd better go down."

"I guess." Reluctantly, Lindsey climbed out of the bed. "I'll get you a clean T-shirt but your jeans will have to do. Mine won't fit." On her way to the cupboard, she bit her lip at the sight of their underwear discarded on the floor. Bernice couldn't have missed it. She picked them up, handing the lacy bra and knickers wordlessly to Daisy.

She put on the bra and stuffed the pants in her bag.

Bernice beamed fondly at Daisy when they entered the kitchen. "So, you and Lindsey are together now."

"We're officially an item," said Daisy with a grin.

Lindsey watched awkwardly as Bernice went from cheery to weepy in a second. The display of emotion from her old friend left her helpless and it was Daisy who hurried to give her a hug. "Hey, Bernie. I thought you'd be happy for us."

"I am. I've been praying that one day she'll meet someone who cares for her. I'm not getting any younger and she needs... Oh dear, I am going on." She gave a sniff then broke into a smile. "Lunch is on the dining room table."

"Great. For some reason I've worked up an appetite. You hungry, babe?" asked Daisy with a twinkle in her eye.

Lindsey felt herself flush slightly. She was starving.

CHAPTER THIRTY-THREE

Lindsey watched Daisy bounce Isabelle on her knee as the child screamed with delight at the two robot-dogs performing tricks. It had been fun programming in their antics, frivolous but fun. When Daisy and Isabelle disappeared into the garden to catch butterflies, Lindsey turned to see Kirsty looking at her curiously.

"I've never seen you look happier, Lin."

"I don't think I've ever been so content. I've everything I thought I'd never have," Lindsey replied, her throat tight with sudden emotion.

"Daisy's great. You're a lucky woman."

"It's early days for us."

"Yes, but you're besotted. Blind Freddy can see that," said Kirsty then added with a glimmer of her old mischievous self. "And she'll make a good mother. Isabelle adores her."

Flustered, Lindsey walked over to put the dogs away and hide her face that must be glowing pink. How had they leapt from dating to a family? "Get back to work," she said gruffly.

Laughter tinkled from Kirsty as they settled back down to the invitation list. As much as she tried to concentrate, Lindsey began to daydream. It was a month since they had begun to date officially, the quiet life that had insulated her for years now gone. Her dull existence had been shaken up like a snow globe, laughter and vivacious energy swirling over her like clouds of snowflakes and glitter.

They had developed a routine. Daisy came out to Lindsey's place on the weekends, while Lindsey stayed at Daisy's apartment when she visited her town lab. At first it had only been one day during the week, but in the last fortnight, Lindsey had stayed Tuesday and Thursday nights. Apart from a couple of movie dates, a day at the beach and a night out at a bar to meet Daisy's friends, they were content to stay at home. And more and more of Daisy's clothes seem to have made their way into her wardrobe.

This Saturday she'd asked Kirsty over, ostensibly to finish planning the company's first major function, but she really wanted to show her the house and have her meet Daisy. She couldn't deny her thrill of Kirsty's awe when she showed her the robots. Though she knew it was a little shallow, to impress her childhood friend was important. She needed her approval.

And she wanted her to like Daisy. She was relieved there were no worries there. They immediately got on like old friends and Isabelle charmed both Daisy and Bernice as soon as she stepped through the door. She scampered like a whirlwind through the lounge until she spied the robot dogs. From then on Daisy took her in hand, keeping her occupied while they organised the invitations.

She sighed as she viewed the list. So much for a small event! The launch of their new line in robotic software was growing by the minute. Nearly three hundred guests. As it was their first public function, Kirsty had persuaded her to host a dinner at City Hall the Saturday night before Christmas. Though Lindsey dreaded the thought of such a formal affair she hadn't argued, not wanting to put a damper on the proceedings. Her staff's enthusiasm for the idea was overwhelming. As Kirsty was proving to be an excellent organizer, Lindsey was only left with working out the invitees, seating arrangements, and preparing the speakers' program.

By midafternoon when they were finished, Lindsey tossed her pen onto the desk with relief. "I'm glad that's over."

"You did well. I thought you were going to give up a couple of times and sneak off to your lab."

"Not exactly my area of expertise, I'm afraid," Lindsey said, yawning.

Kirsty chuckled as she scooped up the papers into a bundle to put in her briefcase. "Well, everything's sorted now. I'll get the invitations into the mail tomorrow. All you have to do is sort out your speech."

"Good, then let's go out to the patio for afternoon tea."

Once settled into a deck chair, Lindsey watched Daisy approach from the gardens with Isabelle. With her face flushed from exertion, her hair wind-blown and feet bare, she had never looked so attractive. Then she looked up and her gaze engulfed Lindsey. Any lingering doubts about the strength of Daisy's commitment to their budding relationship vanished. Her unguarded eyes were bright, shining with love.

Caught up in the moment, Lindsey smiled back at her and then coughed self-consciously when Kirsty murmured beside her, "She thinks the world of you."

"I can't believe she's dating me. She's very popular."

"You always did underestimate yourself, my friend. She's the lucky one and she knows it."

"I've had a lot of lonely years," Lindsey said wistfully. "But now for the first time in my life, I feel there might be a happy ever after for me."

Tears filled Kirsty's eyes as she reached over and brushed her fingers down Lindsey's cheek. "Oh, Lin. I wasn't there to support you. Let's never make that mistake again."

"No, we won't. Now let's stop being so maudlin and have a coffee. Isabelle is going to love Bernie's chocolate biscuits."

"She's a sugar fiend so I'm sure she will. What's on the agenda for you tomorrow?"

"Ah," said Lindsey with a slight wince. "Daisy is taking me for Sunday lunch to meet her parents."

"Really? Things *are* getting serious. Are you worried?"

"Petrified."

* * *

"Here we are," called out Daisy as she slowed down halfway along an avenue of jacarandas. The suburban street made a pretty picture, with the last of blossoms fluttering off the trees to blanket the footpaths with purple. Lindsey flexed her hand on the armrest as they pulled into a driveway, immediately struck by the differences in this and that of her childhood. The Parker home was a charming low-set brick house with lattice panels and a picket fence, a far cry from her parents' opulent mansion. It looked welcoming with its pots of petunias hanging on the front porch and roses in the front garden.

As soon as they stopped the front door opened and a middle-aged woman, the spitting image of Daisy, came out to greet them. There was no mistaking the resemblance—the likeness was remarkable. The same figure, the same facial features, the same hair and the same smile. Dry-mouthed, Lindsey waited for Daisy to embrace her mother before coming forward to be introduced. It only took a second to realize any fears that their relationship would be frowned upon, were groundless.

Sheila Parker engulfed her in a warm hug and a smacking kiss on the cheek. "Welcome to our home, Lindsey. Come on in."

Daisy took her hand, squeezing it reassuringly as they followed her mother into the loungeroom. A man rose from a chair as they approached, then indicated with a sweep of his hand to the chair opposite after she was introduced. "Take a seat, Lindsey. We've been anxious to meet the lady who's caught our daughter's eye."

Lindsey sat down carefully into the leather armchair, conscious of his scrutiny. Richard Parker was a man who looked fit for his age, with a tanned face, greying hair cropped short and a neat beard equally as grey. Judging by the examination she was receiving, she presumed he would be harder to win over than his wife. However, it didn't take her long to realize while he looked the more formidable of the two, he deferred to Sheila. Her approval given, he relaxed and soon they were conversing like old friends.

The time passed quickly, both parents interested in robotics. It was a pleasure to find people who were genuinely keen to hear about her work and not asking questions for the sake of politeness.

When the doorbell rang just before lunch, Sheila exclaimed, "That will be Meg and family. They wanted to come over to meet you."

At that announcement, a huff of breath escaped from Daisy. Lindsey glanced over at her quickly. From the way her face had tightened, she must clash with her sister. Interested, Lindsey leaned forward in her chair waiting for Meg to appear. The sound of heels clicking efficiently on the hallway floor preceded her entry. Then a stylish young woman swept into the room, followed by her mother, carrying a baby, and a slightly harassed man with a bouncinette and nappy bag. Meg was taller than Daisy, with sharper features and a slimmer, less curvy body. She took after her father, lacking the softness of her mother.

Lindsey rose with a smile fixed on her face.

Daisy placed her hand possessively on her arm. "This is Meg and her husband Evan, Lindsey. And this gorgeous little fellow is baby Aaron."

"We're *so* pleased to meet you, Lindsey. We were wondering if Daisy was *ever* going to bring someone home."

The words were said lightly but there was no disguising the disagreeable undercurrent. Feeling Daisy's fingers tighten on her skin, Lindsey inclined her head and said coolly, "Then I'm extremely flattered to be the one. Your sister is a popular woman. And, might I add, a very smart one." To enforce her words, she took Daisy's hand and kissed it lightly. "Sometimes she takes my breath away."

Meg gaped at her while Sheila chuckled. "Well said, Lindsey. Spoken like a true romantic. You might take a leaf out of her book, Meg. Now, excuse me a minute while I attend to lunch. Would you give me a hand please, Daisy?"

"Right, Mum," said Daisy, giving Lindsey an apologetic shrug before she trailed off after her mother to the kitchen.

Meg went off to change the baby leaving Lindsey to chat with the men. As Evan was a civil engineer familiar with some of her father's projects in the city, and Richard a research scientist, the three of them had much in common to talk about. By the time Sheila called them for lunch, she knew she had gained the acceptance of the men in the family.

Lindsey was pleasantly surprised. When she thought of family dinners, she imagined her mother's lavish meals at a glossy cedar table laid with heavy Georgian silver. Where three-courses were accompanied by appropriate wines and conversation subdued and polite. Where the food was served by a maid in a starched white apron.

Not this meal.

They sat around a plain table setting, with dishes in the middle, and everyone helped themselves amidst jostling and laughter. She found it wonderful. When they settled down to eat, the conversation was fun until Meg asked, "How did you two meet, Lindsey? Daisy hardly would be running in your circles."

Lindsey cocked her head at her in surprise. "My circles? What do you imagine those are?"

Meg shrugged. "We're not exactly the rich and famous, and matchmaking is hardly a serious occupation."

Silence fell in the room. Across the table, Richard was frowning at his daughter and she could feel Daisy go rigid in the seat next to her. With her gaze fixed on Meg, Lindsey placed a hand over Daisy's to calm her and said in a low voice, "I'm afraid I don't go out much so haven't a circle as you put it. And you do your sister a great disservice if you think she can't take her place in any society. She's one of the most sociable people I've ever met."

"She always knew how to suck up."

Lindsey held her anger in check and *tsked* chidingly. "It sounds like you don't know her well at all."

"I know her a hell of a lot better than you probably do."

"That's enough," growled her father.

Daisy gave her sister a sour look. "I asked Lindsey over to meet you all because she has become special to me, so stop being a jerk."

When Meg opened her mouth to retaliate, Lindsey hastily intervened. "It's an honour to be at your parents' table sharing a meal so let's not belittle the experience." She flashed a smile at her hostess. "This roast is superb."

Sheila gave a wry smile. "Thank you. It's nice to have you with us today." She turned to look at Meg sternly and said in a voice that brooked no argument. "It's about time you and Daisy sorted out your differences. Your father and I have had enough of the bickering. Now…you owe our guest an apology, my girl."

Meg opened and closed her mouth, casting a quick glance at Daisy. "Yes, Mum." She turned to look at Lindsey then lowered her eyes to the table. "Sorry," she mumbled.

Lindsey nearly laughed. If it was an apology, it was definitely the least enthusiastic one she'd ever heard. Thankfully, the mood was considerably lighter from then on and Evan appeared much happier. He was a quiet unassuming man and she guessed he must be sometimes embarrassed by his wife's wilful tongue and appalling manners. They were just finishing dessert when the doorbell rang. "Are you expecting anyone, Richard?" asked Sheila.

"No."

Daisy got to her feet. "I'll get it." She dropped a light kiss on Lindsey's forehead before heading down the hallway. Lindsey felt a warm glow at the possessive gesture, conscious the family had watched the interaction closely. Daisy was making it plain that Lindsey was more than a casual lover. From the look of approval on Sheila's face, she seemed quite happy with her daughter's choice.

When a scream and then laughter floated from the front door, they all scanned the door to see who was going to appear. When a girl burst into the room, the family members immediately rose to greet her. "Beth," cried Sheila in delight. "Why didn't you tell us you were coming home?"

"Wanted to surprise you," she said, grinning, then embraced her family one by one. When she came to Lindsey, she looked at her curiously. "Hello. I'm Beth Parker."

Daisy immediately put her arm around Lindsey's waist. "This is my friend Lindsey, Beth."

Beth looked at the arm and broke into a wide grin. "You've brought a girlfriend home? Wow!" She gave Lindsey a wink. "You must be very special. She's soooo fussy."

Daisy rolled her eyes. "That's enough. Now tell—"

A squeal from Meg cut the sentence short. "You've got a bloody tattoo."

"A tattoo," exclaimed her father through gritted teeth, staring in disbelief at the rose on her neck.

"Isn't it a beauty?" said Beth breezily, pulling her collar to the side for a better view. When no one spoke, she added, "and I've another surprise. He's bringing our backpacks in."

Someone clearing his throat made them all turn to the door. On the threshold stood a scruffy man with blond dreadlocks halfway down his back, dressed in faded jeans and a crumpled pale orange shirt. "Say hello to Oliver, everyone," chirped Beth happily.

A giggle escaped Daisy. She leaned over and whispered in Lindsey's ear, "You're going to be viewed as royalty after *this* surprise."

CHAPTER THIRTY-FOUR

Daisy and her parents joined the queue into the function room, excited the big night had finally arrived. Lindsey had become progressively quieter as the launch approached and yesterday when she had come over for dinner, she looked ready to have a panic attack. Taking her in hand, Daisy made her promise to stay out the back until after her speech and let her staff be the welcoming committee.

As the waiter led them to a table directly in front of the stage, Daisy took a moment to admire the venue. Kirsty had outdone herself. The place looked spectacular. Soft lights from the domed ceiling spread a warm glow over tables decorated in the blue and silver of LJF Robotics logo and gleaming with fine silverware and crystal glasses. The room was awash with glamour. The finest formal wear and jewellery in the city. Clearly this was not only viewed as a corporation launch, but an important media event on the social calendar.

There were as many women as men—evidently everyone was interested in meeting Lindsey now she was out of her self-imposed exile. The air was filled with the rich scent of a hundred different perfumes, all mixed to form a strong, heady musk. It was intoxicating.

Once they were seated, she let herself relax over a glass of champagne. She and her parents shared the table with Bernice, Joe and Raylene, Kirsty and Martin, Allison and Noel, and Mac and Rachel.

Lindsey had insisted her house staff attend, though Joe looked like he'd rather be anywhere than here. She was thrilled his romance with going so well—Raylene was proving the perfect partner for him. He was smitten with her, and seeing them together, it was obvious the feeling was mutual. Another matchmaking success, she thought happily.

Martin, though rather pompous, kept them entertained, constantly throwing back his head in laughter. Whatever troubles their marriage had been going through were now over. His eyes would rest fondly every so often on Kirsty, who had that radiant, flawless glow that comes with pregnancy. Daisy tried to imagine Lindsey with him. She couldn't visualize the coupling even if Lindsey had been straight. They were chalk and cheese.

After the main meal was cleared away, the formal proceedings began. The new software was described in detail by the LJF Robotics team, five vibrant scientists who clearly enjoyed what they did. Daisy was pleased they introduced their products in lay language; there was nothing more off-putting as too much technical jargon. When a mobility suit was wheeled in, excited murmurs echoed around the room.

Then the audience applauded loudly when Lindsey appeared.

As soon as she walked onto the stage, a lump formed in Daisy's throat. She looked the embodiment of a highly successful woman in her prime. The simple knee-high black evening dress showed off her body to perfection and the blood-red ruby necklace added panache. Though she must have been nervous, it didn't show. She stood casually at the podium beside the mobility suit, waiting for the applause to die down. For a second, she caught Daisy's eye, nodded, then launched into her speech.

"This suit, ladies and gentlemen, is what we call an Exoskeleton. Or what the kids would say…awesome motorized pants. While some companies target industrial lifting with the technology, our product is specifically made to give mobility to the frail or less-abled. We are continuously trying to find ways to refine the suit, but like any new technology there are plenty of challenges. Energy storage is a problem, the batteries need to be smaller and last longer, the material should to be even lighter, and eventually the design needs to be aesthetically user-friendly. All this will come in time. The suit is equipped with sensors…"

As Lindsey continued, Daisy gazed at her with pride. The woman was awe-inspiring amazing. The speech was well-researched, to the point, delivered with just the right mixture of specialized terms and non-technical explanations.

But then something unexpected happened. As she was wrapping up the talk, she suddenly stopped dead in her tracks. The colour drained from her face. Daisy stared at her, horrified. By the way Lindsey's hands were shaking, a panic attack wasn't far off. She prepared to rush onto the stage. It had all the makings of a disaster and she wasn't going to let her go through it alone.

But Lindsey managed to pull herself together and smiled at someone a few tables behind her. If you could call it a smile. It looked more like baring her teeth.

She swivelled to catch whom Lindsey was acknowledging. A woman in a dark blue evening gown sat bolt upright in her chair, her unblinking stare fixed on Lindsey. The perfect makeup was not able to disguise that she was well past middle-age. Though her face still held some of the beauty of her youth, it was pinched. Daisy had never seen her before, but she did recognize from the press clippings that the man sitting beside her was Lindsey's father, Warren Jamieson-Ford. The woman was most likely her mother.

With insides churning, she waited to see what Lindsey was going to do next. She expected her to bring the presentation to an abrupt close and leave the stage.

Instead, she did the unexpected. She held out her left arm. "So now let's address the elephant in the room, shall we."

A hush settled over the audience.

"This is a prosthetic limb," Lindsey continued. "I lost my arm in an accident when I was twenty-one. Until you experience the loss of a limb, you have no idea how demoralizing and gut-wrenching it is. Globally, there are more than one million people annually, who have amputations. That equates to one every three minutes. You might question the number but it's quite true. Not all are from trauma. Over half are from diabetes and vascular disease: there are sixty-two million diabetics in India alone. And worldwide the number continues to rise. No one chooses to lose a limb or a foot or a hand, but having a choice about how the world sees you afterward is essential. Our company is striving to make that concept a better reality, so that people, especially children, don't have to be ashamed. That they have a limb which functions as near to the original as possible. We will continue our work to bring prosthetics into the digital age so that amputees can become an awesome bionic person rather than someone with a disability. Our mission, through creative and innovative research, is to bring game-changing affordable devices to the world."

The room erupted. After acknowledging the standing ovation with a bow, she gestured towards the back of the stage. "And now I'd like to present our future."

A collective gasp rippled around the audience at the sight of the robot walking out from behind a curtain. If Lindsey wanted to make a grandstand play then this was the way to do it. The atmosphere in the hall was electric as Stephen made his way across the floor to stand beside her. She left him there for a minute, then spoke quietly to him. With a dip of his head, he picked up the mobility suit and carried it off stage. For a few seconds the entire room was silent, then it was as if the floodgates opened. Everyone started pitching questions at her. Daisy couldn't hear herself think for the babble.

Lindsey ignored them, simply giving a quick wave. "That's all, folks. Tomorrow we're having an open house at our town laboratory for you to view our products more closely, so no more talking shop tonight. The bar's open until late and there's music to follow, so have fun."

She appeared calm when she descended from the stage to their table, but Daisy could sense her turmoil. Instinctively, she rose and wrapped her arms around her, pressing her body against the warmth of hers. "Are you okay?"

"Not really. My mother's here."

"I know, I thought it must be her. Just remember I'm with you. You're not alone anymore." Deliberately, she took her head in her hands and pressed her lips against hers.

Lindsey let the kiss linger before she withdrew awkwardly with a rueful smile. "And now I'm out to the entire world."

"Stuff them," said Daisy fiercely. "I want everyone to know you are mine, including your mother. I'm so proud of you."

Lindsey gave her another tight hug before she took a seat beside her. "You're so good for the soul, Daisy." Then she smiled across the table at Kirsty. "Everything looks wonderful. You've done a great job."

"Thanks. I'm really pleased everything is going so smoothly. You stole the show with the robot. Very theatrical."

"I thought it was time to introduce him to the world. Just enough to whet their appetite," said Lindsey with a throaty laugh.

"Where do you go from here with your robots?" asked Richard Parker.

"I'm not quite sure yet. The technology is covered by rock-solid patents, so anything is possible. Did you know Daisy wrote both robots a comprehensive behavioural profile?"

"Good for you, Daisy," said her father proudly.

Then the waiters appeared with dessert, bringing everyone's attention back to food. When a chocolate raspberry torte was placed in front of her, Lindsey stared rigidly at it.

"What's the matter," whispered Daisy.

"Once these plates are cleared away, I haven't any more excuses to ignore my mother."

"Why don't you wait until she comes over?"

Lindsey gave a little snort. "Things don't work that way. She'll expect me to go to her."

Daisy frowned at her. "Then don't."

"I thought of that," Lindsey replied, stabbing the fork into the sweet. "But that will just leave things still hanging. The sooner I face her, the sooner I can get on with my life."

"Fuck her," Daisy mumbled in her ear. "If you're up to it, then let's go upset her night together."

The look on Lindsey's face spoke volumes. Relief, determination, love. She gave Daisy's thigh a squeeze, letting her fingertips linger. "Thank you."

"You're welcome," whispered Daisy, the intimate gesture sending tingles to her centre. She seemed perpetually horny now. As soon as she could, she'd have to get Lindsey into bed.

The party turned noisier as waiters continued to carry drinks around to the tables. In the background a singer crooned on the stage. Lindsey deftly fobbed off invitations to talk as they headed to her parents' table. With a reflex action, Daisy grabbed Lindsey's left hand when a good-looking guy stared blatantly at her lover's long legs. Normally, she only held her right hand. Though the texture of the skin was the same, her artificial hand was firmer with less elasticity. She clasped it tighter as they approached the table, figuring that holding it would make a statement to the mother.

It did.

Ellen Jamieson-Ford stared at their joined hands before rising to greet her daughter. They eyed each other warily before Ellen broke the silence. "How are you, Lindsey?"

"Good, Mother. And you?"

"As well as can be expected. When I heard you were coming out of hiding, I decided to accompany your father." She ignored Daisy and pointed to the chair the man beside her had discreetly vacated. "Take a seat."

Lindsey ignored the command. She leaned forward to her father who also had risen and pecked him on the cheek. "Hello, Dad. Mother, Dad, I'd like you meet my friend, Daisy Parker."

"Hi there," said Daisy brightly, casting off her annoyance with some effort.

"It's good to meet you, Daisy," said her father. "Now I'm sure we can find another seat."

The elderly woman in the next seat rose immediately. "Take mine. I need to stretch my legs."

Daisy nearly groaned aloud. If they sat down, it would be harder to leave quickly. She flicked a concerned glance at Lindsey. By the look on her face, all her crisp optimism had died away. She actually appeared frightened. Hell, the mother must be even more of an ogre than she envisaged. Well, she was going to have a fight on her hands if she thought she was going to browbeat her daughter again. She studied the woman as Lindsey and her father talked.

There was no doubt Ellen Jamieson-Ford had been a beauty in her day. Not even time could disguise that. But she would have had a lot of help along the way to retain those looks. Her face was too smooth not to have had Botox injections or a filler. For all the work, there was a tightness around her mouth that made her look sour.

"You're looking much older, Lindsey," her mother interjected. "And you've cut your hair. A pity. It was your best feature."

Daisy leaned over and tucked a strand of hair behind Lindsey's ear. "Do you think so? I think her hair is fabulous."

For the first time, Ellen looked at Daisy directly. Her lips curled in distaste. "And you are *who* exactly?"

Daisy smiled at her, not allowing her friendly tone to falter. "I'm Lindsey's girlfriend." She glanced around the table. Everyone had stopped chatting and were eyeing them with undisguised interest—the family rift was evidently not a secret. To her surprise, she spied a woman she knew at the end of the table, a mother of a friend from her university days. "Hi, Mrs White," she called out.

"Hello, Daisy. How have you been?"

"Great, thanks. Lindsey and I had drinks with Clarissa and the girls not long ago."

"She told me she saw you. I didn't realize your Lindsey was Ellen's daughter."

Daisy brought her gaze back to Ellen. She was studying her like an insect under a dissecting microscope, probably realizing she couldn't dismiss her quite so readily now they were more on an equal footing.

"Oh, so you do have some sort of formal qualification?" asked Ellen, chuckling lightheartedly as though it was a joke.

"Of course she does," said Lindsey sharply. "She's an anthropologist. She worked with me on the robots."

"Really?" exclaimed her father. His eyes twinkled when he looked at Lindsey. "You certainly got everyone's attention bringing the robot in like that. Now tell me all about it. I had no idea you'd come so far in your research."

And from then on, Lindsey became the centre of attention as she good-naturedly answered all the questions fired at her. Daisy sat back and watched with pride as the shackles of her past gradually, and quite simply, fell away. Ellen Jamieson-Ford receded into the background as a new, confident Lindsey emerged like a butterfly from a chrysalis. When at last they rose to go, Ellen looked exactly what she was: a lonely old woman. If Daisy hadn't been so pissed off with her, she would have felt sorry for her.

"Will you come over to dinner one night," Ellen asked in a low voice as they said their goodnights.

Lindsey was silent for a moment, then replied with a shake of her head. "Perhaps it would be better if you had a meal with us. I know Dad wants to see my lab." She turned to Daisy as they walked away. "What about we say goodnight to the folks at our table and sneak out? I'm all talked out."

"Me too. I just want to cuddle up in bed and tell you how much I adore you and how proud I am of you."

Lindsey squeezed her hand. "Let's go then."

Outside on the footpath as they waited for their taxi, Daisy tilted her head at Lindsey and asked the question that had been plaguing her. "Why haven't you ever asked your father to your home, babe? You see him at your town lab."

Lindsey gave a sad smile. "Because my house has been my sanctuary all those lonely years and I wasn't prepared to share that with him. I love Dad, I really do, but something inside me knows he was part of the problem with my mother. If he had been a real father, he would have stopped her bullying right from the beginning. Parenting isn't about taking the easy way out, it's about keeping your children safe." Lindsey gazed solemnly at her with liquid swimming in her eyes. "My children will be properly looked after."

Daisy blinked, then broke into a smile.

CHAPTER THIRTY-FIVE

The morning light through the window caught Lindsey's leg in a warm glow. Daisy stroked along the length of her outer thigh, not to initiate sex, but to savour the feel of the silky skin. She couldn't remember when she had been so happy.

"Good morning," murmured Lindsey sleepily. "I thought you had enough lovin' last night."

"Never enough. I don't know what you've done to me but I'm addicted to you," Daisy said, shifting until she was nestled against Lindsey. She felt warm and soft. "This is so nice. I was so proud of you last night."

"Really?"

"You were wonderful."

Lindsey rolled over on top of her and gazed into her eyes. "Just remember, everyone I valued was sitting at our table. You especially. You're my world now." She ran her fingers through Daisy's curls.

Daisy strained forward as her mouth was claimed in a searing kiss and a hand squeezed her breast. She loved Lindsey in this dominant mood. She reclined back on the pillows, prepared to be ravished thoroughly. With an excited moan, she spread her legs apart, knowing she was going to be brought to new heights. And she wasn't disappointed.

When her orgasm hit, she screamed out her pleasure. But when the last wave had rippled away, she was so overcome that she couldn't stop tears trickling down her cheeks.

Lindsey tightened her arms around her, concerned. "What's wrong, luv? Did I hurt you?"

"Of course not," sniffled Daisy. "It was just what I needed. It's not that. I want to tell you something."

"Don't tell me you have some dark deep secret," said Lindsey only half-jokingly. "I thought I had enough for the two of us."

"I love you. I only realized just how much last night when you faced your mother. I swear if she ever hurts you again I'll make her pay."

"You love me. You really do?" said Lindsey softly, her eyes filled with hope.

"You bet I do. You set my heart on fire."

"Then live with me, Daisy. Maybe it's a bit too soon but I want to wake up with you every morning like this. I hate when you don't spend the night with me. I want us to be together—a family."

Daisy shyly took her face in her hands and planted a long kiss on her lips. "I want that too but I can't give up the agency."

"We'll work something out. Could you commute from here?"

"There's no reason why I couldn't, though not all the time… it's too far." She moved over and propped herself up on an elbow. "Actually, I've been thinking seriously of employing someone to help with the social workload for some time. Maybe now I should."

"Have you the client base to pay the wage?"

"Oh, yes. We can be as busy as we want to be. We've had to turn people away. Marigold is doing very well financially." She ran a finger down Lindsey's cheek. "I would also like to continue working with you. I've enjoyed it tremendously and I get a chance to use my degree in a meaningful way. I could stay in the city Tuesday and Thursday nights and you could spend those nights in town as well. We've been virtually during that anyhow."

Lindsey chuckled. "This is just what you preached to me. Couples work out their lives through compromise."

"I've found those who are fair to each other have the happiest relationships. Now," said Daisy, sitting up, "let's have breakfast and afterward, what say we get a Christmas tree. The twenty-fifth is only two days away."

Lindsey froze, turned abruptly onto her back, opened her mouth, shut it again then stared fixedly at the ceiling. Daisy watched her silently, wondering what had upset her. She stayed quiet, sensing Lindsey would tell her in her own time. When she dropped her eyes to look at her, Daisy could see the moisture glistering on her lashes.

"Tell me," she murmured.

"We've never had a Christmas tree here. Bernie always goes to her sister for the festive season. I know she doesn't want to leave me but I insist she goes. It's her family time."

"Shit, Lindsey," exclaimed Daisy in astonishment. "You spent Christmas alone every year?"

Lindsey shrugged ruefully. "It wasn't all that bad. Bernie always made a proper dinner with all the trimmings before she left."

Daisy fought back a fresh round of tears. Would this woman ever stop pulling at her heartstrings? Swallowing back the lump in her throat, she peppered Lindsey's face with kisses. "Well, Ms Jamieson-Ford, those days are ended. Now get your butt out of bed. After breakfast, we're going out to get the biggest tree we can find and as many gaudy decorations as we can find to put on it. Then after we finish admiring the tree, we're going to ring a gourmet catering firm and order a very expensive Christmas dinner for the two of us."

"You're not going to cook?" asked Lindsey, digging her in the ribs.

"Only if you want a boiled egg on toast. After we've stuffed ourselves with this yummy Chrissie dinner, we're going over to my parents' place in the evening where there will be games such as charades, with lots of serious family rivalry. Your only task will be to beat Meg who likes to win."

Lindsey gave a throaty laugh. "Sounds wonderful."

Daisy smiled at her. "It will be especially so this year with you by my side." She held out her hand. "Come on, let's start the rest of our lives."

Bella Books, Inc.

Women. Books. Even Better Together.

P.O. Box 10543
Tallahassee, FL 32302

Phone: 800-729-4992
www.bellabooks.com